I0636254

This book is a work of fiction. The characters, incidents, and dialogue are drawn from the author's imagination and are not to be construed as real. Any resemblance to actual events or persons, living or dead, is entirely coincidental.

FIRST EDITION
ISBN 978-0-9952885-4-6

1. Time travel romance 2. Time travel fiction 3. Science fiction 4. Hard Science 5. Suspense 6. Thriller 7. Magical realism

Michael Poeltl

Time travel has always fascinated me. Whether traveling to the future or the past, I'm captivated by the idea that I could correct a mistake or catch a glimpse of what's to come. I love researching and reading hard science dealing with new ideas to achieve time travel.

Still, the limitations of traveling back in time are extensive. Visiting the past is considered virtually impossible, with the second law of thermodynamics holding us hostage to the arrow of time. But for Cleo McCarthy, a twenty-four-year-old graphic designer living in Chicago who had never given it a second thought, time travel comes easily. Well, nothing unwanted ever comes easily, but even an unsolicited gift presents opportunities.

Cleo has no steampunk time machine she steps into, with dials, switches, and levers to work, taking her from one time to another. No modified DeLorean or Phone booth. She can't bring new technology back with her, not even a tattoo painfully etched into her flesh, but she will retain her memories of each future.

Why? Purpose reveals itself as Cleo finds herself burdened with an unlimited number of do-overs, asking, how much time is enough?

Michael Poeltl

CHAPTERS

Trauma
Initiation Day
Time Travel FAQs
Bobby Patel - Take One
Time Travel - The Research
Time Travel - The Trigger
Bobby Patel - Take Two
Bobby Patel - Take Three
White Noise
Conjecture
Pseudoscience
What Comes Next
What Comes After
Rome
Kindred Spirits
Paris
Bobby Patel - Take Four
Barcelona
Home for a Rest
Bobby Patel - Take Five
Toronto
Game Changer
Only Fools Rush In
Las Vegas
Coming Clean
Catch Up
Loose Ends
Damage Control
Check Please
Road trip
A Sleepless Night
Ivanpah
Ivanpah Part Two
Ever After

Trauma

Cleo's body pitches as the plane yaws dangerously left, her head snapping to the side, the seatbelt fastened over her lap, the only thing keeping her from tumbling into the narrow aisle. The plane then dives, and Cleo is momentarily weightless. Her heart lodges in her throat, her stomach floating in her torso. Being weightless for the first time is an unsettling feeling. Cleo relates it to the rickety roller coaster she once rode with her best friend at a carnival. Never again, she told herself. The oxygen masks drop, and she tenses her arms to keep them from flailing and grabs the mask. She secures it over her mouth and nose as the flight attendant had mimed just an hour earlier. The other passengers are screaming and shouting and gasping around her. Cleo can't seem to make a noise. A drink cart barrels down the aisle, crashing into knees and running over feet. The plane attempts to even out but then drops gut-wrenchingly, the seat belt pressing into her lower abdomen. Cleo is terrified that her plane will crash in the Indian Ocean.

She sees her life passing before her eyes, and with it, the clear memory of her purchasing this ticket and her excitement mixed with anxiety over taking this adventure alone. Until this moment, her trip had been memorable. She visited many ancient sites in Thailand, Cambodia, Vietnam, and India. This plane is meant to take her to South Africa to complete her bucket list trip and stay a week with her aunt and uncle on the coast. But that reality seems questionable as the plane lurches again to the left. Much less real than the memories she has made these past four weeks.

A screeching sound of metal tearing fills the cabin. Cleo wants to be home. She wishes she'd never made the trip. Her hands are wet with fear, and her muscles tense against each new tremor. Cleo steals a glance out the window. The wing hangs loose, banging against the exterior of the plane. She feels ill. The plane begins a slow spin to the left. It's spinning like a top. It will fall flat into the ocean. They have inflatable rafts for this possibility; she tries to reason. But they are still thousands of feet in the air. The impact will kill them all.

The image of her decision to book with the tour group, purchase the tickets, buy the outfits, get the vaccines, and pack her bags overwhelms her senses. They filter out the screaming and nervous energy happening around her. The plane is still falling. It's falling fast. The man next to her is throwing up in his paper bag. A woman across the aisle is holding her baby tightly against her chest. It's chaos. It's an end she had never even considered.

She's there, at her desk, in her mind. Or maybe it's the pure oxygen pouring into her lungs, affecting her ability to grasp the moment's truth. Perhaps it's some chemical reaction to her current circumstances. Whatever the cause, Cleo is grateful for the interruption from this nightmare.

She's gripping both handles of her chair, fingernails looking for purchase on the hard plastic finish. She forces her physical reality out of her mind and refocuses on the steps taken to arrive here. She smells the cup of coffee on her desk, feels the keyboard under her fingertips, remembers the sense of freedom this trip would afford her, and sees the flight information begging her to complete the transaction. Just do it, she tells herself. You deserve to see the world. When will you have this opportunity again? Then, as she's about to click the *Book Now* button, she envisions an alternate outcome. The cursor moves away from the button, travels up the right-hand side of the screen to the corner of the open window, and closes the tab. She's altering her memory as if this could change her present. She's experiencing all the sensations of being in that moment and willfully changing her mind.

Initiation Day

Cleo finds herself at home at her computer, the screen displaying the backdrop of her, Bobby, and Trish on a night out. She feels nauseous. She fears she'll throw up. She hasn't thrown up since her first year in college. Cleo's right hand has a firm grip on the mouse. She wants to release it but is finding it difficult to do so. Is she experiencing a Parkinson's symptom? Uncooperative muscles are one of the signs that her young-onset Parkinson's, or YOPD, is advancing. It's the main reason she was planning this trip, as there is no guarantee the disease wouldn't overcome her sooner rather than later. Cleo looks at the bottom of her screen, clicks to open her tabs, and sees the trip she'd been planning pop up with the *Book Now* button ready to click. But she's having reservations now. Why? Because the plane is going to crash, she tells herself. The images of a plane cabin shuddering around her, oxygen masks being deployed, and horrified screams echoing throughout the cabin hijack her senses.

Cleo stands abruptly from her desk, the chair spinning back on its wheels. I was on that plane, she remembers. I was on that plane. She feels disoriented.

Her hand still gripping the cordless mouse, Cleo's knees give out on her, and she crumbles to the hardwood floor. I was on that plane a moment ago. A shiver overtakes her, and she releases the mouse, which tumbles to the floor. That's not possible. She scurries back to her laptop on her knees and studies the bottom right corner of her screen to see the date and time. 2023-01-17. This propels her to a standing position, taking two cautious steps backward. Impossible, she tells herself. That was two months ago.

It's also two in the morning, and she is in the dark, the only light coming from her open laptop. Cleo's hand rises to her mouth, and she gasps for air. "No, I was on that plane," she murmurs. "This isn't real." But then she laughs. It's not a laugh she'd recognize as her own if not for having reacted like this once before. It is the same cutting response she had when diagnosed with young-onset Parkinson's. It's an incredulous, doubting laugh that presented itself without forethought. It was like a spell of protection, a protective reaction to an unspeakable, life-altering realization.

Cleo does the only thing she can think to do and pinches herself. "Ow," she replies to the pain. She rubs her cheek as the throbbing lingers. "What's happening?" She pulls her chair back to her desk, sits, and brings up a news site. The date is the same, mid-January. The stories are those she remembers. Grocery prices are heavily inflated, Prince Harry's tell-all book is causing a stir, Tampa Bay was just eliminated from the Super Bowl playoffs, a Republican candidate is accused of drive-by shootings, it's all there, the proof that she is not on a doomed flight from Kashmir to Johannesburg. Proof she is not under the influence of the pure oxygen rushing into her lungs.

"I know I was on that plane." She can hear the blood crashing against her temples. "I - I remember Cambodia." She pulls up her sleeve, looking for the tattoo from a vendor in Thailand. Not there. Then where are these memories coming from? How can I remember something that hasn't happened yet? She searches her memories and pieces together several adventures with her tour group where they visited ancient temples, sat in on family dinners with locals, and pushed through dense jungle in Quads. She didn't imagine all of that had happened - or *would* happen. Cleo stares at her screen. She reviews the trip details and shakes her head. It's all there. Everything she'd already done except South Africa. Everything she *has* done. And then the plane went down and - wait, am I dead? *Am I dead?*

Cleo picks up her phone and makes a call to her friend Trish. She might not answer, but she must call someone. She must know. 2:30 am. She won't answer. It's a work night — a Tuesday. I'll probably give her a heart attack, thinking something's wrong. No answer. Cleo hangs up. Then her phone rings. It's Trish.

"Hi, sorry to call," Cleo apologizes, a trembling hand hovering over her mouth.

"It's okay. Are you in trouble?" Trish's voice is gravelly.

"No, no, I mean, I - I'm at home; I'm fine. I just woke from a nightmare, and I'm just disoriented. I felt I had to call you." Trish was the first person Cleo told about her Parkinson's diagnosis. She's her oldest and dearest friend.

"It's okay, Hun. Do you need me to come over?"

"Oh, no, I just ... can you tell me what day it is?" Then, maybe Trish could confirm that the universe isn't conspiring to make her crazy.

"Uh, Monday, no, Tuesday now. January 17th?" Trish confirms her fears. Does she fear this reality? She should be grateful she's not on that plane destined for the Indian Ocean.

Cleo is quiet for a moment. "Okay, thanks, Trish; I'm sorry I woke you. I hope Dave isn't pissed at me."

"He sleeps through everything," Trish tells her. "Let me know if you need me, Cleo. I'm happy to come over."

"You're the sweetest, Trish. I'm okay. Just getting my bearings. Love you." Cleo says. Trish says it back, and she hangs up.

Cleo feels better after having spoken to a friend. That means she can't be dead. Still, this nagging feeling that she's already been on the trip that's not supposed to happen for another month is mystifying. She sees herself in her vanity mirror next to the monitor and decides she looks paler than usual.

She has memories of the trip but no physical marks to back them up. Maybe her mind is playing back all the travel videos she's watched over the past year and making them her own. That could be a thing. But, no, the impressions are too embedded. There are emotions connected to these memories. That woman and her baby on the plane. The sensation of floating above her seat. The deep blue of the ocean through the window of the aircraft. The transition from ocean to sky as the plane turned relentlessly in its death spin.

Even the trip itself. Four weeks of traveling abroad. Visiting sites she never thought she'd see, meeting people from all over the world. *It happened.* Of that, Cleo is sure. So how is it she's right back to where it all began? Cleo's eyebrows thread together as she struggles to understand this seemingly impossible trip back in time.

The plane ... she was having an out-of-body experience or something. Her brain took her out of the fear and placed her back here. It felt like an act of protection at the time. Is that the fight-or-flight response? Did she flee to a memory? Was it her brain giving her something to focus on amid trauma? Will it happen again? I guess that depends on whether I click on the *Book Now* button, she thinks.

Maybe I'm psychic? Perhaps I just saw the future. That's troubling. I don't want to know things before their time. That's terrifying. But if it could save my life, then it's not bad, right? Still, she returns to the memories. Could she have witnessed her trip in such detail? It doesn't seem possible, but what about this moment feels possible?

She recalls being brought back to this moment in her mind's eye as the plane went down and feeling the excitement, the keyboard, and the sensations of being on the precipice of confirming the trip. She could smell the coffee that sat next to her now. All of it was so real ... maybe she made it more real than what was happening to her. Perhaps she was sent back to this moment to cancel the flight and not experience the crash.

"No," she tells herself, "This has already happened. But, *Jesus,* am I losing my mind?"

"I know it feels that way," a sympathetic male voice from the recesses of her apartment whispers. Cleo wheels around in her chair, unsure of where the voice originated. She squints in the dim light to see beyond the shadows, her heart pounding against her ribcage. "Your first time is always the most bewildering." Still, no form associates itself with the voice.

"I'm hearing things now," Cleo gasps, "hearing voices isn't a symptom of young-onset Parkinson's." She's well-researched on the subject after receiving her diagnosis.

"It's not Parkinson's dementia either, Cleo," the soft voice reassures her as if reading her mind.

"That was my next guess," she replies, gripping the arms of her chair. She looks to her right, searching for something that might work as a weapon against this soft-voiced intruder. She spies her stapler and sighs.

"You'll be up all night guessing what's happened, Cleo."

"What, w-who are you? Are you, my conscience?" She jokes, but that's just another defense mechanism. She strains against the darkness and spies something moving beyond the small kitchen island.

"No, I'm not your Jiminy. I don't reside inside your head. You're not crazy, Cleo. You're – different."

"I am different. I know that. I've known that since I found out I have Parkinson's."

"Your disease won't define you now, Cleo. You've gone through a tremendous change tonight."

"You know what's happening to me?" An air of desperation enters her voice.

"I do. It happens to very few. And fewer still learn to tame the change and understand it."

"The *change?*" Her eyes are beginning to adjust to the dark. "Will I grow fangs and claws and howl at the full moon?" Humor works to deflect the fear in her heart.

The soft, masculine voice chuckles at this. "No, Cleo, you're not a werewolf. You're a time traveler."

This explanation forces Cleo to slump deeper into her office chair. Time travel hasn't occurred to her, and the suggestion makes her lightheaded. That's not a *change;* it's a superpower or magic or something.

15

Whatever it is, Cleo finds it difficult to relate. Time travel is for scientists and space operas. It's not for someone like her. She experiences a moment of elation followed by fear, and then she feels nothing at all. None of this is happening. None of it is real. Next, the voice in the darkness clears his throat, seemingly allowing her the time to process his absurd claim.

Considering it now, she thinks she could embrace time travel. Then she shakes her head and recalls the documentaries, books, and hard science that says time travel is impossible. Then she remembers all the fiction and movies that say otherwise. It's too big a concept.

"I know you're struggling with the notion, but consider the reality," he tells her as if *reality* is being discussed. "You were on that plane destined for the ocean when you pulled yourself out of that future. You did this, Cleo, not some other-worldly force. *You.*"

"H-how did I do this?"

"Let me explain. We all retain our memories. Not until we're stricken with Alzheimer's or dementia or suffer a head trauma do we lose that connection to our past. The past is an important teacher but also an important portal for those gifted to realize it. We're all, all of us, time travelers, Cleo. But when *you* remember a moment, you remember it with all the inherent emotions, senses, and minutia accompanying it. Not everyone is so lucky to recall so clearly their pasts. But one such as you can recall yours with crystal clarity. This is an essential tool for traveling backward in time. Intention is another. Eight weeks from now, the trauma of your flight drove you back to this moment. You visualized this memory when you decided to take that trip and imagined yourself taking a different path by not following through. You found yourself altering the future by giving yourself another chance."

"I remember feeling regretful of my choice on that plane. It was the most terrifying thing I've ever experienced, or – I guess, will experience."

"You don't have to experience it again if you don't want to. You're here now. So, you can deny yourself that trip."

"That seems like I'd be doing something wrong, like - what do they call it, altering the timeline? Won't that cause a rift in the fabric of time or something?"

The light laughter from the shadows eases Cleo's mind. "The future isn't written as such. You cannot affect the timeline if the future didn't happen."

She tries to put this concept into perspective. "So, I get a Mulligan?" Cleo uses a golf phrase to suggest a redo.

"Yes, in effect. Your ability offers you limitless Mulligans. But you must understand that there are minutiae you must accept with each redo now."

"Like?" Cleo is engrossed in what the voice is explaining, yet unsure she is grasping the full extent of this gift.

"You cannot return to a time before this moment. You are limited to now. That is the golden rule of time travel for those like us. None can venture further back than their initiation day."

"Is that what this is? My initiation day?"

"Exactly. And as with many initiates, I present myself and the rules." His tone is no longer sympathetic but rather more direct. "Today is your present and has only one timeline. The future is accessible only by traveling in a straight line."

"Geez, that's not at all confusing." She finds herself reaching for the stapler.

"Know that you cannot move further into the past than today. It is just the way it is."

"So, I can return to this moment when I'm ninety, and that's fine?" She's thinking out loud.

"Yes, this is your launching-off moment. You will forever be able to return here and make new choices."

"That's -" she shakes her head, "that means I could live forever."

"If that appeals to you."

Cleo stands and paces, not to look for the voice in her apartment but to burn off the anxiety she feels closing in on her. She could live a thousand different lives by making other choices from this moment and returning to now whenever she pleased. "Why do we have this gift of time?"

"It's no more known to me than why someone is born with the gift to paint or arrange music. It just is."

"How many of us are there?"

"Oh, not many. We are less than one hundred."

"H-how did you know to come to me tonight?"

"Our ability creates a singularity. It's harmless but leaves gluey energy within a city block of the event. The energy becomes denser the closer to the event horizon. I've known about this for days; the certainty of your return was promised."

"And you – what, you run the show? You find people like us and invite us into your group?"

"And why not? We are as unlike other humans as a star is to a flower, yet we are all made of the same stuff. Still, our gift does not come without its perils."

Cleo hears the warning in his voice, and it gives her pause. "I don't think I'll ever do it again, to be honest. It's – I don't even know if I *could* do it again."

"That you've done it once, you can do it again."

"How many times have you done it?"

"If I were to count the occasions I've repeated my last forty years, I'd be four hundred years old."

"Four hundred ... That's – so, you've mulliganed on your initiation day ten times?"

"Yes, well, more than that, and found eighty-seven of us in that time."

"Wait, that means I'm two months older than I should be right now?"

"Yes. Remember, time is a *human* concept. It's meaningless to you now."

Cleo goes back to what he'd said a second ago. "Eighty-seven people like us? Here?"

"No, all over the world. I enjoy traditional travel as well as time travel." Cleo can sense his smile and grins herself. "You will notice the energy now too. I didn't understand what it was the first few restarts, but once I did, I had no problem sensing the others and seeking them out."

"So, are you going to show yourself or remain lurking in the shadows?"

No more exceptional looking than any man, he steps out of the corner of her kitchen and greets Cleo with a shallow bow, removing a starkly white hat. An earthy scent accompanies him. Sandalwood, she determines. He may be over four hundred years old but doesn't look a day over sixty-something. He's African American, balding, with a few wrinkles to satisfy his age. He's dressed sharply in a tweed jacket over a crisp white collared shirt. His pants look neatly pressed, and his polished shoes take on a shine from the city lights entering her window. "My name is Franklin," he keeps himself at a distance.

Cleo nearly offers her name, but, oddly, this man already knew it. Instead, she asks at what age Franklin's initiation day was. "Not much older than yourself. I was twenty-five when I wished myself back to twenty-one."

"Is it common to be in our early twenties when we discover this?"

"It appears everyone's initiation day takes place in their early twenties, but some don't realize their gift until they're on their deathbed. But then, imagine their surprise when they wish themselves back to their youth. At twenty-five, I returned to my college days." Franklin takes a step toward Cleo, and she instinctively steps back.

"I'm sorry," she apologizes for this. "It's a reflex. You're a stranger in my home." She sets the stapler down.

"I hope we can be friends, Cleo," Franklin replies. "It can be a lonely life hiding this gift from your loved ones."

"I think I would like that," she says shakily and yawns. "Sorry, I'm exhausted, and it's a work night. I'd love to talk more, though."

"I'll see myself out. My card," he hands her a plastic card with a QR code. "Try not to lose it. Visit the link tomorrow when you have a moment. Set up your account, and I'll contact you soon after to continue our conversation. It was a pleasure, Cleo." He bows again with a hand over his heart, replaces the hat on his head, and leaves her apartment. The hat is a fedora, she concludes.

Cleo locks the door and crawls into bed, mentally, emotionally, and physically drained. She, not surprisingly, dozes off immediately, expecting to wake up with the realization that the last few hours were all a hallucination. Instead, she dreams of a terrible plane crash.

Time Travel FAQs

That morning, Cleo wakes early, the night before playing on her mind. She checks and rechecks the date. None of it was a dream. Not the trip she took, not the time travel. Not the kindly older man in her living room. How about that? She laughs cynically to herself.

At work, Cleo pulls up a new search tab on her computer, hiding it within a brochure design she's currently working on for a restaurant client, and searches *time travelers*. Wikipedia tops the list with 'Time travel claims and urban legends.' Here, she finds many strange accounts of accidental time travel, photographs depicting a modern-day-dressed man circa 1941, supposed cellphones in paintings from the seventeenth century, and those who took advantage of future knowledge in the stock market to make money.

Other links take her to those traveling from the future claiming nuclear war wipes out billions in 2025, a dabbing World War II soldier, the Greta Thunberg photo from 1898 in Canada's Yukon territory, a time-traveling Vladimir Putin, but nothing that could be genuinely classified as proof.

This is disheartening to Cleo. These classic time travel ideas suggest that a person from the future could arrive in the past or vice versa. Cleo's style of time travel seems to be less physical than it is mental and more restrictive. According to Franklin, if she decides to return to her initiation day tomorrow, she must focus hard enough on the moment, and she will blink back to her starting point.

She decides the only way to gather more information on her brand of time travel is through Franklin. She digs in her pocket for the card he'd given her last night and opens the camera app on her phone. She scans the QR code and is delivered to a link that is a blank page with a form fill to add an email address.

She types hers in, taking her further down the rabbit hole. It says, *Welcome, Cleo.* Franklin must have already entered her into the system. She clicks where it tells her to, and up comes a notice that she is leaving this site and would she like to continue. This happens twice before she arrives at a new destination hosted on a darknet address with an FAQ. Cleo's manager stops in to speak with her, and she turns her phone face down on her desk.

"How's the brochure for The Black Forest coming, Cleo?" Asks the tall, stern woman in the pencil skirt, white blouse, and teased hair. She's eyeing Cleo's phone accusingly. Cleo isn't a fan of Barbara's. She may be a little jealous of her height, but Barbara has become more conceited in the last year, making her less likable and could do with being knocked down a peg.

"I'm close, Barbara," Cleo answers, "I'm waiting on the client's revisions to their menu items but started work on the Glastonbury House brochure and -"

"Try to keep focused, Cleo. You're lagging." Barbara straightens up, her air of superiority ever-present, and moves through the other cubicles, sniffing out further perceived inefficiencies.

"You don't know how *focused* I can be," Cleo whispers, smirking and retrieving her phone. The site has timed out on her. There seems to be an excess of security on this website. For good reason, she's sure, but she suddenly feels unsafe being on it. She absently pops a stick of gum in her mouth.

Still, she's curious and returns to the site's FAQ section after jumping through the many hoops to arrive there.

- What happens to the future I left?

Answer: That future no longer exists.

- Is each future we experience part of the multiverse?

Answer: Not in my experience. Each future is like a candlestick. Before you've burned it down, you relight your initiation day with another. The former candle (future) is gone. It resides only in *your* memories.

- If we decide to live longer in the next future, will people recognize us from those other futures we lived in?

Answer: Unequivocally, no. Those other futures are gone, like the candlestick. Each future presents through choice. Your choices, combined with others, create a future that will never be repeated.

- Can I stop my friends or family from dying?

Answer: If your initiation day predates a death, you can affect the timeline however you desire by saving a life.

- Can I return to other memories after my initiation day?

Answer: No, your initiation day is the only time you can return to.

- Why can't we return to a time before our initiation day?

Answer: Undetermined. *Update* The working theory of closed timelike curves lends itself to our gift.

- What is the Grandfather Paradox, and does it apply to us?

Answer: If you were to travel back in time to a point before you were born and kill your grandfather, you would never have been born to travel back in time. Thus, the paradox. No, this does not apply to us, as we can only travel back to our initiation day.

- Can I take winning lotto numbers from one future and apply them to another?

Answer: No, one future's winning numbers will not occur again in another.

- What happens if I die?

Answer: You will be dead.

- What's the point of our gift?

Answer: That is a question we each must ask ourselves. Why does a doctor heal? Why does an entertainer entertain? Why are athletes competitive? Why have we been offered opportunities to relive our lives from a particular moment? Your purpose will present itself.

Okay, that's vague, but Cleo guesses it's the same for everyone. *Why am I here?* Great question. If I'm here to repeat my twenties through eighties, I'd better learn some deep shit like meditation and Yoga and maybe how to win at cards or take up rock climbing. If I can restart my life from this moment every forty years or every twenty-four hours and retain those memories, I could become anything. *Anyone.*

This thrills Cleo, and she shudders as a chill assails her. Why isn't Franklin the *King of the World* in this lifetime? Maybe he has already? The possibilities are endless.

To sum up, she can't jump ahead to the future and is restricted in how far back she can go. Franklin explained that each future is erased when she decides to return to her initiation day. In essence, it never happened.

There is no steampunk time machine she steps into, with dials and switches and levers to work, taking her from one point in time to another. No modified DeLorean or phone booth. She can't bring new technology back with her, not even a tattoo painfully etched into her flesh, but she will retain her memories of each future.

There are many more Frequently Asked Questions to read, and she spends the better part of her morning doing just that, all while under the judgment of Barbara's all-seeing eye.

Less than one hundred others share this gift. That would make it an anomaly. It's utterly rare. She wonders if others from the distant past have enjoyed this same gift. If true, are they still experiencing new futures limited to their time frame? If so, someone whose initiation day was 200 BC is trapped in a time loop and reliving their lives from their initiation day in that era. *How does that work?*

Cleo places her phone down and rubs her face with both hands to reboot her brain. This is all too much. She's no physicist. Oh, but she knows someone who is.

Bobby Patel – Take One

Does she tell her friend Bobby about her latest life event - doesn't she? Franklin hasn't connected again since she signed up on his website, and she wants another opinion on his concept of time travel. Not a *concept*, she corrects herself. It's not some abstract idea; it's a *fact*. It's happening. But she would be wise not to take that line with Bobby, the physicist. Cleo's sure he'll revel in the idea if he and his peers haven't already conceived it in his think-tank. And if so, it would be even more exciting to hear his thoughts on the possibilities attached to this 'concept.'

It's January 19th, two days after her initiation. She hasn't thought seriously about going back. She's scared to try. Time travel feels unnatural still. But, of course, it does. She feels at odds with how comfortable Franklin seems with it, but perhaps that ease comes from experience, making it less terrifying.

"Oh, hi, Bobby, it's Cleo. Hi, I'd like to bounce something off you if you can find some free time in the coming days. I know you're busy with your think-tank, and, oh, congratulations on that, by the way. I know you were hoping for a spot. I hope it's everything you expected: solving the world's problems. Uh, anyway, you have my number. Call me when you can. It's about time travel. The thing I want to bounce off you. Just curious about what you might think of my concept. Okay, thanks. Uh, bye."

Cleo hangs up and feels a warmth rise from her neck and fill her cheeks. She's embarrassed. That was the worst message I have ever left anyone; she berates herself. Bobby is a friend from high school who has won multiple physics awards and scholarships, and now this think-tank honor. He's a genius to the nth degree. The last time she saw him was a year ago when Trish, Bobby, and her got together over Christmas. But she's been in touch over phone, text, and video calls.

"Well, he's not going to call back," Cleo sighs as she moves through the clinic enroute to see her specialist.

There is a distinct scent in the clinic. Hand sanitizer is prevalent. Cleaning products, too. It's too sterile for her. She likes her essential oils. At the doctor's door, she rings the bell and is greeted by the receptionist.

"Hi, Cleo, take a seat. The doctor will be out in a minute."

Cleo nods and obeys. Doctor Ross is a neurologist specializing in movement disorders. He's a nice man, she's decided. Not terribly older than her, he looks in his mid-thirties. She notices her right hand has formed a fist and concentrates on releasing it.

"Cleo, good to see you, please," Dr. Ross motions for her to follow him. They enter screening room B, and Cleo takes a seat.

The doctor sits with his tablet on his lap and addresses Cleo. "So, Cleo, tell me how the last six months have been."

Cleo would love to tell him about the time travel but doesn't want him to think she's losing her faculties. "I've had a couple of instances where my hand tends to ball up and tremble the last two days."

"Okay, is that the extent? Brief tremors and muscle contractions?" He puts his hands out, palms up, urging Cleo to offer him her affected hand. She does, and he massages her palm, looking for whatever he's looking for. She nods yes; this is the extent of her muscle's betrayal thus far.

"Contractions are a symptom of the disease," he begins, wiggling her fingers on her right hand, "You say it's happened twice in as many days?" She nods again, telling him it had just happened in the waiting room. "Does it hurt?" she nods again. "With your young onset, it's likely limb-dystonia. Cramping and spasming of the hand." He asks her to resist his push and pull of each finger. Then, she is asked to mimic gestures he performs with his hand. She thinks she does an excellent job of it. "It's worth a DaTSCAN to check your dopamine." He looks up at her, releasing her hand. "To stay ahead of it," he winks, and she feels protected.

"How soon could that be done?" She cradles the affected hand in the other.

"I'll have Beth call you once the details are finalized. It shouldn't be more than a month."

The doctor then shines a tiny light into her eyes and asks if she's keeping up with her weight training and balance exercises. She appreciates the notes of spearmint on his breath and assures him that she is. She takes great pains to be proactive against this disease.

She thanks the doctor and nods at Beth as she exits the clinic. She can still hardly believe she's been diagnosed with such a devastating disease at such a young age. Yet, she's equally intrigued at how this appointment went slightly differently than the one in her original timeline. Minutiae, she thinks, make all the difference.

On the sidewalk enroute to the bus stop, Cleo's phone rings, and it's Bobby.

"Hey, McCarthy," Bobby's voice carries his trademark casual confidence, referring to her by her last name as he has always done. "So, what are you doing? Writing a book?"

"Hi Bobby, no, what? Why?"

"Well, the time travel concept you mentioned. You're writing a book, or your interests have far exceeded your intellect," he laughs. Bobby has always been this way. Confident, intelligent, sarcastic.

"Oh, right, *funny guy*. Always the funny guy." She replies to his sharp wit. "I think it would be a 'choose your own adventure' book more than a novel."

"I loved those books!' Bobby says, and Cleo smiles, envisioning little Bobby at nine years old, dark curls falling over his hazel eyes, lying on his stomach, knees bent, and feet kicking behind him as he devoured the pages.

"You're too cute," she says with the image in mind. "Anyway, I woke up a few days ago and wrote down this idea. When I reread it in the morning, it still made sense to me, and I wanted to run it by you," she lies.

"Let me have it. I have twenty minutes before I need to be back at it."

Cleo hadn't expected to explain it over the phone; she had hoped to meet at a coffee shop or pub, but if this was her chance to gain some new perspective, she decided to give it a shot. So, she arranges her thoughts and presents them as clearly as possible.

"Okay, um, does it make sense to you -" Cleo starts but is cut off by Bobby. "Let me preface this by stating I'm not a time travel theorist."

"Just let me get through it. You're the smartest person I know, and I want your opinion," she realizes her mistake in offering a compliment, but perhaps it will feed his ego to her benefit. Bobby is silent.

"You're going to let me complete a sentence?" She waits.

"You have eighteen minutes."

"You're an asshole."

"The smartest asshole you know." Bobby corrects.

"I'm never going to live that one down. Okay, so one day, you're, say, in the midst of a traumatic event, right? And you wish yourself out of it by recalling a memory of a past event to mostly soothe your nerves while your plane falls from the sky. Then you find yourself in that memory. You're there and not in the tumbling plane destined for a watery grave. You've transported yourself into the past."

There is no hesitation in Bobby's answer. "What I know about time travel theory is that going forward is more realistic than going backward," Bobby starts. "What with the speed of light and yada yada yada, sorry, that will take more than the sixteen minutes we have left to explain to a layperson. But that's the thinking on time travel. If it's not completely disregarded as a science, then it's a *maybe*, and that's a big maybe, that we might one day travel into the future. But the past is a no."

"So that's it? You're just killing the idea there?"

"Let me think. I'm sure I can explain it to you." There's that confidence. "Because time doesn't share the multi-dimensional freedoms our three spatial dimensions do; moving in any direction you like in the physical world, one would have to curve space-time to travel backward, which means theoretically, that you could only go back to when you first realized it was possible. Any further back than that, and I don't know, the universe might collapse in on itself." Bobby chuckles to himself and then falls silent, presumably contemplating his explanation. "I mean, time is a straight line, McCarthy. It has a current like a river. One directional. Turning it would take all the energy in the universe. It's just inconceivable."

"What you said about only traveling back to when you first realized you could, though. I dreamed that, too. You travel to your memory in the past but are denied going any further back than that one day, that memory," Cleo says, pacing within the bus shelter.

"Well, going back at all is unsupported, so it's a moot point. That said, it's interesting that you would have dreamed the science that says you can't go beyond a certain point. So, that's curious. Still, traveling back in time is a no, so the whole argument is lost."

"That *is* interesting, though, that I got that part right," Cleo says, her mind returning to Franklin's explanations.

"Sure, maybe you picked it up from a documentary you watched or, more likely, a B-movie."

"You suck," Cleo tells him. "I watch docs."

"About serial killers and unsolved murders," he knows her so well.

"Then how did I come up with not going backward in time beyond a certain point?"

"I can hear the hamster on the wheel through the phone, so I'm going to research your little conundrum and get back to you, McCarthy."

"I appreciate your time, doctor asshole," she says lightheartedly in response to the insult. "Maybe we'll get a drink soon."

"Well, I can't predict the future, but that sounds achievable," Bobby replies. "I'll let you know when I'm back in Chi-town."

"Bye," Cleo says and stops her pacing. He'll find someone more qualified in time travel theory and get back to her. He's good like that. He always follows through.

She remembers when she told him about her young-onset Parkinson's. Bobby became an expert on the disease. His outlook wasn't rosy but wasn't as grim as she'd feared. He's been an absolute comfort over the past few months. He'll humor her and get the facts even if he believes it is just a nonsense dream.

Bobby had said something that corresponded with what Franklin had told her: that time travels in a straight line. That and the shared idea that attempting to travel beyond her initiation day would be impossible gave her goosebumps. Franklin and Bobby's parallels have made this somehow more real for her. What had happened two days ago had actually happened!

"I should do it again," Cleo whispers to no one. "If I do it again, I'll know for sure."

Time Travel – The Research

That evening, Cleo sits in front of her thirty-two-inch TV and searches for documentaries, movies, and television series with a time travel theme. The list is staggering. The couch she's sinking into is from her last year in college when she'd rented a house with a few other girls. It was *previously loved* then. In fact, none of her furniture is new, save the mattress on her bed. Nothing is cohesive. The Art Deco dining table is her prize piece, given to her by an uncle renovating his condo uptown. She believes the other chairs in the living room are vintage velvet. Her desk and office chair are from the thrift shop up the street, and everything else is from the nineties. Not an exceptionally stylish nineties either. Very neutral. But everything has been thoroughly cleaned and restored to the best of her abilities – besides, she'll buy new furniture when she can afford a house.

While surfing what the television can offer, Cleo also searches for books on time travel with her tablet, and the list is equally immense. Should she watch and read all of these? Will they all share a commonality where time travel is concerned? Will they be rooted in scientific thought or based solely on the author's imagination?

Cleo decides against the undertaking but is inspired to rewatch Back to the Future, where the science of time travel is lightly touched on in the movie, so the experience isn't triggering.

She frees a bag of popcorn from its box and places it in the microwave. As the kernels begin to pop, her thoughts return to attempting it again. If she concentrates on that same memory, she should appear there. But then, according to Franklin, this timeline will have ended, and her phone call to Trish, the doctor's appointment, and her conversation with Bobby will all disappear. *Poof.* They will only be memories for her.

Whatever I decide, I must share this with Bobby in each timeline. He will help me make sense of it. The microwave wails, and she removes the inflated bag of popcorn, sits on her couch, and pulls a blanket over her lap. She starts the movie and takes pleasure in the lighter side of time travel.

An email interrupts her distraction half an hour into Marty and Doc's adventure. She frees her phone from the blanket. It's Franklin. She recognizes the darknet address.

He wants to talk. She replies that she isn't in the mood. He responds immediately, curious as to how she is dealing with her newfound gift.

"Currently, I'm not dealing with it," she responds.

Call me, he asks and gives his number. She decides she will. He is, after all, the only other person she knows who shares her gift. It would be silly to ignore him.

"Hi, Cleo," Franklin sounds animated.

"Hello," she replies.

"You sound withdrawn. Are you okay?"

"I'm confused, scared, curious, angry," she offers with a dark, comedic edge, "but not okay."

"I don't want you to fear your gift, Cleo. On the contrary, I want you to rejoice in our abilities. We're living proof that closed timelike curves occur in nature. Are we rare? Absolutely. But not impossible."

"I read that in the FAQs about the timelike curve, but I don't really know what it is," She replies coolly.

"Stephen Hawking would be scratching his head over our ability," Franklin continues, undeterred. "Hawking was sure time travel was impossible, stating that the laws of the universe would be such that they prevent any possibility of us. That any probability of creating a paradox in the timeline would go against universal laws "

"But if our futures disappear when we step back to our initiation day, then there is no possibility of a paradox, right?"

"Exactly, Cleo. What physicists fail to see is that time travel is far more intricate than the arrow of time or a singularity warping spacetime. With it comes new laws that govern time travel. That we still exist in this physical plane tells us that these new laws work within the parameters of the natural laws controlling our day-to-day."

"Are you a physicist?" Cleo wonders. Franklin laughs lightly at this.

"I've tried more than once to master physics but lack the necessary intellect. I can't retain the mathematics required to imagine how we can use this gift without suffering any of the accepted consequences."

"I have a friend who is a physicist. He works at a think-tank. He's brilliant." Cleo shares. "I've mentioned our condition to him - in theory. I haven't told him this is happening to me, just that I had this concept of time travel."

"And he's looking into it?" Franklin sounds cynical.

"Yes, and he mentioned not going back beyond a certain point, too," Cleo leaves the answer hanging, unsure how to finish her reply.

Franklin breaks the silence. "But, to what end? I don't see how it can help us."

"Knowing is enough. I'm having a difficult time believing my own story. If he can give me some science to back up our gift, it would make me feel more at ease. I won't return to my initiation day unless I get something I can hold on to."

"Remember, we can offer no proof to anyone. No letters we write in the future will reach anyone. That future is no more. No one can travel with us by holding our hand," Franklin pauses, "trust me. I've tried."

Cleo sits up, the blanket falling to the floor, pausing the deployment of a popcorn kernel into her open mouth. "You've tried bringing another person back in time with you?" She senses there are many more layers to peel back concerning Franklin's experiences than what he's shared in the FAQs.

"My wife, Marla ... in another life. We were both so old. She knew everything, and she agreed to come back with me. So, I began the process, hugging her tightly, and returned to my initiation day ... without her." Cleo remains quiet as he recounts his heartbreaking story. "The worst thing about it is knowing that life had never truly happened: that my wife and I hadn't fallen in love and that only *I* will be privy to those memories."

"That's an awful story, Franklin. I'm so sorry." Her hand settles over her heart.

"It is one of my rules as laid out on the website." His tone has turned to stone. "Don't fall in love. Unless you're willing to die for that life, you will carry the memory of a future that never really happened."

Cleo feels gutted by this admission and selfishly imagines herself in his position. Could she bear it?

"The only real future is the one you perish in." Franklin asserts. "I sometimes still wish I'd chosen to stay with her in that life. But that life cannot be repeated."

"Have you not tried to find her again and again?"

"Each time she slips through my fingers," silence. "Perhaps a love like that is only meant to be experienced once," he defends. "I'd have happily died in her arms. But, instead, she haunts my memories and remains out of reach in each new future scenario."

A stillness permeates the atmosphere. Cleo's blood runs cold. She's been in love once, but it was unrequited. To experience reciprocal love is the envy of all. To be so connected to another person must feel like magic. Now, would she ever know such love? Not if she were to become like Franklin. Not if she were to commit to time travel.

"I'm sorry if my story has tainted you against our gift. It is not something to be taken lightly, but it is a *gift*, Cleo ... and a choice."

"Then I choose not to."

"And that is your prerogative. But don't deny yourself the incredible opportunities to live other lives. Learn and experience things you couldn't in one lifetime."

"I'm getting a mixed message here," Cleo tells him.

"I am only warning you off certain pitfalls. Love is one of them. I was lucky to have lived a full life like that with the woman I loved. I know that. But repeatedly living in timelines where she exists out of reach is torturous."

Cleo picks up that he's alluding to the minor details of each new future we tackle, meddling with the outcomes. That's why you can't bring a winning lottery number back with you or make the same person love you. "I'm going to wait to hear more from my friend. I'm not jumping into this without some research behind me."

"That's smart, Cleo. Whatever you decide, I only mean to educate you. What you do with that information is up to you. Be cautious with whom you share this, however. You may want to live and die in this life."

"Right," Cleo feels very much at odds with her gift. That she may fall in love or decide to keep her distance from others only increases the unease she feels. "I'll keep it limited to my friend, the physicist."

"If that goes south, you must return to your initiation day. That way, you will have killed that possible future."

Franklin sounds deadly serious, further embedding the apprehension she's experiencing. "I'll be careful, Franklin. You can trust me."

"The others are counting on you too, Cleo. We're all in this together."

"I understand," she doesn't, not really. The implications of time travel and killing future timelines are too new for her to truly understand. Closed timelike curves and the arrow of time feel like advanced stuff. But if she doesn't understand it, she isn't going to jump, and that's that.

FRANKLIN

Franklin hopes he hasn't complicated the issue for Cleo with his sad story as he walks to his car from the restaurant where he'd been chatting with Cleo from his private booth. It's never far from his mind and forever in his heart. It was a difficult lesson and one he wouldn't wish on anyone. Moreover, it distresses him to think she never truly existed – his wife. *That* Marla and that entire future blinked out of existence once he jumped back to his initiation day. That it has been so challenging to reconnect in any meaningful way with her in his other lives has broken him.

He enters the back, passenger side of the car, and is asked, 'Where to, sir?' Franklin knows he's lucky. Luckier than most. His lifestyle is lavish by others' standards. But he remains humble in spirit. He doesn't trust himself to drive at his age. Macular degeneration in his left eye prompted him to acquire a driver. A shame as he loves to drive.

They travel to the lakeshore community of Winnetka, where his home faces Lake Michigan off Sheridan Road. Pretentious? Perhaps, but it is what he aspires to in every life. Financial security to manage all the international travel when searching for those like him. His career as a financial analyst has always succeeded in producing this lifestyle.

Cleo is an interesting girl, he ponders. But there is something more to her; of this, he is convinced. Perhaps this friendship will uncover the riddle that has plagued him all these years.

Time Travel - The Trigger

She jumped. Cleo jumped. She's back at her computer. It's January 17th, 2023. This time, the sick feeling in her stomach erupts onto the floor beside her desk. She stumbles to her feet and fetches a glass of water and paper towels. When she's completed the cleanup, she spies Franklin standing in her darkened apartment, and they have a new conversation.

"I'll always be here when you return to your initiation day," he explains. "I was here the first time; therefore, I will be here every time."

"I-I don't know how I got back here," Cleo starts, anxious over having come back. "I was on the bus, what, three days from now, going to see my friend, Bobby, the friend I told you about. Or I will tell you about. Or, I guess I'll have to retell you about him since that future is a burner." Oh my god, this is ridiculous, she thinks.

"Did something happen?"

"Yes, the bus was cut off by some yahoo in a burgundy pickup truck," she explains breathlessly, "we hit a light pole. I remember standing, ready to get off at my stop, and then I was thrown through the air."

Franklin clears his throat. "When you returned here the first time, were you experiencing a traumatic episode?"

"Yes, I was in a plane plunging to earth on one wing." She says this matter-of-factly as she rinses her hands in the kitchen sink.

"Ah, then trauma is your trigger. When you experience trauma, you will almost always return to this memory by default."

"Wait, so if I cut myself, I will end up here again?" Cleo is drying her hands on a tea towel.

Franklin laughs lightly at this. "I doubt a cut will trigger you. No, more a life-threatening scenario."

"How do I stop that?"

"You'll have to work on that. See a psychiatrist."

"But you told me to be careful -"

"Yes, yes, you don't have to explain all that," he waves off her concern. "Mention that trauma brings you back to a memory you'd rather not relive. They will give you tools."

Cleo is beyond frustrated by this unforeseen hurdle. She was about to get somewhere with Bobby on time travel. He said he wanted to speak to her in person. Now, she has to go through it all again.

"You've only lost three days," Franklin approaches cautiously to appease her. Unfortunately, Cleo's energy is not conforming to Franklin's soothing tone.

"Yes, but those three days were about to produce information." She's pacing between the kitchen and living room, frantically rubbing her hands together.

"Three days is nothing; believe me, you can refocus. It's not like you just lost ten years," Franklin's tone begins to produce the calming effect as intended.

Cleo sees how this might work in her favor. She's learned a lot in the past three days and retained all of it. Now, she can offer Bobby a more detailed explanation of her concept and get a little further.

"I think I can make it work," she says, and Franklin visibly relaxes his shoulders. "Still, we need to catch up."

Cleo tells Franklin of their initial meeting, the event that triggered it, Bobby, and how she wouldn't jump back to her initiation day until she had more information. Now that she has, she will approach Bobby again, but with a better understanding of what's happening to her.

Bobby Patel – Take Two

Bobby isn't answering his phone and not returning her messages. This is unexpected, and it goes on for days. Finally, Cleo realizes she must return to her life and start living again. She goes to work, creates marketing materials for clients, takes lunches with coworkers, and spends a night in a pub with a potential suitor from a dating app. All of this is background noise to the question racing through her mind. *Where are you, Bobby?*

Cleo's hand tightens into a fist on her way home from the bus stop. It hurts this time. Her muscles are staging a mutiny and flexing their independence. She tries to assert control over the action, but whatever is supposed to carry the message from her brain to her hand is glitching.

Cleo grasps her right hand with her left, hoping to massage the muscles into obedience. The idea that this will happen to her entire body one day is unfathomable. To her throat muscles, complicating swallowing. What kind of life will that be?

Doctor Ross has mentioned medication that will help ease the spasms, but from her own research, she's discovered that Parkinson's is a relentless bitch bent on turning your muscles against you. But that could be years away. It's why she took that trip. There is no guarantee of a tomorrow where she has complete control over her body.

But that's in the past now. The future past. A possible future that only she remembers. God, it's all so frustrating.

Cleo is getting nowhere with her hand and thrusts it into her jacket pocket. Twenty-four and already experiencing the effects of young-onset Parkinson's. It's not enough that she will be battling this disease for the rest of her life, but now she's a time traveler too. It's ludicrous, really, and she barks out a laugh.

January is not her favorite month. The chill, once you've caught it, is difficult to shake. With Parkinson's, Cleo has an increased sensitivity to the cold. As a result, her limbs sometimes get and stay cold and can even ache. It's early days for that, but she read the symptoms, and sometimes that's enough to convince her it's happening. Steam billows out of her mouth as she sighs against the pain in her fist.

Suddenly, Cleo senses a presence as if emerging from a mature maple growing out of the sidewalk. She turns, and just as quickly, it vanishes. She shrugs it off, but not before the sound it made recalls a memory. What did they call that when an old television was on a channel with no transmission signal? Static noise, or white noise. A blurry blizzard of static noise dipped behind the maple tree as if following the kid with the headphones set to Deafen. It wasn't like it just resided in her head. Instead, it filled the space around her.

The incident forces a shiver, and she feels the need for a hot bath.

At home, she runs the bath and checks her laptop for emails. Two from her parents she should answer sooner than later. They worry she's living in Chicago while they're an hour and a half away by car. They worry about the disease. That they won't be available to help when she needs it. So, Cleo downplays her symptoms to keep them from worrying.

Nothing from Bobby. Trish sent a link to a Parkinson's patient's YouTube channel, *PD Patty*. She'll look at that later. She usually sends informative but lighthearted links Cleo can feel good about. Trish is the best. Cleo follows everything Michael J. Fox on PD as well. At twenty-nine, he was diagnosed young, too, just five years later than her. Fox is PD's celebrity ambassador.

Her hand has released its grip on itself, and she shakes it out. Pins and needles follow.

Cleo slides into her scalding bath, allowing the heat to seep into her bones. As she closes her eyes, the snowy image returns to her memory. She recalls how it willfully slipped behind the tree when she took notice as if the kid with the headphones had a ghost attached to him. Cleo's memory of the event sharpens, and she tries to put a form to the snow.

Her eyes open as she considers the familiar silhouette. *Was it human?* She saw the tree trunk blur as the rest moved behind it. She sits up in her bath and rubs her eyes, steam enveloping her.

Admittedly, Parkinson's can affect a person's eyesight. Blurred vision and even visual hallucinations are well documented. But that's in cases where the disease is well-established in the patient, and other symptoms are rampant. Moreover, she's only just begun this journey. Oh, she hates that term: *the journey,* as if she should look forward to it.

Cleo doesn't connect her vision to the disease; she decides. No, whatever it was, it was there. It was focused on her but attached to that kid. She shivers despite the hot water.

She will address this sighting with Franklin.

Cleo shaves her legs next. She notices her hand tremble and wonders how long before she is considered disabled. Will she let herself get to that point? Will she jump back to her initiation day each time her Parkinson's worsens? What kind of a life would she have once it's fully entrenched? Perhaps this gift of time travel will help her live better in the short window she has before things get worse. And to jump again and again, avoiding the inevitable.

But that's what Franklin's doing, too. He's evading death by living his life over and over and over. She supposes that's what the others are doing, as well. But each must have their reason. Whether that reason is merely to cheat death as long as possible or to learn as much as they can is anyone's guess.

Cleo's phone rings, and she puts the razor down, picks up her phone, and presses it to her ear. "Hello, Trish," she says, moving a collection of bubbles to the side.

"Hi, Hun," Trish sounds like she's been crying. "I've got some bad news, awful, really," her breath is shaky on the intake. Cleo suddenly feels sick to her stomach. Trish isn't a crier.

"What's happened, Trish? Are you okay?"

"No, well, *I'm* okay. I'm not hurt or anything," she explains, "it's Bobby, Cleo. He's dead."

This doesn't feel real. She can't process something like this right now. It can't be true, but why would Trish lie to her? She wouldn't. And not about Bobby being dead. No way. So, that leaves her with the real possibility that Bobby is gone. Or maybe she got it wrong.

"You're wrong," she exclaims. "You're wrong, Trish."

"I wish I was, Hun. Ben, his brother, just called. It's been three days. They're having the funeral next Saturday."

"No," she loves Bobby. He's one of her oldest friends. A trusted friend. One who also may hold the answers to her new ... development. If he's gone, then she's lost all of that.

"I'm sorry I'm giving you this news over the phone, Cleo, I'm not in town but thought you should know right away." She sniffs on the other end.

'How?" Cleo manages as if it mattered.

"Ben said it was a fluke incident at a corner store. A robbery. Somehow Bobby got shot," something catches in Trish's throat. Cleo can hear the pain in it.

"Oh, Trish, oh, Jesus," Cleo cries now. They share a moment of grief over the phone and cry together.

She thinks; I don't want to live in a world without Bobby. I can't. She knows how much she leans on him even though they don't live in the same zip code. How could this life rob her of him?

She jumps.

Bobby Patel – Take Three

January 17th, 2023, Cleo is beside herself. She's confused over whether the nausea she feels is because of the jump, Bobby having died, or both. Whatever the reason, she races to the bathroom and empties her stomach. Soon after, she explains to Franklin what has happened and her terrible loss. He is at her side, consoling her.

"Because it happened in one future life doesn't mean it will happen in this one," he relays. "You saw that in the original jump."

Cleo nods yes. "I know, it's just so raw. I need to call him." She stands and looks frantically for her phone. Franklin lifts it from her desk and hands it to her.

She calls Bobby, and despite the late hour, he answers.

"Cleo, is everything all right?" Bobby sounds a little stunned. Cleo falls onto her couch and exhales. "Was that a sigh?"

"I just needed to hear your voice," Cleo tells him, then laughs at herself. "Is that weird? It's weird. I know it is." A smile is stamped on her face.

"I won't argue with that. I don't have the vocal stylings of a James Earl Jones or anything," he laughs tiredly.

"What are your thoughts on time travel?" She decides not to waste a minute of her time with him. Bobby is alive and being his witty self, and it's three in the morning.

"Have you been into your pot cookies?"

"No, it's – I have a thing. I have to know what you think." She's up and pacing the apartment.

"It can't wait, huh?"

"No," she insists. She explains what's happening to her and how it came about. She's decided to hide nothing from him. She describes the three futures she's already experienced, even the most recent in which he dies. Bobby isn't fond of that one, and he tells her so but lets her continue mostly uninterrupted.

"It's your lucky day, McCarthy; it just so happens that I attended a think-tank conference on this subject."

"No shit," Cleo leans forward, back on the couch, and Franklin motions for her to put Bobby on speakerphone. She obliges him.

"Your theory wants to combine the concept of a closed timelike curve and the arrow of time. You say you remember your future memories, but memory is irreversible. To say we remember the past, not the future, is based solely on the only fundamental irreversible law: the second principle of thermodynamics. Simply put, if you removed yourself from that future, your memories of it should not exist.

"Even if you were experiencing a closed timelike curve, in theory, you wouldn't return to the past with memories of the future."

How in the shit is he this coherent at three in the morning? "But I do have memories of them, Bobby. I remember the month vacation, the plane going down. I remember my bus accident, I remember you being dead, I remember them," she defends.

"This plane will go down when?" Bobby asks.

"Uh, well, if things were to pan out as they had in the other future, then on March 17th it would crash."

"But, to your point, even minuscule changes mean that there's no guarantee this future will go that way," Bobby states.

Cleo suffers a sudden conflict of conscience. "Wait, should I warn the airline that the plane will crash?"

"No, if there's one fictional rule I think is worth observing about time travel, it's that you don't bring future knowledge to the past."

"But it's the moral thing to do," Cleo looks at Franklin as she says this. Franklin shakes his head.

"Yeah, but what if the next Adolf Hitler is aboard that plane? Your warning could unleash a monster upon the world." Bobby's point is taken.

"Right, and that rule is included in the website FAQs," Franklin adds.

"Website?"

"Yes, I created a website on the darknet to offer a set of instructions to those like Cleo and myself," offers Franklin. "To help them navigate the difficulties of time travel."

"Can I see it?"

"I don't see why not," Cloe looks at Franklin again, who shrugs. "But, be warned, it's not scientific. Franklin's no scientist, but he has a lot of experience to draw from."

"Experience trumps theory every day of the week," Bobby admits.

They take Bobby through the site, read the rules together, and Franklin answers his questions as best he can.

"What is written is learned information but holds no scientific merit," Franklin admits. "As Cleo said, I'm no scientist. My years dedicated to time travel are all I have to pull from."

"What I'm struggling with, Franklin, is the math. Mathematics would explain time travel to the past with your memories intact if possible. Furthermore, it has explained the potential for time travel to the future through Einstein's time dilation if we were ever to travel at the speed of light or even 99% the speed of light. So, the simple fact is that if the math isn't there, it's pretty much a moot thought," Bobby takes a breath. "That being said, you're both telling me you are living proof that this is happening. But the proof is locked in your own experiences. So, I must take it on faith that what you're telling me is fact."

Bobby can be heard scribbling on a whiteboard with a squeaky marker. "That we developed mathematics to understand our universe means that mathematics was applied to the creation of everything long before we ever discovered it. That means scientists at the end of the universe have already looked at traveling to the past and said, nope. Not today. Not ever."

"So, God is a scientist?" Cleo teases to lighten the mood.

"If there is a God, there's no question he s a scientist," Bobby says, becoming increasingly more invested in the conversation.

"Are you a Creationist?" Cleo jokes.

"The longer I spend in a think-tank, the more I realize that none of this could have just popped into existence without a plan. It's all too precise. It's all too perfect."

"I guess that makes me the mole on the face of a Ms. Universe," Cleo is being playful with her old friend and missing him more and more.

"What about the futures we've lived? How can they live now only in our memories?" Franklin asks.

"In your example, there are no shared futures. Each future path you take, you take alone. Only *you* will ever know it. Everyone else in your life, Cleo, me, your parents, wife, kids, we'll know only the future you chose to expire in."

"Or does everyone experience life alone?" Cleo poses. "Do I exist at all in your future? Am I just a thing you play off while navigating the world alone?"

Bobby makes an amused sound. "That's deep. That's think-tank deep, McCarthy."

Cleo ignores the compliment to stay on track. "What's that saying?... Everybody *dies* alone. Maybe everybody lives alone, too."

"Time travel has expanded your mind," Bobby declares. "If I needed proof, there it is. McCarthy: Designer turned Philosopher."

"I wish you could experience what we experience, Bobby," Cleo says, her tone more somber, more suitable for the discussion.

"I'm not sure I would want it, Cleo," he replies to her surprise. "I'm afraid it would drive me crazy. The nuanced differences to each future. You might find I won't remember you the next time you jump back."

"I hope that doesn't happen." She says earnestly. "It was bad enough you'd died in one. That's why I came back."

"That's sweet, McCarthy. Maybe you live out this future, and we don't take that risk again."

"I think I can do that," she says with a genuine smile.

"Good. Because I'm enjoying this life," Bobby laughs, and Cleo joins in. Franklin doesn't.

FRANKLIN

Bobby interests Franklin immensely. His sharp wit and sharper mind will significantly assist in understanding their gift. Though he'd previously studied physics, he admits his mind is not wired to retain or even understand it. What was it Einstein said? *'If you can't explain it simply, you don't understand it well enough.'* Or something to that effect. Bobby seems gifted with the ability to dumb down highly complicated concepts.

Yes, Bobby is a patient young man, and if Franklin's not mistaken, he should be of great help in solving his own riddle. But, it's good to keep some things secret, not to come off as sinister - lord knows his thoughts would sound the part if spoken aloud. But a friendship is, after all, a two-way street. So, while he helps Cleo understand her new gift, he'll stay close in the event the two of them can explain the riddle presented to him so long ago in more straightforward terms so that he may act.

Well, enough of that, he thinks, and wishes Bobby well as they end the call.

White Noise

After saying goodbye to Bobby, Cleo asks Franklin to join her on the couch. "Aren't you tired of jumping from life to life?"

"Honestly, Cleo, I should have ended it with my wife." His head hangs low between his bony shoulders, and he rests his elbows on his thighs, a slight bend to his long spine.

"The truth is, it's very addictive. To cheat death and keep learning is an opportunity relegated to very few in my experience. So I don't know if we should deny it." His head shakes.

"But what happens to Bobby and everyone when we jump? He said he's enjoying his life. Is it fair for me to leave this future, and he blinks out of existence?"

"It's not so dire. Everyone turns up in the other futures one way or another."

"I don't know," Cleo is on the fence, "I feel like I'm the only one playing a role in my life now. It's like other people are just there to fill space while I live my life. What effect do I have on their lives? What's the point -"

"The point is for you to live as many lives as you can," Franklin answers abruptly, his fingers interlaced and forearms still resting on his thighs. "It's not about them. It's about *you.*"

"You can't believe that. Not after the future life with your wife. She deserved to know you like that, and now that's gone." Cleo says, all at once embarrassed for bringing it up.

It takes Franklin a moment to compose himself. "I believe we have this gift to live for ourselves *because* of that life. It was a lesson. It was a hard lesson, but I learned it. Now, I have passed that lesson on to you and the others."

Cleo wonders whether he genuinely means what he's saying when she suddenly senses the white noise return, pinpointing its origins beyond the window that oversees the street below. Cleo stands suddenly. She can hear the static fizzling accompanied by a blur of activity, again unsure whether she's imagining it.

Franklin slowly rises, eyes locked on Cleo.

"What is it you're not telling me, Franklin?" She asks slowly, captivated by the blur that embodies the white noise.

"What do you hear, Cleo?" He asks carefully, rising from the couch slowly. "Be very specific."

"White noise," she tells him. "It's..." she swallows hard, eyes narrowing, "like the presence of a snowstorm attaching itself to me."

Darting her gaze toward the couch, she sees that Franklin doesn't flinch at the description, leading Cleo to think he knows about the white noise.

"And does it speak to you?"

"No, what? It's just white noise." She whispers, feeling frozen in place. Is it gait freezing – a symptom of Parkinson's, or is she afraid to move for fear of what the thing buzzing in her ears and blurring her vision might do if she stirs?

"They emit every frequency across all spectrums of audible sound." Franklin offers, crouching in front of the couch.

"How do you know that?" her eyes dart back to him.

"Because I have captured the sound and run it through a series of EVP recorders. That's Electronic Voice Phenomenon. What's also called a Spirit Box for ghost hunters."

The hairs on Cleo's arms stand on end at this description. "I'm not saying the white noise is emitted by ghosts, only that an EVP is a means to gather information on them." He insists.

Cleo relaxes as the presence disappears, replaced by the early morning sun reflecting off the windows of the building across the street. The tension in her legs lessens, and she crumbles to the hardwood. Her heart is pounding, and her head hurts.

Franklin takes a tentative step toward her. "The blurring of space-time you saw, I've seen them too. I needed to hear your explanation to ensure you saw what I've seen. Heard what I've heard." He sits on the couch, hovering over her, Cleo rising on her palms, looking up at him.

Franklin looks like he's attempting to tame a wild animal, his hands defensively leaning into her. She sits up.

"Maybe you should mention that on your website," she says, exhausted. "It might have helped had I known static blurs would be dropping in on me occasionally."

"I'm afraid that may do more harm than good. Cleo, you're the only other gifted individual I've met who has experienced these phenomena."

FRANKLIN

So, Cleo is gifted not once but twice. First, the ability to time travel, and second, to act as a receiver of the messages he's convinced are coming from another time or place.

He must stay close. That means he further embeds himself into Cleo's life. That will include Bobby. The more that is revealed, the more Franklin realizes that these two may hold the key to his future – deciphering his age-old riddle through their combined efforts. If what he hopes has truly begun, then it won't be long before they piece his puzzle together, and he can act.

Conjecture

That morning, Cleo is at her specialist to attend the appointment she took two lives ago. Two lives ago, she repeats to herself. It's absurd. But it's her reality. That's been proven now. No question. She can travel back in time. *Suck on that, Universe.* She smiles as she sits in the waiting room, but it's a pained smile.

Dr. Ross goes through the motions with her, checking reflexes and motor control. He's not unhappy with her six-month checkup, but Cleo brings up the issues she's been experiencing with her hand.

"Should I just start on the medication?" she asks as the doctor manipulates her right hand.

"It's only happened twice ... this functional disability?" Cleo nods. "And it hasn't lasted long?" She shakes her head.

"Maybe five minutes at most," she replies. "But I just – I don't want it to get worse." Her gaze falls to the floor.

"Cleo, you know how young-onset Parkinson's works. It will progress, but keep up with your exercises and stretches, and if the occurrences become more frequent, we will review medicating on your next visit. Okay? Keep a journal of each event." He gently places her hand on her arm, and Cleo looks up. "I don't want to start you on something when you're only experiencing very occasional involuntary movement and tremors."

"Why?" Her voice cracks.

"Because the medication is hard on your body. It can lead to other issues. Cleo, you're experiencing mild dystonia right now, but putting you on Levodopa or something similar could lead to more severe issues like dyskinesia." He looks her in the eye. "You're managing the disease right now. You're doing wonderfully." He lifts his tablet from the small desk, and his fingers work madly at it.

"Do you think in another life they've found a cure for it?" Cleo asks, wondering if she jumped back endlessly and researched 'Parkinson's cure,' she would one day end up in a life that had eradicated it.

"Conjecture isn't my strong suit, Cleo, but when I feel we need to implement medications that improve your quality of life, I will. *Trust me.* That said, I don't see a need for them at the moment. Besides, a cure could be just around the corner. Stay positive. This disease could be cured in your lifetime." He assures her, still working on the tablet.

In your lifetime, she repeats in her head. It's a death sentence as far as she's concerned. She's only twenty-four. With young-onset Parkinson's, your life expectancy is only another thirty years. It needs to be cured next year so she can live a normal, long life.

"So, we'll see you in three months, Cleo. Beth will call you with an appointment time. Keep a journal of your episodes. As detailed as possible. We will address all your concerns and consider treatment plans if necessary then."

"Thank you," Cleo says more out of a sense of civility than gratitude, standing and exiting the office, nodding to Beth at reception. Then, walking toward the bus stop, she considers her question to Dr. Ross. Maybe in another life they will have cured her disease. But to jump that much without knowing ... she feels suddenly spent.

On the bus ride home, she nearly nods off. In her apartment, she decides to take a bath, where she further contemplates how to live a life that is slowly robbing her of her freedoms. If she wasn't granted this gift of time travel for a greater purpose, like saving a plane full of people from a terrible death, she should at least be allowed to use it for personal gain. And not for monetary reward but just to rid herself of Parkinson's. It's not a lot to ask. Besides, as the FAQs stated, a winning lottery ticket in one future will not occur again in another. The details of each timeline prevent such events.

Cleo receives a video chat from Bobby and takes it. She disables the camera on her end but can see Bobby clearly. His handsome, dark features look quizzically through her screen.

"No video share?" Bobby asks, screwing up his face as if that will persuade her.

"I'm in the tub, Bobby. I'll spare you," she replies, sinking further into the warm water. "But it's nice to see you. Your beard looks distinguished."

"I'll just have to imagine yours then," he laughs. But, of course, no one thinks Bobby is as funny as Bobby does.

"I'm happy you called. Is this a social call, or have you found a scientific way to prove my gift?"

"Always business before pleasure with you, McCarthy," Bobby replies with a playful smile. "I have asked my colleagues about your gift, without mentioning my friend thinks this is happening to her. I didn't want to come off as crazy."

"Of course not,"

"So, we talked about the arrow of time. That's the second law of thermodynamics in action. Where from order, you get disorder." Bobby is animated on screen, sets his phone down, steps a few paces back, and illustrates an example on his whiteboard. "An instance of this is when you whisk an egg to make your omelet; you've added disorder into the closed system that was the initial egg."

"I get thermodynamics," She's read up on them since their earlier conversations in other futures. "But now I'm thinking breakfast for dinner," Cleo jokes.

"Let me get through this, McCarthy," he says with amused disdain, "Entropy is an important consequence of thermodynamics. Just as an arrow is loosed, it travels in a single direction, which we witness as time. You can't expect an omelet to turn back into an egg. The second law of thermodynamics, *nature*, traps us in this straight line."

"There's a *but* coming, I hope," Cleo says, listening more intently.

"*But*, in the quantum realm, they did manage to de-age a qubit one-millionth of a second through a computer-generated model. I know it doesn't sound like much, but that they did it at all is a first step. It's the equivalent of pushing back the ripples in a pond, returning them to their source."

Cleo is quiet for a moment, searching for the point. "So, you're saying it's not impossible."

Bobby laughs. "Right, *you're* not impossible, McCarthy. In a million years, someone might manage to travel back in time with their memories intact of a future that will collapse on itself the moment you exit it."

"A qubit is what?" She attempts to filter through the nonsense.

Bobby releases an audible sigh, puffing out his cheeks like a blowfish. "A normal computer uses a basic unit of information called a bit that is either a 1 or 0. A quantum computer uses qubits which are both 1s and 0s."

"Why?"

"To enhance their processing speeds exponentially," he says dryly. "But you don't need to know all of this. I'm happy that the qubit was de-aged - or traveled back in time in a quantum computer. It means it can happen on an infinitely small scale, so maybe it could happen to you."

"It *is* happening to me, so thank you for your research. I mean it, Bobby. It helps me come to grips with this."

"I always said you were one of a kind, McCarthy."

"So," she deflects, "you don't think we're living in a computer-generated program, and I'm some kind of blip?"

"That's a subject for another time," Bobby rubs his eyes.

"Let's get that drink soon," she insists, and Bobby agrees.

"I'll be in your neck of the woods in two weeks; my parents are having a thing. I'll call you to arrange a meetup. Enjoy the rest of your day, McCarthy." Bobby winks and disappears.

Cleo is left with the knowledge that the most intelligent person she knows thinks she's not impossible. That's more than she can say for her ex-boyfriends.

Pseudoscience

"I've held seances in the past to draw out the phantoms," Franklin says as he unpacks his equipment in Cleo's apartment. "Your static blur." He struggles with a tripod. The three legs fall to the floor in unison with a crack, and Franklin jerks back, clearly agitated.

"You never told me – did you have any success?" Cleo is hopeful for an affirmative. It's late, and though she is optimistic this equipment will bring her more answers, she's hesitant to know more.

"Nothing, no," Franklin's expression is grim as he wrestles with a cord. "That's why I was excited to hear you had experienced them the other day and heard the static they emit."

"Static is what, again? All frequencies happening all at once?"

"Yes, static is just background radiation leftover from the Big Bang, and when you aren't in range of something stronger, like a radio or TV signal, that's what you get, static. White noise." Franklin passes Cleo the untied cord and motions for her to plug it in.

Cleo does so and asks, "And this equipment is supposed to do what? Sort through the noise and pull a signal?"

"If the phantoms are trying to communicate with us through all that noise, the EVP should filter out all the crap and give us some structure," he lifts a small box from a case on the couch.

"I know what Bobby would say about this," Cleo says, standing. "Pseudoscience." Franklin waves the comment off.

"He would also disregard your claim about the white noise, but we've heard them. He hasn't." Franklin affixes the EVP box to the tripod. "But your Bobby is a scientist, and science will only get you so far. There's a quote I love from Nikola Tesla: *If you want to find the secrets of the universe, think in terms of energy, frequency, and vibration.*"

"And he was a scientist!"

"He was," Franklin straightens up to address Cleo, "but he was also a very spiritual man. Another quote of his is even more appropriate for what we're facing: *The day science begins to study non-physical phenomena; it will make more progress in one decade than in all the previous centuries of its existence.*"

"Deep," Cleo admits. "Fair to say he was ahead of his time."

"So," Franklin has completed his setup and takes a few steps back to review his placement, "we'll leave these here." His hands frame the room. "I'm going to ask that you push this button," he waves Cleo over, "when you see the blur interrupt space-time. Let it run and ask direct questions such as Who are you? What do you want? Are you here to help me? That sort of thing."

"And supposedly, they will answer?"

"If they want anything more than to merely observe you, I suspect they will answer," he pulls on his coat and wraps a scarf around his neck. "If they don't, your experience will be much like mine. Whatever that might mean."

"Do you think they might be from another time?" Cleo moves a rogue strand of hair from her face.

"Perhaps," he places his crisp, white fedora with black band - wholly unsuitable for the weather - over his receding hairline. "The honest answer is that I don't know. I hope they will give you more than they've given me."

"Well, maybe this stuff doesn't work on them?" Cleo suggests, opening the door for Franklin.

Franklin turns to her, and she catches a hint of garlic on his breath, briefly wondering whether he fears the white noise vampires. "As I said, I've held seances, employed Ouija boards, motion sensors, taken thermal photography, paid psychics, and mediums, but none penetrated whatever realm these phantoms reside in. And to be fair, I've tried EVP too. I trust you will have better luck."

"I'm a little nervous. Isn't this how the ghosts in Poltergeist pulled the little girl into the television?" Cleo wipes her sweating palms on her sleeves as a chill overtakes her.

Franklin releases a sharp chuckle.

"Well, what if they *do* answer me?"

"Then you will know immediately. Watch the video I sent you. It will explain how everything works. This is the best of the best in EVP technology. It will assess the responses buried in all that static and deliver them as distinct words."

"Maybe they don't speak English?" Cleo's mind is running through every possibility as to why this might fail.

"Typically, with ghosts, they tend to know the language of the places they're haunting. Whatever these beings are, I suspect they are far more advanced and would be learned in the language of the places they are frequenting."

"Good point," Cleo nods, and Franklin excuses himself. "I'll text you if I get anything." Then, she is alone, and the sensation casts an unwelcome shadow overhead. She rubs her upper arms and walks toward the equipment situated between her living room and kitchen. It's silhouetted against the window as the lights from the adjacent building bleed into her apartment. This was the last place she experienced the white noise outside this window. She palms the window. It is ice-cold. She pulls her hand away and places it in her front pocket.

"What are you?" She asks into the night. "Why me? What am I meant to do with this ... gift?" She flips on the EVP, and the white noise discharges from it as if searching through a range of frequencies. Cleo jumps back, a hand at her mouth and one on her chest. She drags her hand away from her face slowly. "W-what do you want with me?" She stammers.

The static forms words, "Find - us," the 's' in us carries on for a few seconds, and then the static returns. Cleo takes three steps backward. She doesn't see a phantom, as Franklin refers to them, but she has no question they are using the EVP as a medium.

"W-who am I to find? How?" Her face flushes, and she feels vertigo encroaching.

"Us ... him," the static replies. It sounds terrifying, and she fights off another chill, but a *Happy Birthday* greeting through an EVP would sound chilling, Cleo reasons. She wants to push the button to record this session but fears losing the connection.

"Who are you?" Cleo hugs herself tightly.

"Others," the static voice answers, and she approaches the EVP, pushes the button Franklin had pointed out, and steps back quickly. "Others? Who are the others?" Nothing. "I can't find someone if I don't know who you mean?" She waits, the hairs standing upright on her forearms, but there is no more. Her teeth are chattering, and she closes a hand over her mouth to stay the chatter. Then her window blurs and she yelps into her hand, moving back, catching her heel on the foot of her couch, losing balance, and dropping hard to the floor. She bounces her head off the hardwood and blacks out.

What Comes Next

"I need a vacation," Cleo tells Bobby. "I need to get away." They are at a pub in Chicago's South Loop neighborhood, waiting for Trish to arrive two weeks after her EVP incident. The atmosphere is picking up as the college crowd shuffles in in groups of desperately underclad young women for February and young men who have clearly been pre-drinking.

Bobby nods to where the frigid draft swoops in from the open doors. "I remember those days," he says as if it were a decade since they'd graduated.

Cleo looks at him like he's crazy. "We graduated like three years ago."

"You did," Bobby corrects her. "I just graduated last spring."

"All the more reason you shouldn't feel so far removed from this lifestyle. And no one forced you to get your Masters," Cleo says, filling her mouth with beer. The numbing effect of the alcohol is starting to relax her. She feels it in her face first, then as it travels to her extremities.

She hasn't had a night out in ages. After the scare with the white noise and the resulting concussion, she has been more present for work and nothing much else. The phantoms hadn't returned, and she had Franklin remove the equipment from her apartment with little to no explanation. Finally, he obliged and didn't push. She's grateful for that. She'll tell him what happened eventually, but for now, she wants to feel normal.

"Oh, I failed to mention another time travel scenario eerily like yours. I don't know why it slipped my mind," Bobby says animatedly. His fingers drum down on the sticky table. "There is a theoretical physicist who has the most amazing back story," he waves his hands in front of himself to refocus, "anyways, he has developed the math for what he calls a ring laser," He looks at Cleo with an intensity that almost scares her.

"Ring laser, that sounds very sci-fi," she replies with a nervous chuckle.

"Crazy sci-fi, but with the math to theoretically back it up. It's based on Albert Einstein's theory of general relativity that says anything with energy also has gravity, even if, like light, it's massless." Bobby rearranges four coasters on the table to have them create an open square. "This ring laser is basically four mirrors set up on the four corners of a square, and the lasers are fired around them forever. This physicist likens these circulating beams moving the space within the square to a stirring spoon moving the coffee in a cup." Bobby's finger circles the interior of his makeshift ring laser. "So, the spinning space inside the ring laser is being twisted, and if you have enough energy behind the spinning, it will twist space-time into a loop. So, you could create loops in time by circulating laser light."

Cleo snaps her head back and shakes it. "I'm not using laser light to do anything. How's that anything like what's happening to me?"

"Hear me out, McCarthy, Christ; you only ever want the punchline."

"Sorry ..." she draws out the apology and motions to the server, ordering another two pints. "Please, continue,"

"You're not even going to remember this conversation, are you?"

"That will be my last drink. Promise," she holds three fingers up as if she were an Eagle Scout, grinning.

"Okay, this is where it becomes more like your situation in that you wouldn't be able to travel further back in time than when the closed timelike curve or loop was created." He leans in and smiles widely at her. "Like *you*, McCarthy! You can't travel further back than your, what did you call it? Your Big Day?"

"Initiation day," she corrects him and leans in, smiling maniacally back. Their faces are inches apart, and she can smell his cologne and the beer on his breath. The pair produce a tingling sensation in her chest.

Bobby doesn't lean back; he leans nearer to Cleo and bumps foreheads with her. She pushes back with hers, and they laugh. Bobby kisses her forehead, and they part.

He's never kissed her before. She decides she likes it.

"We'd briefly discussed the timelike curve, but when reviewing it in more detail, I read that part about not being able to jump back beyond the invention of the machine or initiation day in your case. Then it hit me. That's just how you explained it to me."

"Huh, I guess Franklin knows what he's talking about." She lifts her fresh pint, and they clink glasses.

Trish pulls up a seat next to Bobby in the booth, brushing snow off her shoulders and removing her winter wear. She shoulders Bobby over, and he shifts to make room.

Cleo notices she's looking at her with a mischievous smirk and then winks at her. "Sorry I'm so late," she drawls. "The kids refused to acknowledge their babysitter tonight. It was exhausting. What did I miss?" She asks with a raised eyebrow.

Cleo realizes Trish must have witnessed the forehead kiss. That would feel awkward any other time, but she's just nicely buzzed and couldn't care less. She grabs Trish's freezing hand, and Trish kisses hers as if absolving her of any wrongdoing. Trish leaves her hand in Cleo's and squeezes.

"We've solved time travel over our first pint," Cleo explains giddily, "what should we cover next?" She looks back at Bobby, who waves at the server and points at Trish.

They order a few hot wings, a large salad to share, and a Gin and tonic for Trish. When Bobby excuses himself for the bathroom, Trish leans into Cleo across the table and asks the burning question.

"So, Bobby kissed your forehead? What was that about?" She leans back to give Cleo space to tell the story.

"Oh, I don't know, nothing, I guess," Cleo explains unconvincingly.

"Stop it; that wasn't nothing! It was *something*. Something I may remind you, we had decided a long time ago never to do." She's right. As the Three Amigos through high school and then visiting each other tirelessly through their individual college experiences, Trish and Cleo vowed never to make a move on Bobby. But she hadn't made a move; Bobby had.

"You're not angry with me, are you?" Cleo asks innocently. "I mean, we're full-blown adults now. You're married. It was harmless."

Trish reaches across the table, and Cleo takes this as a request for her hands. Trish holds both of Cleo's in hers. "Oh, I'm only interested, Hun; I'm not calling you out on the vow," she laughs. "That was ages ago," It was.

"And you're happily married, right?"

"Right, yes, of course. Is he gone on business more than ever? Sure. But we're happy."

"Besides," Cleo continues, "Bobby was just being affectionate. You know how he can be. If he's not a sarcastic asshole, he's playful. It's just been too long between visits."

"Then I'll expect my forehead to connect with his full lips at some point tonight." They laugh at this and part as Bobby returns.

"Jesus, was it always this dark in here?" He slides next to Trish, and she polishes her forehead with a napkin, winking at Cleo. Cleo laughs out loud. "Seriously, I nearly missed a step going down to the bathroom."

"It's always been dark, but I don't remember it being this crowded," Trish adds, taking a cautious sip from her glass. The food arrives, and they devour it over lighter conversation.

Cleo catches herself staring at Bobby in a different light. A fire in the corner illuminates his large, caramel eyes. His light brown skin glows as she watches his strong, now bearded, square jaw chew slowly. Of course, he's handsome; she and Trish have always known that. But they kept him at arm's length to avoid losing him to a breakup. Is that what *Bobby* wanted, though? He'd never been included in the vow they'd taken as fifteen-year-olds. It seems suddenly outdated.

Cleo makes a satisfied groan as she considers new possibilities with Bobby. Both Bobby and Trish hear her and look at one another, laughing. "Good wings, McCarthy?" Bobby asks comically. She's slightly mortified but nods her endorsement. She hopes they believe it was only the wings responsible for the outburst.

At the end of their night, Bobby and Cleo hug Trish goodbye. Cleo came with Bobby in his rental car, and he agreed to drop her off. Trish winks again at Cleo, arching her brows and making a kissy face. This only serves to make Cleo blush.

In Bobby's car, Cleo lets the hum of the street below her lull her into an even more relaxed state. She bends her neck loosely to look at Bobby's upright posture at the wheel and smiles giddily. Could she invite him up to her place for a nightcap? How would he take it? The thought sends more tingling sensations through her body.

The moment arrives when Bobby is pulling in front of her building, and she tries to act casual, as she would have in past scenarios like this. "Wanna come up for one more?"

Bobby notices the nervous energy that carries the question over her teeth and past her lips. She's sure of it. The delivery was too direct. There was no silliness to accompany it. But - shit, had she raised an eyebrow? Bobby nods and tells Cleo he'll park in the visitor's spot. The tingling intensifies.

In her apartment, she excuses herself to the bathroom. "You know where the hard stuff is. Help yourself." She splashes cold water on her face and looks intensely in the mirror. She's okay. It's okay, she tells herself. Whatever happens, happens. When she exits the bathroom and turns the corner to join Bobby in the kitchen, he has two glasses on the counter with the bottle of Jägermeister next to them.

"Don't be shy," she tells him, "Jäger doesn't scare me. Pour away." She stops and notices the way Bobby is looking at her now. Hungrily. He's resting both hands on the island countertop. Leaning in and narrowing his eyes, he licks his lips.

"What's stopping us, McCarthy?" He asks boldly.

"Stopping us from what?" she knows damn well what.

"Come on," he pleads. "Come here." She does, and as she rounds the island, Bobby pulls her into him at the waist and bends to kiss her. She accepts his kiss, and they sink deeper and deeper into it. It feels like years of pent-up sexual energy is being released. Finally, she pulls away briefly enough to take his hand and lead him to the bedroom, where they expend the remainder of that energy.

What Comes After

The next day, Cleo realizes Bobby has left her apartment in the night. That's fine, she thinks. He didn't have to wake up here. She recalls the passion of last night and wonders if he would be interested in repeating it. He lives four hours away by car. Would they try for a long-distance relationship? Was this a one-night stand?

The questions have her out of bed and into the kitchen. She sees the bottle of Jägermeister and the two unused glasses on the counter and smiles. She fills one from the tap and drinks it down thirstily.

This is what it means to be alive, she thinks. As she goes to put the glass down, her hand trembles. Her grip on the glass tightens, and she holds her trembling wrist with her other hand. This scares her, and she shouts at her disobedient muscles. The bottom of the glass hits the counter hard and shatters. Then, her grip tightens into a fist, crushing the glass in her hand. "No!" She shrieks.

The trembling ceases, and her hand releases the shards of glass. Some remain embedded in her palm and fingers, and through tears and painful squeaks, she pulls them out one by one.

Blood is everywhere as she recognizes a memory trying to surface. It's the one where she's sitting in front of her computer that night, reconsidering the trip. She shakes her head no; she won't let this minor trauma trigger a jump into the past. She's accomplished so much now. She's learned so much, and then there's Bobby and what happened. No, no, she tells herself to stay present, and the memory fades.

Cleo moves to the bathroom, pulls a towel from its place, and rinses her hand in the sink. Next, she wraps the wounded palm in the towel and applies pressure. She hopes she won't need stitches. She sits on her couch and squirms against the pain still in her Christmas-themed nightshirt, now spotted with blood.

A text comes through, and she retrieves her phone. Her heart jumps at the sight of Bobby's contact. She taps on the chat and reads.

Hey, Cleo, it reads. That's weird, she thinks. He rarely calls her by her first name. But maybe the intimacy shared last night is forcing a change. She can live with that.

Listen, Oh, *shit*, she thinks. *Listen?* That's not good. **Last night was a long time coming, no pun intended.** Is he being funny or indifferent? **You know me. I'm not a relationship guy. It's just not in my DNA. I hope that's not going to be a mindfuck for you. But I think you know me better than anyone. I don't want to put words in your mouth, but I want to**

be straight with you, Cleo. We're friends. If you want to make that 'friends with benefits,' let's have that discussion. But you know better than to get mushy with me. At least, I think I'm right about that. Cleo's heart is in her stomach, and a wave of anxiety overcomes her better sense.

What Bobby is saying is true. She knows who he is. So why is she so disappointed reading this text? He'll be a bachelor his whole life. It's his plan, so why does she think she could change him? She cherishes their friendship. Is that in ruins now? She couldn't be happy without Bobby in her life. *This was a mistake.* That's what he's telling her. She knows it, too. It was a mistake.

Her hand is pounding, the wounds amplifying her heartbeat. She peels back the towel and counts three significant cuts and four small ones. She thinks she sees tiny glass shards brightly burning under her skin. It's gruesome. Blood continues to pool in the larger gashes. She turns away from the scene and forces herself to read the remainder of Bobby's text.

Last thing I want is to mess up our friendship. It means too much to me. Xo. But it *is* messed up, she thinks. They'll never be like they were. Not anymore.

Tears run down her cheeks and soak the collar of her nightshirt. But then, something catches her attention by the window, where she sees the blur of the white noise buzzing, sending vibrations through her body.

"No!" She screams at the image, gripping her hand tighter. The static noise emits its obnoxious sound through her phone lying on the dining table. She feels a deep regret taking hold. Sleeping with Bobby was a life-altering mistake. Cleo feels that in her bones, and these lacerations will render her useless at work for weeks. And now the phantoms have returned. The memory of January 17th – nearly three weeks ago, surfaces with perfect clarity and purpose. She surrenders to the image, wishing the morning away, allowing herself to jump.

Back at her desk, she breathes in the coffee and instinctively checks her hand. No puncture wounds, no blood. She bends her head to her desk and cries. Weeps. She'd lived, and now she had to start all over.

When she regains her composure, she swallows her nausea and acknowledges Franklin. "I know you're here, Franklin," she manages through her grief. "We've done this a few times." She hears footsteps emerge from the kitchen.

Franklin asks, "How long?"

"Maybe three weeks." She blows her nose and dabs the tissue under her swollen eyes.

"I'm sorry, Cleo," he offers. "It's never easy to jump. Were you in distress?"

"I made a terrible mistake with a friend," she admits to him.

"You won't make it again, of that, I can assure you," Franklin's tone is calm and comforting.

"I learned a lot more about our condition. Our gift," she wants to tell him how right he was about the closed timelike curve and about the ring laser, how the puzzle was starting to come together.

So she does. She explains what she's learned and the EVP experiment he and she set up in her apartment. Then, she reveals her conversation with the phantoms through the EVP.

"That's fascinating, Cleo. Thank you for telling me this. They have been silent for me, but it appears they are desperate to talk to you." He sits on the couch, and Cleo joins him.

"They said they wanted to be found," Cleo explains, "referring to themselves as others. Does that make sense to you?"

Franklin takes a deep breath through his mouth and looks at Cleo. "Others..." it comes out as a sigh. "No, nothing comes to mind." His brows raise, and he scratches his five o'clock shadow. He stands next, pacing the hardwood in the dark.

"The EVP worked for you," he reasserts. Cleo nods. "And you say they answered 'Him' when you asked how you should find them?"

"Yes ... I mean, I think so. There was still white noise accompanying the words." Cleo is still somewhat preoccupied with her recent jump. It's a mindfuck, to use Bobby's description of their ruinous one-night stand. Is she really creating a closed, timelike curve or loop to achieve this?

"They couldn't be referring to other people like us, could they?" Cleo wonders aloud. "The white noise."

Franklin turns abruptly to face Cleo, his eyes burning with an intensity she has not seen. "Why would the phantoms want us to find the others? I've already done that."

"Maybe you've missed some?"

"Of course, that's certainly possible," Franklin openly admits, his slender fingers rubbing at his dimpled chin. "But if there are others, they could be anywhere in the world."

"Then should you go looking again?"

"I'm one person, Cleo," he says, returning his attention to her. She watches a plan take shape in Franklin's expression and shakes her head no.

"I have a job. I have a *life*. I have to be here," she says, anxiety rising.

"You can take vacations, can't you? I need you, Cleo. They need you. Maybe the phantoms will disappear if we find more like us. I'll pay for you to travel if you will agree to it."

"Where?" The memories of her passenger plane plummeting to an icy grave assaults her memory.

"You could go anywhere you choose. You just need to trust your intuition. When you sense a heavy energy, follow it. Let it be your guide. It will lead you to others just as your initiation day singularity led me to you."

"H-how will I know what that feels like?"

"You will feel suddenly heavier as if gravity is turning on you. It will be a gentle nudge at first. So, you will need to intuit it. But once you've established the sensation, you can follow it."

"And then I feed them your speech?"

"Something like that. I'll prepare you. Lead them to the website, and then I'll take it from there."

"Rome," Cleo says definitively. "I'd like to see Rome." Her heart soars at the realization that this is happening. Perhaps her purpose mirrors Franklin's. To travel the world in search of others like her. She could see every corner of the globe, experience every culture, and taste every culinary delight. She could do it all.

"Rome," Franklin grins widely. "Then let's get you a ticket to Rome."

FRANKLIN

Though he feels for Cleo, her most recent jump has given him a recruit to help locate others like them. It is a portion of the riddle he is trying to unravel. Perhaps Cleo will be more than just a new friend.

She'd told him he'd lent her his EVP machine to listen to the phantoms. She has an excellent start, which should prove helpful in understanding the puzzle he's been presented with.

Her friend Bobby has researched their gift extensively and given him much to ponder. His theories seem to align with what science suggests might take a traveler back in time. He feels closer than ever to revealing the riddle he has yet to decipher.

Rome

Rome. Cleo can hardly believe it. She's walking the open ruins where Emperor Trajan's column still stands, erected to celebrate the Roman victory in the Dacian wars. Her feet retrace steps ancient Romans once took. Umbrella pines line the streets, offering shade to those seeking it and pine nuts for your pesto. The link to the past here has a depth all its own. Chicago is a newborn compared to Rome; it is the eternal city. The subway has been simple to navigate as there are so few lines. Each time the Romans attempted to expand, they ran into ruins. She places sunglasses she purchased from a tourist hut over her eyes as the Roman sun warms her skin under the new leather jacket she acquired at the airport. It's not hot, but the February sun teases the summer months ahead.

Franklin had explained to her his rules of tourism for the time traveler. First, buy what you need when you arrive at a destination—no need to carry luggage and look the part of a tourist. It's best if you blend in. The places a singularity might take you may be difficult to maneuver if you're seen as anything but a local.

Cleo senses nothing more than the euphoria she's experiencing being here. Even when she'd decided to travel to Asian countries in her original timeline, Europe had always been a close second. So, having taken that tour of Thailand, Cambodia, Vietnam, and India in that life, Europe made sense in this one.

Franklin also mentioned the importance of learning the language, if possible, before traveling abroad. After spending three intensive weeks before taking this trip on an online course, Cleo considers her Italian quite passable. She found in high school that Spanish came easy to her, and she's retained much of her four years of classes. Italian didn't seem so different.

Rome is a very walkable city, she's decided. Perhaps it is her youth, but she finds navigating the streets and bridges easy. She has been to the top of Castel Sant'Angelo to enjoy a wonderful meal with an inspiring view of the city, the River Tiber, and the Vatican's St. Paul's Cathedral. There, Cleo enjoyed wine with lunch in the company of an over-eager seagull watching patiently from the narrow vertical aperture in the ancient, fortified wall.

She is truly on vacation and immerses herself in the experience. Yet, Cleo frowns over the fact that each destination she experiences will live only in her memory. As much as she wants to snap pictures with her phone, she knows they won't return to her initiation day with her. She wonders about the human brain's capacity to store memories. How many times could she start again and recall each life?

As she moves through the Trajan forum, she runs her palm along a marble block that had fallen with its pillar long ago. Time stands still in a place like this, she thinks. The past is tangible here. You can taste it in the food, wine, and water. The endless garbage bags that pepper every residential street and their combined scent are off-putting, but as she understands it, garbage pickup has been the bane of Rome's existence for decades—that and the constant transit strikes she is currently experiencing. Still, Rome's romantic side prevails in the parks, fountains, cafes, and restaurants serving classic Roman fare. The scent of pizza and coffee are equally present day to day and keep her ravenous.

Cleo spent a fair bit of time in the airport before taking the train into the city, where she bought three outfits, pieces she found most representative of what Roman women were wearing. She's glad she did. The women here are dressed beautifully, and with her tall, lean frame and dark black, shoulder-length hair, Cleo blends nicely. Her pale complexion hints that she is not a native Roman, but plenty of ex-pats live and work in Rome.

Hours later, crossing over the River Tiber on one of the many extravagant bridges, she pauses to look down at the rushing waters. She breathes in the cool air through her nose, filling her chest, holding it for a moment, and then releasing it through her mouth. She is full of gratitude for this opportunity. Whether anything comes of finding another time traveler, she is confident that this experience and those to follow will be life-changing.

As she turns to continue her approach to the Piazza San Pietro, St. Peter's Square, where the faithful and curious gather to listen to the Pope's sermons, Cleo feels a peculiar tug in her gut. She places a hand on her stomach and prays she's not having an adverse reaction to her breakfast. Then, she remembers Franklin's description of encountering a singularity. *'You will feel suddenly heavier as if gravity is turning on you. It will be a gentle nudge at first.'*

Can this bizarre sensation be her intuition telling her another traveler is nearby? It feels different from the nausea that accompanies her with every jump. She decides to meet the sensation, turning back on the bridge, retracing her steps, and remembering that the closer she gets to the event, the heavier gravity will feel.

Could she be so lucky to have found someone on the brink of their initiation day three days into her trip? It seems unlikely, with Franklin having found less than one hundred in his four hundred years. But perhaps they are more common than he thinks. Cleo feels the pull of gravity on her shoulders next, and it nearly topples her over in front of a group of young, black-robed Vatican priests moving quickly across the bridge. First, she feels the breeze they leave in their path, their ankle-length cassocks swooshing past her. Then she feels a force drag her along in their wake.

There is a singularity amongst them. As much as they look alike: black hair, olive skin, silver crucifixes swinging from their necks, one is not like the other. A smile follows the inside joke as she tries to keep up with the gravitational pull, nearly tripping on a raised cobblestone. She realizes she's still gripping her stomach, but the nausea has disappeared, replaced by this weightier sensation bearing down on her.

Cleo feels dizziness enter, blurring her vision. It's like when the white noise blurs space-time. She's not enjoying this. A wave of warmth envelops her then. The scent of the city disappears, and she feels as if a forcefield has descended upon her. In his more detailed telling of the symptoms attached to this experience, Franklin explained that calm would eventually overcome her the closer she came to the singularity.

Cleo pushes back her shoulders and straightens her neck. She continues to follow the seven priests as they blaze a path over the bridge and turn abruptly left. A homeless man watches with great interest from his station beside a low-lying bush against a stone wall. Cleo has pulled away from the priests and toward the impoverished man. It's not one of the young priests experiencing the singularity. It's this man brushing his beard with a plastic comb missing too many prongs to be useful.

Cleo lands in front of him, slamming into the dry grass with her knees, startling the displaced man. "Scuza," sorry, she says, embarrassed over her clumsy approach, head feeling heavy again.

"Andare via." go away, he mutters, flinging his hands at her. Cleo's head is down, and her palms push against the earth. She studies the man's ruined footwear. "Risparmia una moneta?" Spare a coin? He asks, changing tactics to take advantage of the intrusion. Cleo barely pieces together his Italian.

Looking up, she wonders how a man like this would master time travel. He smells of garbage. Cleo gets to her feet, but the weight of the space is still upon her. Something is going to happen here, she thinks. He mumbles more, shuffling forward with his palms upturned, but it is incoherent in any language. Still, she places two euros in his hands.

"Sai chi vive qui?" Do you know who lives here? Cleo asks in broken Italian. The corner is well stocked with wooden pallets forming two make-shift walls, a filthy blue tent, what appears to be a couple of bags of clothing, a hibachi, and several blankets.

He pounds his chest and says, "Vivo qui," I live here. This is difficult for Cleo to accept. That this drifter might jump back to this spot from a future she can only guess at seems unlikely. Does he have the capacity to visualize this moment in time to make it his initiation day? And how awful is his future if this is where and when he would prefer?

"Dammi di piu," Give me more, he insists, pulling rogue beard hairs from his black tongue. Cleo looks into his dark, chestnut eyes, trying to find some common ground.

"Io sono, Cleo," I am Cleo, she asserts, pointing at herself. "Come ti Chiami?" What is your name? The man's head tilts like a dog's might at a question. It's very possible he no longer knows his name, she considers. How on earth will I ever express to him his gift or pull any information from this person?

"Sono senza nome," I am without a name, he tells her. "Sono senza posto." I am without a place. He taps a gnarled finger against the soiled earth beneath him. That statement sends an unwelcome chill through her.

"Uh, viaggi nel tempo?" Do you travel in time? Cleo asks, curious about how he'll answer. But he cackles loudly and turns one rotation as if explaining how he might do that. Cleo smiles sadly at the man. Perhaps he's not the source of the singularity she's sensing. She moves through the space while the little man looks on in amazement. Cleo feels strange being so forward, but she must know. Something is about to happen.

The stone wall only comes up to her chin so that she can see the raised green space beyond. A couple sits at a bench, a woman reads on a towel, and a man walks with a grey pug. Several others are moving along the sidewalk, approaching and departing the bridge. Cleo feels the weight of the singularity upon her again. Her sight blurs, panicking; she stumbles from the displaced man's plot and rounds the sidewalk, moving up into the green space.

Cleo's head is spinning now, and she kneels on the grass. A large umbrella tree places her in shadow. Then everything changes. Her vision rights itself, the spinning disappears, and gravity pulls back. She stands surveying the area. She's looking for confusion on the face of the time traveler. It's not the couple engaged in a kiss. It's not the man walking the pug. The people on the sidewalk move energetically, undeterred by the effects of time travel.

The woman on the towel, however, is throwing up.

Kindred Spirits

There is a chill descending upon the city now. A wind pushes past Cleo as she tentatively approaches the woman seated on her towel in the park. She is recovering from vomiting a moment ago, her gaze thoughtfully evaluating the landscape, blanket, and book. Cleo pulls a tissue from her purse and kneels next to the woman.

"Mi scusi, posso offrirle un fazzoletto?" Pardon me, can I offer you a tissue? She asks in a gentle tone. The woman looks up at Cleo and shakes her head, her large, blue eyes assessing her. She's frightened. I get that, Cleo thinks. The woman's expression illustrates confusion. Seated on a towel in a park or not, your initiation day is no picnic.

"I – I don't speak Italian," She replies weakly. "Uh, non parla Italiano?" she accepts the tissue and wipes her mouth. Cleo is glad not to have to explain this in Italian.

"I'm Cleo," she tells the woman who looks two or three years younger than her. She notices that the young woman has an English accent and wears a colorful spring jacket and jeans. She's heavier than Cleo and taller, too.

"I'm, uh," her pretty eyes widen as she struggles to recall her name. "I'm Doris," she says, slowly processing her whereabouts. "Thank you for the tissue."

"I'm going to tell you something, Doris," Cleo starts sharply. "Something that may shock you at first, but it will make sense when you realize you're not where you were a moment ago."

"You know where I was?"

"I know you weren't here," she nods slowly, forcing Doris to nod as well, mouth agape. "You were in another time. Maybe years from now. You remembered this moment and returned to it. Didn't you?"

"I -" Doris looks down at her hands, her tight, blonde bun pulls against her forehead as she furrows her brow. "How?"

"You're a time traveler, Doris," Cleo says. "So am I." She places a calming hand on Doris' shoulder. "We are drawn to each other's initiation day. Someone visited me at mine, and I'm here, with you, for yours."

"Initiation?... I'm not a *time traveler*. That's impossible. No one can do that. I'm not that." She scans her whereabouts again, a panicked expression overriding the confused calm of a moment ago. Cleo's hand squeezes down on Doris' shoulder in an attempt to ground her.

"Where were you a moment ago, Doris?"

"Dreaming, I guess," she wants to make sense of it. Of course, she does. Cleo remembers the terror and confusion of her initiation day.

"No, you weren't. You were living your life until some trigger sent you back to this moment, this memory," Cleo explains. "You're not losing your mind, Doris. This is happening, and I'm here to help you navigate it."

"I was playing with my daughters in the front garden," she says as if removed from the memory. "A lorry lost a wheel," tears well up and fall from her round, rosy cheeks. "Oh, my god, my girls," she looks like she's about to cry out. She stands abruptly, hands trembling, and Cleo stands with her. Doris' head is turning this way and that as if she needs to return to that life, that memory.

"No, no, no, the lorry, it came at us," she's crying and shaking now, and others are starting to notice. Doris is gripping Cleo's leather jacket at the lapels.

"That future never really happened," Cleo tells her to settle her nerves. Something clearly devastating had occurred. Doris looks directly into Cleo's eyes.

"What do you mean?" Her grief is palpable. It's starting to make Cleo uncomfortable.

"Whatever just happened - that future is gone. It's like it never happened because you're here now."

"My girls," she says, no more comforted by the thought that her future never happened. "What do you mean?"

"I mean, you have a chance to prevent that future now. You remembered yourself back to this moment to start again," Cleo explains. "It's really just that simple."

"What?" she asks absently, her head shaking imperceptibly. Then, she refocuses. "We can do that?" She's still a mess, but Cleo seems to be getting through to her.

"We can, you and me and others like us." Cleo looks around them and decides to take this conversation to a more private venue. "Gather your things, Doris, and let's go somewhere to talk. You have a lot to learn about the rest of your life."

Doris does what's asked and follows Cleo, who pulls her into Pizzeria Da Marco, where they sit beside the Coca-Cola machine. A server takes their order of a Margherita pizza and sparkling water.

Cleo explains Doris' new reality as Franklin taught her, with the hum of the Coke machine concealing their conversation. Doris nods a lot and doesn't touch the pizza when it arrives. She's upset to have lost the life she'd built but encouraged to start again.

Cleo reminds her that the life she had lived beyond this point, beyond her initiation day, resides only in her memories. That the accident that took her children's lives so violently never happened. None of it had.

"Then, you're saying I never had Emilia and Page? I was never pregnant. I didn't stay up all night with them. I didn't breastfeed them. I didn't cry my eyes out when they went to daycare." A tear tracks down her plump cheek.

"That future is gone." Cleo reiterates.

"But I remember them. I remember everything."

"I know," Cleo says empathetically. "I remember my other futures, too. It's fucked up. I know that." She takes up Doris' limp hand on the table in hers and squeezes. "You will always remember your children, your husband, your life then, but they won't. We live and die alone, you and me. Our realities aren't anyone else's." Cleo added this information from her own realizations with Franklin and Bobby. "Emilia and Page are living their own lives in another future."

"A future I'm not a part of? But how?"

"I don't know that. I imagine you are a part of it, or how would they exist? It's new to me, too. Take this," she hands her Franklin's plastic card with the QR code. "This link will take you through a series of web addresses. Please don't lose it. When you access it, a man named Franklin will contact you. He will help you understand."

"The one who was there for you on your initiation day?" Doris is eyeing the pizza now. Perhaps her appetite is returning. That's a good sign. Cleo nods and finishes her water.

"When you experience trauma as you did with the truck bearing down on your children, you may jump again," Cleo tells Doris. "When you do, I will be there. I don't exactly know how, but I will be."

"Because you were here originally, you would have to be as long as I'm jumping back." She seems to have understood the pseudoscience connected to time travel. Cleo is impressed. "And if I want to return voluntarily?"

"Recall that moment from memory and all the fundamental sounds, smells, and emotions you experienced." Cleo releases Doris' hand. "I've done it a few times now. It doesn't seem to get any easier, but it isn't difficult."

"I – I don't know how to thank you. If you weren't here for me -"

"I'm staying at the Grand Hotel Palatino a block from the Colosseum on Via Cavour." Why not? It's expensive, but Franklin's credit card will never know it had been used when she jumps again. "If you want to talk further, contact me there." She looks at Franklin's card in Doris' hand. "Please visit that link as soon as you can."

Doris smiles reservedly at Cleo, who returns the social queue. "You'll be fine," she assures Doris. "It's not as strange as you'd think."

With that, Cleo stands and reminds Doris to eat the pizza. Then she leaves Doris and the noisy Coca-Cola machine behind. Will she ever hear from Doris again? Hard to say. She doesn't know how much longer she will stay in this life. This future. She's done a good thing. She has made a difference in someone else's life.

Cleo walks Corso Vittorio Emanuele toward her hotel with the sun behind her and countless new futures ahead. She thinks she will have a late dinner tonight; the pizza will keep her sated for a few hours more.

She considers Doris' time trigger and feels a kinship. That they share trauma as their trigger may not be unique, but it's made her struggle more relatable. They are kindred spirits.

Cleo marvels over the extraordinary complexities of the universe. It's funny to think of how little people actually know. This is evident in her gift. Time travel, one of the most paradoxical ideas ever conceived, fits neatly into the blueprints of the world. She cannot affect change to the greater timeline. The universe won't allow it. We all live our lives alone, affecting only our bubble, only our own life. We live alone, and we die alone.

The following six days are uneventful in so much that Cleo does not come upon another singularity, but meaningful in that she has experienced incredible moments from the Trevi fountain and its roasted chestnut vendors to the Colosseum, Roman Forum, the Vatican, and the exceptional Roman people. It has been an absolute thrill for her.

A day trip to Florence also paid dividends, seeing Michaelangelo's much prized *David*, the wonderful merchants on the Ponte Vecchio, or Bridge of Gold, and enjoying the afternoon in the restaurants sipping wine while avoiding a passing rainstorm.

She imagines living a life like this forever. She adores travel and can see herself taking Franklin up on his offer of sending her all over the world to locate others like them. It's not a bad gig.

Paris

She thought the phantoms would be happy, having located one of the *others.* But white noise fills her head while the space in front of Cleo churns in a blur of activity. It's making her feel more light-headed than in past occurrences. She ought to have brought Franklin's machine with her, she admits. The noise has taken on an angry energy. She thought she might be safe in another country, but any hope of that happening is washed away in the flood of static noise assaulting her senses.

Paris has been as inspiring as Rome these past five days, and she's felt at ease with no incidents involving the white noise. But now, it has returned with a vengeance.

Cleo is up and out of bed with her hands clasped over her ears to dull the sound. She's unsteady on her feet as the blur seems to bubble and engulf the television on the opposite wall. Then, as quickly as it appeared, it was gone along with the noise. Cleo tentatively lowers her hands and blinks hard at the space no longer stirring in front of her. She must have left the TV on last night.

She falls to her knees and cries in disbelief more than fear. With the return of the white noise, Cleo calls Franklin, who is currently in Sweden on a similar quest.

She is audibly shaken by the event, and Franklin picks up on this. "I don't understand," Franklin reacts to Cleo's experience. "I thought we were doing good by them." Of course, he's referring to the phantoms.

"I'm scared, Franklin," Cleo declares, her voice rattling in her throat. "Maybe I should buy one of those EVP things. At least then, I'll have some idea of what they're saying?"

"I'll arrange it, Cleo," Franklin offers in his calming tone. "Are you going to stay in Paris much longer?"

"I haven't had any luck yet, but as you said, the more populated a city, the better the chance." She's nowhere near wanting to leave this beautiful city. She's staying in old Paris, taking in the cultural landmarks and exceptional art occupying every city nook. It had been going so well—cafes, chocolate croissants, wine, the Louvre, the Eiffel Tower, and walks along the Seine. Even with a dusting of snow, the city is alive with people and vibrant energy.

"If it's going to happen there, it will happen soon," he confirms, his voice warm and confident. "Give it another week, and I'll order the unit for delivery to your room in the next twenty-four hours. Remind me where you're staying."

Cleo gives him the address and name of her hotel on Rue St-Louis-en L'Île. She's staying on the Island that nearly butts up to the Île de la Cité, which boasts the Notre Dame Cathedral. She loved the idea of being so close to such a powerful icon of the faith. Not that she has any catholic leanings, but we all share a history, and it's the history of things that stirs her. Nevertheless, she regrets that her gift will not allow her to travel beyond her initiation day and to a time where she can watch history unravel first-hand.

"Let the front desk know you'll be receiving a package in the next day and try to enjoy yourself," Franklin tells her, "You've still much exploring to do, I'm sure."

"The Père Lachaise cemetery this afternoon," Cleo relays, "I'm not sure I'm in the right headspace to visit that anymore."

Franklin laughs heartily at this. She likes that she can make him laugh. "Then I have a tour of the Catacombs tonight," Cleo says, encouraging more laughter from her friend and fellow time traveler.

"How has your time in Sweden been?" She checks her text messages as she listens to Franklin's reply.

"Nothing to report yet. I can still hardly believe your luck in Rome. I've spoken to Doris twice, and she's considering a new and unrealized life path. As much as she misses her once-future family, she has decided to take up environmental studies. I encouraged her, of course. She has the rest of eternity." Franklin is a nurturing time-traveling figure in the lives of so many now, Cleo considers. He must be exhausted.

"I thought she'd try harder to regain that future," Cleo says, smiling at a text from Bobby.

"She understands her options," Franklin starts, "there's a very slight chance she'll end up in that position again. Although, of course, if she does decide to have children in a new future, she can name them Page and Emilia again, but they won't be the same."

Cleo considers this and feels Doris' loss. Though it sounds as if she would have lost the girls to the truck bearing down on them in the future she jumped from, accepting it must be a difficult ask. "So, she's doing okay?"

"She's processing, as you did, as we all have had to. Making positive choices is an important part of moving on and accepting your gift for what it is."

Cleo and Franklin say goodbye, and Cleo prepares for the day ahead. A sudden tremor attacks Cleo's left hand in the shower. She drops the shampoo bar and attempts to steady the hand with her other. Limb-dystonia, she recalls the doctor calling it. But in the left hand this time. That's odd. Minutiae, she thinks. But she had been expecting this. If her different futures are any indication, this is overdue.

She slides down the wet tiles of the narrow shower to a seated position, rubs at the muscles in her palm, and practices deep breathing. She thinks she should jump every few weeks and never experience this again. The trouble is the repetitive nature of each future life in that short period. Explaining everything to Franklin, learning languages, choosing travel destinations – though that part she never tires from. If she could do it as Franklin has, live forty years at a time and then jump, it would be less tedious, but how long can he sustain her travel in one life? How long before she is run ragged?

Cleo decides to walk to the Père Lachaise Cemetery after having lunch at the hotel's restaurant. Unfortunately, her walk is interrupted by a light drizzle. She is prepared for this with an umbrella bought at one of the many souvenir shops that pepper the city. She muses that this will be the final blow to the snow that fell a few days earlier.

Cleo waves down a cab as the wind picks up to avoid the discomfort of wet feet and legs. It's not warm out, and this breeze is testing her windbreaker as the temperature plummets. "Père Lachaise, merci," she tells the driver. It takes only another ten minutes to reach the handsome gate at Menilmontant. Cleo pays the driver a generous tip as she does for everyone offering her a service. It's her way of saying she's sorry when she inevitably jumps, and this future disappears with all its people and their complex lives.

She stands at the threshold of the cemetery for a moment. The rain has stopped, and she looks up. The stone walls that surround this place are high and thick. The cemetery closes at five-thirty. A graveyard that closes. That's a foreign thought, but she has little experience with cemeteries in general. Although, upon entering the place, she can understand why it would close.

A seemingly endless run of raised tombs lines either side of the broad walkway, and as she scans the terrain, she notices that this is far from the only walkway in this massive cemetery. So much history and architecture. She would never cover it all in the four hours she has left, but there are certain tombs she wants to see. Namely, The Door's frontman Jim Morrison, Chopin, Oscar Wilde, Georges Seurat, the post-impressionist painter, and more recently laid to rest, Marcel Marceau, the mime who coined his performance art: the art of silence. Interned in 2007. The cemetery has always been a place to lay France's most accomplished artists to rest. Morrison was an exception.

Within the walls, Cleo feels safe. As an artist herself, she has always wanted to visit this place with so many revered corpses adorning its landscape. Her attempts at painting and life drawing in art college left much to be desired, so she decided to take on a more reliable path with a paycheck and benefits. That is her sensible side. Graphic design allowed her to be creative using skills she could master, so she dropped art college after six months and focused on graphic and web design. She still considers herself an artist, just not at the level of those laid in Père Lachaise. Few are. She wonders briefly if a graphic artist could earn a spot here.

As she moves up Avenue Principale within the cemetery, she passes several others walking the gravel and cobblestone paths. She stops at several tombs to look through their tiny stained-glass windows or run her fingers along the stone carvings. As she finds her way to Jim Morrison's grave, far removed from Principale, she is underwhelmed by the scene. His is just a stone laid upon the cold earth between several tombs looming over it. As if he were an afterthought – which, in fact, he was. Still, it seems a sad commentary on the placement of an outsider of Morrison's talent.

She steps over some foliage to secure a better look at Jim's grave and notices a man seated, cross-legged, behind one of the larger tombs but facing Morrison's. Next, Cleo feels the pull of gravity and positions herself to slam against the ancient tomb and not fall on top of this man. He's a time traveler; she knows immediately. The singularity is on top of them, and she feels the push on her whole being; kneeling, she places both bare hands on the cold undergrowth. It crunches beneath her weight, and the man turns to her, eyes wide open. He sees how she's struggling, stands, and, with the same motion, throws up beside Morrison's stone.

"Mon Dieu," My God, he mumbles, not appearing overly upset over his reaction to time travel. Cleo wipes a bit of vomit splatter from her left cheek. The young man uses his coat sleeve to remove any lingering vomit from his mouth and chin. He turns back to Cleo and apologizes.

"Je suis vraiment désolé." I'm so sorry, he tells her and bends, offering a napkin. Cleo waves him off with a kindly smile.

"Parles-tu Anglais?" Do you speak English? she asks, hoping to avoid muddying her way through the French language despite her consistently studying it and practicing on everyone who will listen. The man nods.

"Oui, uh, yes, I speak English," he says with a heavy accent. Cleo smiles brightly now and stands to meet him. She is not much shorter than he is and dressed better for the weather.

"You're a time traveler," she cuts right to the point, and the man nods as if he is well aware of what he is. "I'm Cleo," she introduces herself with a hand to her chest.

"Hello, Cléo, Je Suis Stephan, uh, I'm named Stephan," he replies and clears his throat with a hand to his chest. "I'm not surprised to see you, you know?"

Cleo is taken aback. "I-Is this not your first time? I mean, traveling like this?"

"Non, it is no. And this is not our first meeting," he smiles despondently. "I have been here," he counts on his long, slender fingers, "neuf fois." Nine times.

She knows she looks shocked but supposes she's looked like this at least seven times to Stephan. "I'm sorry, this is new to me," she explains. "I haven't met someone I've supposedly met before. But, *God*, it's confusing."

"I explain," he says, motioning that she sits on Jim Morrison's stone. She does, noticing a small amount of graffiti adorns the long slab of concrete. "This moment started for me twenty years ago today. It's my Birthday," he says with the saddest smile Cleo has ever seen.

"But, twenty years ago," Cleo starts and realizes it's only been twenty years for Stephan, not her. "Oh, you're twenty years into being like me, a time traveler."

"Oui, uh, yes, and I have been back nine times. So, I know you very well, Cleo." His sad smile has not left him.

"What is your trigger, Stephan? Is it your birthday?" She asks, assuming she has heard this answer eight times before.

"Oui, my birthday is not a good time for me," he tells her. "I'm afraid to say, Cleo, that I am very sad on my birthday." He pulls up next to her on the slab and sits with his fingers linked and hands resting on his knees.

"Then sadness is your time trigger?" She decides. Stephan tilts his head at her and then, understanding her meaning, nods again.

"I've tried and tried to live better, Cleo, as you have asked. And this time, I stayed through my twenty-first and twenty-second birthdays." He speaks in his accented English well, but a growing sadness now affects his speech, and he swallows thickly. "I cannot," he clears his windpipe, "I cannot seem to get past twenty-three."

Cleo places her hands on his and squeezes. Stephan looks up at her quizzically. "Oh, Stephan," she says, her heart breaking. "What is keeping you from moving beyond twenty-three?"

He looks at her with conviction, the corners of his mouth pulled down, and then there's that sad smile. Tears flow gently, and Cleo feels as if she might cry. Instead, she pulls him into her, and they hug for a long while. His familiar way with her has made it easy to connect to his sadness. With her chin resting on his shoulder and

Stephan crying into her chest, she realizes how difficult it must be for him to relive this each time. He must consider his inability to move past his sadness a failure. Something awful, whether real or perceived, is sending him back to this time, this place.

"Have you addressed your sadness in the other futures?" She feels oddly maternal toward Stephan.

Stephan pulls away softly and wipes his face with his sleeve again. "It is my head," he tells her, tapping the ball of his palm against his temple. "It all goes sideways eventually."

"Oh, Stephan," Cleo doesn't know how to approach this. Is the decline of his mental health in each future leading him to jump?

Stephan licks his lips and drags his hands across his cheeks, removing the wetness. He coughs out a laugh and shrugs. "I do not know what else I can do than what I have done." His accent seems thicker now.

"Why here, Stephan? Why this moment?" Cleo asks, looking about the space, wondering whether she should take a psych course to better deal with the various people she will meet.

Stephan watches her. "I'm a hopelessly dark soul, Cleo," he tells her, swallowing gruffly. "I love places like this. I fantasize about death. I think about suicide all the time. It is my prevailing thought. I didn't even understand that I was the only one at eight years old considering killing myself. My therapist was the one who explained to me that it was not a normal thought. I can not change. I never do."

Cleo's heart plummets to her stomach, and it feels like a gut punch. Her hands land on his knee. "Oh, Stephan, you don't go through with it, do you?"

"Neuf fois," nine times, he says sadly. "As I lay bleeding, I come back here to this time. It's all I can envision. It is where I belong."

"The living don't belong in a cemetery, Stephan; they visit them," Cleo's gaze catches his, and he shakes his head.

"Oui, if I was like *you*," his hands find Cleo's, and she notices how cold they are. "Maybe you will visit me?"

"I'm older than you by, like, a year in real-time, so that means I go first!" She insists, attempting humor. "There has to be a pill or a coping technique to help you live a full life." Her eyes track his.

"Non. I will always try to end myself. I know that now. Each time, I end up here. If I step in front of a bus, I blink back. I cut myself, and I return. I hang myself. I am back before I feel the rope tighten." He's wringing his hands now.

"There must be a *reason*, Stephan. There is a purpose to experiencing our gift -"

"Gift?" He says sharply. "You call it a *gift*, but I only want to stop it. I am in purgatory, Cleo!" His voice is straining now. "I want to stop it! I want to stop!" He stands abruptly and charges out of the hidden knoll past the tombs and into the avenue. Cleo is momentarily stunned by the speed at which he exits the conversation. Then she stands to follow, only to find that he has disappeared amongst the many stone statues and tombs. She experiences a chill as a gust of wind enters the cemetery. She rubs at her forearms and silently walks the remainder of the Père Lachaise cemetery.

"I expect we will meet again, Stephan," she says to no one, rubbing her hands together to remove the chill in her fingers. Rain begins to fall again, and she opens her umbrella as others rush to the cover of trees.

She'll skip the Catacombs, she decides. No more talk of death and dying today.

Bobby Patel - Take Four

The following day, Cleo receives the EVP machine at her hotel. She wonders whether the phantoms will be angry with her for failing to reach Stephan. She imagines that's how it's gone all nine times he's jumped. She's sad for him. It's awful to be tormented from the inside out and feel helpless to change it. She knew a boy in high school who took his life. He'd struggled with social anxiety and depression since he was twelve, she remembers. So, the news of his death wasn't surprising to anyone but forced the issue of depression in schools and more assistance in managing it.

Cleo opens the box on her King-sized bed and pulls the unit out. It's a replica of what Franklin had set up in her home. She skims the instructions and locates the 'on' and 'record' buttons. She takes a moment to breathe. She feels the anxiety build in her chest over attempting a conversation with the white noise.

If they don't want to talk, who is she to push the subject? She wonders. Will turning on the EVP be an invitation to the white noise? Should she stay put and order room service until she experiences another instance of the hair-raising event?

A shower first, she decides. Then breakfast. After that, she can focus on the task at hand. Breakfast arrives, and Cleo tips the server handsomely. Poached eggs atop sliced avocado on a cut and buttered croissant. Baked new potatoes fill out the meal, and she pours herself a coffee from the carafe. It takes her all morning to shower, dress, and eat breakfast. She knows she's stalling. She watches the pigeons outside her window as they hop along the stone sill. The view beyond them is more interesting still. The ancient city sprawled out before her.

Next, she turns the EVP on and sets it atop her dresser. She doesn't bother with the record button yet. Instead, she turns on the radio at her bedside so as not to feel alone. She sits at the desk provided and reviews her phone for messages.

Bobby has responded again. Her body reacts to the text with the memory of their night together in that distant, alternate future. She feels flush. She reads the text.

McCarthy, when are you coming home? We miss you. Let's get together for a drink soon. She loves reading that he misses her and wants to connect in person but is wary of how a night out with him will end. If she sleeps with him again, will she jump right away? She expects to return home in the next few weeks after visiting Barcelona. That was the plan she and Franklin had hatched. After that, she's considering jumping every few weeks to prevent her Parkinson's from advancing while locating the others, as requested by the phantom noises.

Her radio begins to fizzle with static as the station she's listening to degrades into the familiar white noise. Her gaze immediately lands on the EVP machine next, her hand rising to her chest to calm the anxiety. Its yellow light is flickering, and the space around it is beginning to spin. She slides off the bed and quickly taps the record button. Standing between the radio and the EVP, Cleo considers questions.

"Who do you want me to find? Who are the others? Are they other time travelers?" She stands stock still. Her hands now clenched into fists at her thighs.

The EVP is cycling through frequencies to pull something recognizable from the static. Then, the answers come in quick succession.

"Find ... Others. YES!" the replies feel like they are being fed through a metal grinder, and Cleo sucks her lips between her teeth to stay off the uncomfortable sensation of metal on metal.

"Am I doing it right?" Cleo asks, her tongue running over her top teeth.

"Merge..." the white noise insists. Cleo senses the urgency in the message, but one-word answers aren't going to get them far.

"Merge? Is that what you said? Merge what?"

After a moment of static that seemed to hold its structure, they reply, "Us...."

"T-The others? The others need to merge?" Cleo is hoping she's piecing it together. "Merge like, become one or...?"

"MERGE!" they shout, and Cleo flinches. It's as if they think she is too thick to get their meaning. "MERGE..." They say again. It's a pained screech, and she senses they are desperate to merge. How that will be accomplished is another story.

"You have to explain what you mean by *merge.*" She demands, nearly stomping her foot on the carpeted floor.

"Him..." they say in a calmer tone. "Him ... merge."

The only him she can think they're referring to is Franklin. The only him they have in common. "Do you mean Franklin? You want to merge with Franklin?"

"HIM!" they screech as if that were going to crack the mystery of who 'him' is. This is like texting, she thinks. There is no modulation in the tone beyond loud and screeching and screeching at a lesser volume. She wishes she could have a conversation over the phone. Face to face might scare her silly.

Then, as if sparked into action by her thought, her phone joins the cacophony of white noise and blinks on her bed. She moves slowly toward it, picks it up, and sees Bobby's text there. "Bobby," she sighs, returning to the EVP.

"Is the 'him' you're referring to, Bobby?"

It seems like an eternity as the phantoms attempt a reply. The white noise picks up in volume and then falls rapidly. She fears she will lose the connection before an answer is given.

Cleo places her head against the EVP. The radio has returned to its pre-programmed station, and her phone has ceased blinking. The EVP is struggling to produce an answer; she can feel it. "Tell me," She whispers. Cleo strains to hear, but the phantoms are gone, and all that remains is the white noise.

Cleo hits the dresser with both palms, rattling the EVP and lamp atop it. She points at the EVP and says, "fuck that! How long are you going to string me along?" Frustration bubbles to the surface. She turns the EVP off and paces the room.

"'Him' can only refer to two people, Franklin or Bobby," she insists. "Franklin is a time traveler, and Bobby is a physicist. I don't have anyone else in my life that some otherworldly phantoms could be asking for. I don't!"

Cleo pours another coffee and snaps the cup up, still pacing. Maybe she's had enough coffee, she thinks. She feels wired.

Whatever the barrier is between the white noise and Cleo, it must be difficult to penetrate. So, she decides to call Bobby.

"McCarthy! Are you back?" Bobby sounds ecstatic about the call. That's not the Bobby she remembers, but new futures and all that.

"No, still in Europe," she tries to sound laid back. "I have a question I need you to field for me."

"Never been to Europe, McCarthy; I can't tell you where to get the best pastries," he says light-heartedly—still the sarcastic one.

"Yeah, yeah," she says, brushing off his nonsense. She recalls that she hasn't approached him in this future about her time travel and doesn't feel she has the time to dive into it now. "Let's say someone wanted to contact me from another dimension or something. How would that work?"

"How would they do it?"

"Yeah, how would that happen?"

"I don't know, McCarthy, through a head injury? Are you suffering voices you can't explain?" He's not taking her seriously. She can't really blame him.

"It's a serious question, Bobby," she snaps. "Sorry, but it's for a book I'm considering writing. You're the physicist; you can break it down for me, right?"

Silence. Then he says, "Inter-dimensional conversations, huh? That's a new one for me, but I can take a stab at it." That's the Bobby she knows. "Are we talking about, like, multiverse dimensions here or the fourth dimension, or...?"

The fourth dimension is time, Cleo remembers. So, if the phantoms are time travelers, that makes the most sense. "Time," she tells him.

"That's a curious thought," he yawns. Shit, she thinks, it's only five in the morning back home. She should have considered that first, but did he not just try to contact her?

"What makes time a dimension anyway?" Cleo interrupts. "Isn't it just a concept for us humans to know when we'll be late?"

"Time is more than a tool to measure the duration of events or the intervals between them, McCarthy. It's a dimension because, along with our three spatial dimensions, we move *through* time. So space and time are inextricably linked." Cleo remembers this lesson from one of the past Bobbys.

He continues, "No matter which direction you move in space, you're also moving through time. Even when you're not moving through space, you're moving through time. Time is the constant."

Cleo appreciates the explanation but wants him to answer her initial question and asks it again. "Okay, so how would someone be able to communicate from one time to another."

"Future to past or vice versa?" Bobby asks. It's a good question, Cleo admits.

"It could be either," she replies.

"I mean, you could look at what they did in Back to the Future and write a note that's mailed to a place and time in the future, but you can't mail a letter to the past. I mean, not without a time machine," he sounds less than convinced of these examples.

"Yes, but this is a conversation, not snail mail. It's not even texts or emails. It's someone talking through dimensions."

"And how do you propose they do that? Through the phone? Analog or digital?"

"White noise," she tells him. "Frequencies."

"Huh. That's cool. So, a person from the future is reaching out into the present through radiation from the Big Bang." He's not posing it as a question but, rather, working it out in his head.

Cleo loves to watch him work out problems. Like when he studied the symptoms and treatments for her disease, she would watch him intensely from across the table where he would furrow his brow, make clicking noises with his tongue, narrow his eyes as if they were attached to a microscope, and he was studying Parkinson's at the cellular level. But this is just a phone call, so she imagines his handsome face squinting over the complex problem she's put to him.

"That's ancient energy. White noise would permeate every time period, so it makes sense it might act as the conduit to exchange information through time."

"I can hear the hamster on the wheel, Bobby," Cleo says, quoting him from an abandoned timeline. "If I were to say that space blurred when the audible communication came in, does that help or hinder?"

"You say it's a conversation, so you would be asking and answering questions in real-time?"

Cleo confirms this, and Bobby sighs. She can hear the air moving past his teeth, a hand over his mouth. "Listen, you've piqued my interest, McCarthy. I want a couple of days to ponder. You don't have a deadline looming for your first book, do you?"

Cleo laughs. "No, but I am at a crossroads and would appreciate a quick turnaround." Cleo laughs again, and Bobby joins in.

"All right, I'll see what I can do," Bobby assures her. "Go easy on the pastries, McCarthy, and if you're not clocking in at over twenty-thousand steps a day, then you're doing something wrong. Talk soon."

"Thanks, Bobby. Au revoir." Cleo falls to her bed and lays there, considering the many conversations she's had with Bobby on the subject of time travel. If he can offer her a plausible theory that the phantoms are reaching out through the fourth dimension, then perhaps she will have a better chance at decoding what the white noise is asking of her.

Cleo feels better with Bobby involved. Franklin is great, but she'd rather rely on a close friend, and Bobby is one of the best. She looks at the time and realizes she will be late for her tour of the Rodin Museum if she doesn't leave now.

The concierge puts her in a car, and she only just makes her group tour. The French sculptor is renowned for his piece The Thinker, which adorns the tranquil and expansive gardens. Cleo has longed to see this in person, and now she has. But there is so much more to see.

The Gates of Hell are on display outside also. This massive bronze sculpture is said to depict a scene from the Inferno, the first section of Dante Alighieri's Divine Comedy. It's an impressive piece, Cleo thinks, staring at the many tormented souls and demons that range in size from six inches to three feet. The gate itself rises eighteen feet and is twelve feet wide.

"Abandon every hope, who enter here." This quote from the Divine Comedy was Rodin's inspiration for the door. Looking upon the characters depicted certainly illustrates the statement with terrifying effectiveness. It's darkly beautiful in its extraordinary craftsmanship. She learns that several casts have been made of the gates and now adorn foreign museums worldwide.

She walks the grounds and finds a bench to rest at. The museum isn't jam-packed today, and the weather is not conducive to outdoor activities, but she needed to see these sculptures. She will be leaving for Barcelona in two days.

Barcelona

There is so much to see in this city. Cleo has her itinerary and will head to the Sagrada Familia Basilica first. Designed by Antonio Gaudi over a hundred years ago, the Basilica is still unfinished. Gaudi put the heart into the city with his organic architectural style. It's unlike anything else, and Cleo, with her artist's soul, is thrilled to see as much of it as possible. Next, she will visit Park Guell, which he designed, full of mosaics and organic architecture, and the residential building La Pedrera, where gates of twisted metal akin to wild vines adorn the property.

Upon arriving at the Sagrada Familia, she is awestruck by the sheer size of the structure and the carvings and statues that embellish it. It is like no other Basilica in the world. The organic lines wandering to the heavens in their textured twists and turns make it seem like the cathedral is growing out of the earth. And as much as it does not resemble other Basilicas, it is unmistakably a Basilica.

Cleo bends down to pet the massive concrete turtle near the entrance, supporting one of the many pillars on his shell. Gaudi included animals and trees in his design to speak to the beauty of God's creations. To put them on display, and rightly so, Cleo thinks, alongside the saints and profits of the bible. She supposes she will get a kink in her neck after this tour, rolling her head and rubbing at the base of her skull. "It's so going to be worth it," she reminds herself, stepping inside the massive, open space.

In this surreal depiction of a Catholic Basilica, pillars are trees that reach incredible heights, their branches moving off in every direction to support the Gothic arches, while stained glass carries bursts of color that command your attention as they reach from floor to ceiling, dispersing light throughout the open-concept Basilica.

Cleo can hardly believe her eyes. It is a living thing, this place. Or, at least, the reproduction of a living thing. It is a petrified forest. It is a church. It is a place of worship both to nature and the God who supposedly created it. Cleo turns in space with her eyes set on the ceiling and feels a sense of vertigo. She seeks out an empty pew and sits, her head heavy on her shoulders.

She wishes she could share this with someone. Trish would love it here. Bobby would appreciate the architecture but not the faith. But she's on a mission as well. This isn't just a sightseeing trip. It's not a vacation. She fears sensing a shift in gravity wherever she goes now. It would be a terrible interruption to this experience, she decides. But at the same time, she could certainly appreciate someone jumping back to this place to start over. That would be inspired.

After two hours inside and another half hour roaming the exterior, Cleo has escaped any scenario where she feels the singularity encroaching upon her day.

That evening, she takes her dinner at her hotel, the Gran Hotel Barcino, in the Gothic district of the city. She orders the Catalonian favorite, Paella. It's delicious. Then, feeling adventurous, she wanders through the streets where medieval structures tower above her. She rubs her neck distractedly. "So much to see," she whispers.

When she finds herself in a narrow alley with a subtle incline, she is greeted by a server at the door of a bar named Craft. "¿Le gusta la música en vivo, señorita?" Do you like live music, Miss? He queries, armed with several menus. Thankfully, Cleo has Spanish training from high school, and with a little in college, she can ascertain what the handsome young man is asking.

"Si," she tells him, nodding. He hands her a menu and leads her into the bar. It is all stone, wood, and atmospheric lighting inside. He shows her past the busy bar area, turning sideways to slip through the tight arrangement of tables, and moves right to descend a few steps into a shallow basement with a curved, bricked ceiling, stone walls, and a small stage at the rear. The space is barely fifteen feet wide and maybe thirty feet deep. She adores it.

"Un trago para ti?" Would you like a drink? He asks. Cleo pieces the question together and nods, pointing at the San Miguel beer at the top of the menu's drink list.

"No voy a comer, gracias," I won't eat, thank you, she explains, handing him back the menu. He nods and returns, not two minutes later, with her pint. She is seated at the back of the basement on a wooden bench at a small table where the largest cockroach she's ever seen has joined her. She laughs out of fear, but at least it's not a rat, she tells herself. She shoos it away with her coaster, and at first, it is resistant to her pleas, but once the coaster makes contact, the roach crawls into a gaping hole in the mortar. Cleo experiences a shiver and sips at her beer.

It's open-mic night at the bar, and she watches and listens as several would-be musicians belt out classics. Her favorite is the young English student who sings a perfect version of *Back to Black* by Amy Winehouse, with her brother playing guitar and the bar's owner on the drums. It seems that most of the customers speak English. Perhaps this is an English pub? Whatever the case, Cleo appreciates this moment for what it is: exceptional, unique, and a remarkable bit of luck.

The night sees two more San Miguels and one distressing development in that when the music stops; white noise bleeds through the speakers.

Cleo watches as the owner tries to turn the speaker down and even turns it off, but the static interference persists. Cleo looks on in horror as the man's face contorts, and she reads his lips, *'What the fuck'.* He pulls the cord next, and still, the white noise permeates the basement. The owner scratches his head as he looks at the wall jack with a half dozen cords dangling. He thoughtfully touches each plug, looking fearful of unplugging anymore.

"Merge ... Us...." Cleo hears as plain as day, her heart in her throat. The voice, as always, is androgynous. It is coated in static. She looks about the other tables, wondering if they, too, heard the words. But they show no more surprise than over the constant white noise occupying their headspace.

Cleo's palms begin to sweat, and she rubs them on her jeans. Her drink is half full in front of her, but she wants to flee.

"Him ... Merge ... US!" The screeching accompanying the last word causes Cleo to jump in her seat. Then, with a hand on her chest, she asks again, "Who is 'Him'?" She says it not in a whisper but in a normal, albeit frustrated voice, confident no one else will hear her over the speaker.

"BOB ... BY!" The speakers shriek at her. Then, the white noise stops, and an audible sigh from the other patrons replaces the sound. Cleo feels stuck in her seat. She is rigid. It said Bobby, she reflects. That's big. That's fucking huge! Next question: why Bobby? But there is no noise to ask. These phantoms seem to be stalking her now. But if they give up the answers required to complete the task they are so desperate for her to support, she's good with their stalker status.

Back at Gran Hotel Barcino, Cleo showers and dresses for bed. Any buzz she might have caught from the three beers earlier vanished with the arrival of the white noise. Nothing is as sobering as a shot of adrenaline.

Cleo enjoys a well-deserved sleep after a long day and wakes with renewed energy to face another full of uncertainties. But what's certain is her trip to Park Guell. She walks to the underground, picking up breakfast at a café to eat on the train. It's sunny and seventy-two degrees. That will be the high for the day. From the final stop at Avinguda del Santuari de Sant Josep de la Muntanya, Cleo discovers the remainder of the walk is aggressively uphill.

When she reaches her destination, sweat glistening on her forehead, pulling at her many layers to let the cooler air in, she turns to take in the view. It is expansive. She can see straight to the Mediterranean Sea from up here. Cleo refocuses on the gardens. The grounds embody an elaborate freedom of form and textures, creating a kind of organic unity with the landscape. The luxurious colors in Gaudi's mosaics offer a visual smorgasbord, and as she moves through the gardens, taking her time to absorb the cornucopia of visual interest, a heavy feeling besets her.

"Oh, come on," she pleads, shoulders slumping, her backpack in freefall. She slings it onto a bench that winds like a serpent along a short, mosaiced wall. She sits and practices conscious breathing. She scans the park's upper level and sips from her water bottle. The weighty sense of gravity is upon her. Someone near here is about to jump back to this moment from some alternate future.

Europe has not disappointed with its populous cities full of both locals and tourists alike. Cleo feels her stomach flip-flop and wishes the sensation away. Her Spanish is similar to her French but better than her Italian. She should be able to talk this one down if she can find them. On the other hand, so many people are moving around the grounds that she worries she will miss the event.

She stands to follow the tug of gravity, which pulls her along the lengthy, twisting bench to her left. She narrows her eyes, panning the scenery, her hand on her stomach. She goes down the double staircase, past the iconic mosaic lizard, and onto the lower level. Her vision is blurring now. Or is it space-time? Where she focuses her attention, the blur follows. Or is she to follow the blur? She rubs her eyes and turns left, traveling a minute along a new path flanked by more exotic and tropical trees and plants.

There, seated on one of the planters that separate this path and the one running parallel to it, is a woman staring at her hands as if they were not her own. Or, perhaps, her own, but much younger.

"Has viajado una distancia para llegar aquí," you have travelled a distance to get here, Cleo says forcing the woman to look up. "Si," she replies.

"¿En qué año te fuiste?" What year did you leave? Cleo asks, hoping the question will snap the woman out of her dazed state.

"¿Qué año?" What year? The poor woman is utterly clueless. "El año es... 2055," the year is 2055, she explains. She thinks it's still the year she just jumped from.

Cleo shakes her head slowly with an empathetic smile. "No, el año es 2023. Eres un viajero en el tiempo y yo también," no, the year is 2023, you're a time traveler and so am I," Cleo explains. The woman slides off the stone planter and takes several steps away from Cleo.

"Eso es imposible," That is impossible, the woman stutters, now frantically looking around her, one slender hand gripping the stone planter. Her dark eyes complement her skin tone and short curls. Her full lips are parted, and the fear in those beautiful eyes makes Cleo feel like the bad guy. A passing couple steals glances as they move past.

She approaches the woman with her palms forward to appease her. "por favor, ten calma, ten calma." Please, be calm, she repeats. "You're here; that is a fact," Cleo forgets her Spanish.

"I am here," the woman speaks English. Cleo takes a deep breath. She studies Cleo's clothes and hair. She must look very different from someone arriving from 2055. Then she smiles brightly, "Estoy aquí," I am here, she repeats and approaches Cleo. She takes Cleo's hands and pulls her in for a hug. It is a long hug in which the woman's fingers grasp Cleo's jacket as if the tactile sensation makes this more real. Finally, Cleo breaks the hug and pulls back. The women's noses are almost touching.

"What happens in 2055?" Cleo asks in a whisper, fearful of the answer.

"It is a terrible place," the woman explains in her Catalonian accent. "Spain is under a terrible dictatorship. Most of Europe is. There is famine and sickness," her voice cracks, and she cries, her fingers pulling at the shoulders of Cleo's coat as though thankful for touching another human being.

"That future is gone now," Cleo tells her, fighting off a shiver over the woman's description, "That future only lives in your memory. It will never repeat itself. None do. Do you understand? You get to start over from this point, as does the rest of the world."

The woman nods emphatically. She's smiling through the tears. She can't believe her luck. "I need to visit mi familia," she says. "I have to go," she studies her surroundings again, and Cleo takes her by the wrist as she moves to leave.

"You can't tell anyone about your gift," she tells her. The woman's expression falls as her neatly trimmed brows knit together in confusion.

"Gift? Is this - I can do this again?" Cleo nods at the question and then explains everything. She leaves Sofia with Franklin's card and an extended hug and, now exhausted, leaves Park Guell and hails a cab to take her back to the gothic district.

That night, Cleo has nightmares over the beautiful woman's hellish future. It sounded to her like a textbook description of what the world will face if climate change is not seriously addressed in the next few years.

Home for a Rest

After another two days in Barcelona, Cleo makes the call to return home. Besides what she's wearing, Cleo drops the clothes bought during her trip in a donation box and takes the train to the airport. She is resting comfortably in her roomy first-class accommodations on the Dreamliner-787, settling in for a nap when she receives a text from Franklin.

You've done remarkably well, Cleo, he starts. **I've heard from two of the three travelers you've identified. I look forward to catching up in person when you return.**

She responds with a smiley emoji, a tired one, and finally, a sleepy face. Cleo doesn't expect Franklin to hear from Stephan since she hadn't the chance to give him his card. She pulls the eye mask down, wriggles into the mattress, pulls the sheet up, and tries to forget she's on a plane.

Cleo sleeps nearly the whole flight, catches a cab from O'Hare to her apartment in the South Loop neighborhood of Chicago, and orders dinner. She experiences jet lag as her body is confused over whether to sleep more. When she's eaten, she rests on her couch with a movie for company.

Cleo senses a tightening in her right hand as it begins to tremble. The troublesome symptom has her standing to shake out her arm. She presses the hand back, stretching the forearm, but the hand lurches forward and balls into a tight fist. Cleo cries out of fear and frustration until the seizure passes.

Exhausted, she falls back onto her couch, rubbing tenderly at the affected limb. Such *bullshit*, she tells herself. "Why am I letting this happen? I should jump before it gets any worse."

She appreciates that jumping back every couple of weeks would rob her of a full life, but what would a full life for her entail? With her Parkinson's inevitable march forward, Cleo knows her life has been weighed and found wanting. Still, wouldn't it be nice to experience love, marriage, and children? Of course, but that life isn't for everyone, and she needs to accept that it won't be for her.

The following day, she returns to work, where she is met with hostility by her manager, Barbara, who is in fine form today, wearing her favorite expression, a grimace. Cleo overhears Barbara berating a co-worker for her untied shoe and another for wearing a baseball cap to the office before she enters Cleo's cubicle. She's an HR nightmare, but no one has the guts to complain. Cleo included.

Cleo is still reeling from a sleepless night as her body argues it's still on European time. She's in no mood to listen to Barbara's whining about things that don't matter and finds herself rising out of her ergonomic office chair to look her manager in the chest. While Cleo is nearly a foot shorter than Barbara, she can still see over the other cubicles on the marketing floor with their graphic and web designers pumping out materials to propel their clients above their competition. The scents of coffee and angst permeate the space.

Cleo's eye twitches. She fears that it's her Parkinson's acting up, then realizes it's just stress playing itself out. Barbara is still blathering on about the Hamlin account when Cleo snaps.

Barbara is swiftly silenced as Cleo lifts her leg and sends her foot plummeting down on Barbara's naked toes with the heel of her boot. The silence lasts until the trauma travels to Barbara's brain. Then, finally, she cries out, eyes bulging from her ferret face, hands grasping to either side of the cubicle. Cleo laughs cruelly at this. Seeing the uber-composed Barbara flinch like this is a treat. She watches the others rise from their cubicles to take in the show.

"What – what is wrong with you, Cleo McCarthy!" Barbara shouts, confusion and pain playing out across her features, reaching for her bruised foot. But Cleo stomps on the other one before she can, laughing harder and harder out of exhaustion and grim satisfaction. All or nothing, she decides.

Barbara is stunned a second time and then releases another tortured howl. Cleo can't believe she's doing this.

145

She's never been a violent person. She has surprised herself. "If you're looking for inefficiencies, *Barbara*, look in the mirror!" she shouts at her manager. "You're the inefficiency on this floor!" Barbara is bent over so Cleo can look her in the eye. "We're not a bunch of robots, *Barbara!*" Cleo spits out her name like poison. Then, she decides to humiliate her manager further. "And your tits are fake! Fake, fake, fake, and everybody knows it!" Her mouth is full of saliva, spittle flying everywhere as she shouts down her manager. How far could she take this fantasy? How far should she?

Cleo gathers her belongings and marches past Barbara, who is leaning against Cleo's desk, inspecting her toes and confirming those now gathered around her cubicle saw the whole thing. She will certainly lose her job for this. In addition, she'll likely be charged with assault and battery. But in the back of her mind, she'd always known she had an out.

Her ride home is uneventful save the thoughts occupying her mind over the day's bizarre outcome. She can hardly believe she did what everyone on her floor had always fantasized about doing. She can't stop smiling and giggling when she thinks of Barbara's expression after the first boot dropped. It was like watching videos of people falling. So hilarious, and even though you know you shouldn't laugh, it's impossible to stop.

Once the adrenaline wears off, Cleo realizes she will have to jump for this sin. She can't afford to lose her job and possibly go to jail. So, she will jump and burn this timeline. She realizes this is the sort of thing that could become addictive with time travel, facing down your enemies. But Cleo reasons she hasn't any other enemies, so this is the only time she'll allow herself such a guilty pleasure. God, that felt good, though.

She calls Franklin and explains what she's about to do, and though he sounds slightly frustrated over the news, he understands the need.

"I feel we're so close now to understanding what the phantoms are asking of us; it's a shame we have to take this step back," he tells her.

"I'll memorize the message and get you up to speed when I return, and I'll put everything we've learned to Bobby again, and maybe he'll be able to build on what we've discovered." Cleo's embarrassed by her actions but explains that this could be good. She knows the more information she can offer Bobby at once, the more he has to work with straight away.

Bobby Patel – Take Five

The jump, accompanying nausea, and recap with Franklin went swimmingly, Cleo thinks. On her way to work in the morning, she considers what she'll tell Bobby this round. It's not necessary that he knows about her time traveling – not really, she'd rather query him on the white noise voices and get a better handle on that. The mystery behind what they're asking her to do is what's driving her and Franklin now.

She's well aware that they've been so engaged in trying to do the phantom's bidding that they never stopped to ask whether they should. As a result, they don't really know what they're asking of her or the consequences. She and Franklin are going on short, segmented bits of information. Cleo wonders if there isn't more to the conversation that isn't getting through and if Bobby could help boost the signal.

Cleo nods at her coworkers, amazed they have no memory of her altercation with Barbara, who is watching from the staff kitchen doorway. Cleo smiles to herself, shaking her head, thumbnail between her teeth, picturing the expression on her manager's face after the first stomp.

Cleo avoids making herself a coffee in the kitchen while Barbara stands imposingly at the open door. She pulls up the familiar files at her desk and then checks her emails.

At lunch, she calls Bobby, who tells her he is in town and hopes to get a drink with her later. Perfect, she thinks. She will pose her questions then.

Cleo pores over her wardrobe at home to pick the perfect outfit for her evening with Bobby. Why does she care so much? She won't sleep with him again. She's made that promise to herself. Instead, she will have one drink and ask him to research her white noise. That she's jumped again means she must present her concept more clearly and purposefully to Bobby.

Still, she wants to look nice for him. She can't deny how she felt after he explained he was not interested in a relationship. She was hurt and upset even though she knew who he was. Cleo shakes her arms, wishing away her feelings for Bobby beyond friendship, but that is easier said than done.

At the pub, Cleo arrives first and secures a table next to the fireplace. In anticipation of Bobby's arrival, she orders them a pitcher of beer. She'll have one glass. Bobby is never late, so she expects to see his lean, muscled frame enter the front doors within the next five minutes.

Contemplating the menu, Cleo hears white noise escape the speakers above her. They are turned low, but she can make out a few words as they tumble down to meet her. Not words - numbers. "35 ... 57115 ... 47." Cleo pulls the cutlery from her napkin and rifles through her purse for a pen. She writes the repeating numbers down, hoping the pauses between aren't where other numbers ought to be.

"Closed ... Curve...." It says next. These are words the phantoms have not spoken before, and Cleo recognizes as part of the phrase: Closed timelike curve. However, the middle word is missing. The message has been fragmented, she realizes. Perhaps she hasn't been receiving the whole message all this time. This excites her, noticing the hairs on her forearm stand on end.

Cleo jots down all the words she remembers hearing since the white noise began. YOU. FIND. OTHERS. US. MERGE. HELP. BOBBY. YES. CLOSED. CURVE. 35. 57. 115. 47. "Jesus," she says aloud, "it's like a word jumble."

With her head bent over the napkin, Cleo is surprised when the chair across from her is pulled out, scuffed loudly across the worn, wooden floor, and Bobby drops himself into it. She looks up in a daze and smiles back at a grinning Bobby.

"You ordered!" He says emphatically, pouring himself a glass from the pitcher. Cleo folds the napkin and places it in her purse.

"Help yourself!" She insists while Bobby sucks the two inches of foam from his glass. "Never did perfect pouring a pint," Cleo reprimands him, shaking her head comically.

Bobby adds more beer to his glass and says, "You know how much I love head." Cleo nearly blushes over the memory of their night together but manages to laugh instead. "Besides, this way, you eliminate the acid in the alcohol."

"Your knowledge pool continues to impress," Cleo teases.

"Hey," Bobby starts, "ever been to Toronto?" He picks up a sticky menu and drops it with a frown. Then, he snaps up his napkin and watches as it pulls apart on his sticky fingers. Next, he dips his fingers into his water glass and dries them on another napkin.

All the while, Cleo has been watching. "That's quite a system you've got there." She drinks from her glass.

"Is it too much to ask to have someone wipe down a menu with umpteen drinks spilled on it?" The way his wavey hair is bouncing, Cleo pictures him running along a sandy beach and then shakes her head, closing her eyes hard.

"Have I been to Toronto? No," she answers his question, wetting and wiping her menu off with another napkin.

Bobby looks at her as if he's forgotten he'd asked. "Oh, right, good."

"Good?"

"Yeah, wanna come with?" Bobby gulps beer and licks his lips. "I've got a conference there in two days. So we're staying right downtown at the InterContinental. Loads to see there, too. We could check out the Royal Ontario Museum, The Ontario Art Gallery, the Hockey Hall of Fame, and the CN Tower."

"Wow, you've been?" Cleo feels a familiar sensation rising in her chest. Bobby is asking her to come along on a business trip. Would they share the same room? The same bed?

"I went back in college twice," Bobby shares. "It's like Chicago, but not as big."

Cleo deliberates for one point two seconds before answering. "Sure!" She says, her voice rising. Smooth, McCarthy, she lectures herself. "I mean, if there's room, uh, in your room."

"Yeah, sure, I'll book two queens," he insists, tracing a line up the condensation on his beer glass with his index finger.

Cleo feels the sensation leave her chest at the mention of two beds, but a trip to Toronto sounds like a blast. "Perfect," she replies. "Did you want to get anything to eat?"

Bobby looks scornfully at the offending menu and tentatively picks it up again. "I could go for some pizza," he says, holding the menu at arm's length as if it might reach out and slap him.

"Pepperoni?" Cleo asks, knowing that's all Bobby will tolerate on his pizza. He nods, and they order.

"So," Cleo starts, clearing her throat, "Can I bounce a physics question off you?"

"If I can bounce a design question off you," he says with a wink.

"Huh," Cleo doesn't field many of those outside of work, but she supposes that's Bobby's point. "Okay. I don't have to ask if it's going to be an imposition." Her hands raise defensively.

"No, no, McCarthy, I'm just fucking with you," Bobby assures and gestures for her to lay it on him.

She explains her concept for a book that includes communication coming from different times through white noise. "Static is just radiation left over from the Big Bang, right? It's everywhere and in every time, so maybe it could carry a message?"

Bobby leans back, running his fingers through his thick, dark, unruly curls. "McCarthy, you never cease to amaze me," he's smiling brightly. Then, leaning forward, he slides his forearms along the table, gripping both sides. "You're asking me if this idea is plausible?"

Cleo nods. "Why not? You work at a think-tank. If anyone is qualified to answer it, shouldn't that be you?"

Bobby picks up his beer and drinks. "You have a point," he admits. "That has a time travel element to it. I hate to go there -"

"That's what's stalling me," Cleo breaks in. "I don't know how to make sense of it."

"Okay. You want to know if communicating through time is possible, and if so, how?" Bobby gets it. "Using white noise – frequencies," he clarifies.

"Yes," Cleo replies. "Now, *go.*" She leans back, crosses her arms, and smiles at Bobby. He laughs.

"Okay. All right, McCarthy," he's nodding and takes another sip of his beer. "We're talking about CMB, or, to the layman," he motions at Cleo, eyebrows raised, "the cosmic microwave background that proves the hot Big Bang theory. This peaks at 160.4 gigahertz." He stops and asks if she's impressed yet. Cleo nods. "The peak frequency is where vocal sounds find their maximum effectiveness."

"So, tuning into 160.4 on a device would offer the best reception from the background thingy?" Cleo posits, playing dumb.

"Nice, McCarthy, I'm glad you're paying attention," Bobby says through his smile, where unnaturally white teeth gleam in the light of the fire. "Yes, the background *thingy* that you're interested in, the white noise, offers the best reception at 160.4."

"But you can't tune into JAZZY 160.4 on your FM radio," Cleo points out.

"No," Bobby attests. "You'd need an antenna booster to increase your range."

"Might an electronic voice phenomena recorder do that?" Cleo asks with great interest.

"A what now?" Bobby seems not to have put any time into ghost-hunting at the think-tank.

"It listens for messages from beyond the grave," Cleo explains. "I know, I know, silly, but could it pull that kind of frequency?"

"If it's an enhanced receiver, I guess so. But you mentioned it's coming through speaker systems, too. So if that's the case, something else would be at work."

"Like?"

"Uh, shit, McCarthy, I don't know. I mean, white noise is white noise. If voices are coming through at any frequency, then fine. It doesn't have to be at 160.4 gigahertz. It's science fiction. Do you even need to explain it?"

"I'd like to."

Bobby sighs. "I thought we were just catching up tonight, not grilling me for information."

155

Cleo reaches out and takes his hand in hers. "It's *killing me*, Bobby. I need answers."

Bobby recognizes the look in Cleo's eyes, and she hopes he remembers the power it's had over him in the past. "Let's say your character is hearing voices in every frequency white noise puts out." He says, yielding to her wants. "Could these be coming from another time? Maybe. As you said, the cosmic microwave background has existed since the beginning of time and will remain so until the universe collapses in the Big Crunch."

"Right, so it's in every time," Cleo states, taking a drink from her glass.

"Right, so could a message from a hundred years ago or a thousand in the future end up in this moment through those means?" His expression has become dire. "A frequency changes when traveling from one medium to another, but would it change from one time to another? Radio waves travel at the speed of light, and if there are no obstructions to travel through, it will travel forever." She can sense that Bobby is no longer in the pub with her; he's somewhere else entirely.

He pulls a pen from his pouch and a notepad from his shirt pocket. He begins to scribble equations you only see in movies, and Cleo becomes increasingly impressed by her friend's intellect.

"Frequencies are vibrations that make up all of reality at the quantum level. Almost anything is possible at the quantum level." He looks up from his pad, staring directly into Cleo. She feels the intimacy of his gaze.

"McCarthy, you're the most interesting thing that's ever happened to me." He says it like he means it. Like it's a compliment. Cleo blushes. "If you go with a quantum explanation for your book, you don't need to offer more "

"Then frequencies create vibrations?"

"The opposite, actually," he responds. "Vibrations create frequencies. But audible frequencies are carried through the atmosphere, so I'd say what your character experiences originates from the quantum realm. If traveling through time. Time can act differently at the quantum level and theoretically be carried over vast distances of time, presenting in your character's timeline as white noise."

This explanation spellbinds Cleo. "Then, if a person discovered a way to communicate through time, it would be at the quantum scale?"

"Yes," Bobby replies. "The math is beyond me, but I could put it to a colleague." He closes his notepad and slips it back into his shirt pocket with the pen.

"Bravo, Bobby," Cleo says, lifting her glass. Bobby raises his and they cheer with a clink. They drink and refill their glasses.

"That should suffice for your book's explanation, but now I'm curious and want to take it further. If I discover anything more substantial, I'll let you know."

"Thank you, Bobby. I mean it," Cleo says, handing the menus to the server as she places their pepperoni pizza between them. "Now, let's eat."

Toronto

As Bobby navigates the 427 highway and moves east along the Gardener expressway from Pearson International Airport in his rental car, Cleo marvels at the CN tower rising above the city center. There is not as much snow as she had expected, and Bobby reminds her that Chicago is not far removed from Toronto's latitude and shares a similar winter.

As they enter the city, Bobby takes the Lower Simcoe Street offramp, and they travel north past the CN tower and Roger's Centre, where the Blue Jays play. After some gridlock, they reach their hotel and check in. Bobby's charm is not lost on the woman at the front desk, and before Cleo knows it, they've been upgraded to a premium room.

Bobby's conference is at the InterContinental Centre, and they stay in the hotel of the same name situated above it. Cleo watches the buzz of activity within the building and feels unworldly for not appreciating what an international city Toronto is. Bobby finishes with the front desk and leads her to the elevator. They rise eighteen stories, and when they enter the room, Cleo doesn't even notice the bed as she rushes to the tall, corner windows where their view displays the CN Tower, Rogers Centre, and even the Scotia Bank arena, where the Toronto Maple Leafs play. It's so much of the city all at once that Cleo fills with anticipation.

"Oh, shit," comes from Bobby, and Cleo turns to see what's happening. He's staring at the King-sized bed. Then, finally, he looks up at Cleo and says, "I'll fix this, McCarthy."

Cleo lays eyes on the sheer size of the bed and shrugs it off. "It's *huge*, Bobby; we won't bump into one another." Then, spinning back to her view, she says, "I don't want to risk losing this!"

"If you're good with it, I'm good with it." As he says this, Cleo wonders if he'd be good with them bumping into each other under the covers. He was undoubtedly game in her alternate future. But she doesn't want to mess up this timeline. She's enjoying it.

"Did you want to get a drink? They have a pretty sweet bar downstairs," Bobby suggests.

"Don't you have any work-related parties tonight?" Cleo brought her best dress in case.

"We do, but not for another three hours. So I say we get a drink in us and wander. It's not too cold out." This is true. The temperature is five Celsius or forty-one degrees Fahrenheit, and anyone born and raised in Chi-town should have no issues going out in that.

In the hotel's Azure bar, they order Smokey Manhattans and sit at an elevated corner where Cleo has a panoramic view of the popular setting.

"Do you see anyone you know?" Cleo sips at her drink while Bobby scans the expansive room.

"Nah, but I don't want to get into conversations with colleagues right now. That's what the reception party and next two days are for." He looks at Cleo, and that familiar sensation rises in her chest. "Let's just pretend to be tourists," he says.

"I *am* a tourist," Cleo laughs, settling into her comfortable chair's rounded back. Jazz plays over the speakers, and she fears white noise will begin fizzling through them at any moment, spoiling the mood and putting her to work.

They skip the walk and order dinner at the bar with a bottle of red. Bobby explains how everything is being expensed through the think-tank. No limits were set. He has free reign with their credit card and suggests a night trip up the CN Tower tomorrow.

They return to their room to dress for the reception party. Bobby showers and re-enters the room with just a towel wrapped around his waist, water dripping from his hair. Cleo makes a face. Bobby shakes his head, forcing droplets to scatter all over the room like a dog might. Cleo screams and pushes him back into the bathroom, her hands connecting to his taut, damp chest.

"Can you throw me my undies and shirt if you can't tolerate my nakedness?" Bobby asks, laughing. Cleo retrieves these items from the bed, where his clothes are laid out neatly. "Turn on some music, will you?"

Cleo places her phone on the clock radio and streams music from her playlist. She felt light-headed after the bar, where she ate only a small salad. A violent static erupts from the clock radio as she tends to her hair. Cleo flinches. Then, she moves to the radio to listen more attentively. "Do it again..." it demands, and she has no idea what this means.

"Do what again?" Cleo whispers, fearful of Bobby overhearing her converse with the radio. "Do what?"

"Do it again...." Then, a long silence, "Must find .... Like us...." Cleo has now collected all the words the white noise has uttered on her phone. She opens the Notes app and adds these words to the jumble. Some have not been revealed before. This gives her goosebumps, thinking she's getting closer to understanding the entire message.

Seconds later, the static is replaced by Cleo's music. She breathes a sigh of relief. Bobby resurfaces from the bathroom, less naked and dryer than before. She can't let on that she preferred his earlier state of undress. She won't ruin this future if she can help it.

"You look nice, McCarthy," Bobby throws the compliment effortlessly into the air, but Cleo catches and holds onto it, a mock curtsey and bow to establish humor.

"It's my finest apparel," she says in her best imitation of a British accent. "I'm sure you'll clean up well once you've completed your ensemble." They both laugh.

"If I look half as good as you, I'll be happy," he says, slipping on his pants. So much praise, Cleo thinks. There is no sharp sarcasm to cut the compliments. *Who is this person?* She studies him briefly, sizing him up, remembering the small changes Franklin and Bobby alluded to from one future to the next. The same minutia that says you can't bring a winning lotto number into another future could also alter a person. He's still Bobby, but a nicer, gentler, more attentive one.

The reception is jam-packed with Bobby's peers. The most apparent difference between him and them is the age gap. The room is expansive and filled with high-top tables to put your drink on, with trays of appetizers being served in an endless loop. Cleo takes advantage of the shrimp cocktails and cheese trays.

Bobby introduces Cleo to three physicists he adores, one woman and two men. Each is smiling, but Cleo gets the sense that myriad other, more critical calculations are taking place behind their eyes. Still, they seem genuinely happy to meet her.

As the night continues, the numbers drop dramatically from hour to hour. By eleven o'clock, she and Bobby leave the mostly abandoned room and return to the eighteenth floor.

In the room, Cleo again is drawn to the windows where the tower is lit up, along with all the other buildings within view. Lake Ontario isn't frozen, but the water from the Great Lake reflects the city's lights, creating an atmospheric picture. Cleo considers taking a photo with her phone.

Bobby sidles up next to her with a glass of wine from their minibar. She takes it, looks up at him, and smiles. It's not lost on Cleo that this moment has the potential to become an incredibly romantic one. Would Trish egg her on to make the first move? Regardless, Cleo senses Bobby is way ahead of her.

She wonders if he'd asked for a King-sized bed. Perhaps this has been a less spontaneous and more carefully planned invitation to Toronto. Is this some elaborate date? Cleo experiences the now familiar sensation not only in her chest but lighting up in other regions. Still, she tells herself, she won't let sex complicate their friendship. It's not worth it. Bobby is too important to her.

They cheer by tapping their glasses lightly together as a tremor rises from deep within her. Her knees begin to shake, and then her hand. Her right hand. The one that has been acting out in most of her alternate futures. It's Parkinson's again. *Fuck*, she thinks. Now? She grasps her wrist with her left hand to steady the involuntary trembling. Bobby notices her symptoms and peels the glass from her fingers before she snaps the stem, injuring herself.

"It's okay, Cleo," he says in a whisper to calm her nerves. He leads her to the couch, lowers her into it, himself with her, and wraps a reassuring arm around her shoulder.

Cleo is overwhelmed by his kindness. It's not that she thought him incapable of this level of care, but she's never experienced it in such close quarters. Emotion overcomes her, and she leans into his chest and cries. She feels comfortable sobbing into his chest, shaking uncontrollably now more from the emotional release than the Parkinson's. She cries for herself. For her future. She has no future with this disease, she's decided. Who would want her? Who would want to go through this day-to-day if they didn't have to?

"I'm here, Cleo," Bobby whispers into her hair, squeezing her tighter. He's too good to be true in this life, she thinks, but she is not letting the thought consume her. She feels safe in his arms. She's always felt safe with Bobby. He hands her the box of tissues on the side table, and she takes a half dozen, blowing her nose and wiping her face.

"Thank you," she mumbles into the tissues, his lips pressing down on her head. She lifts her face to his, and Bobby looks as though he's been crying too. His eyes are puffy and red. Cleo raises her now steady hand to his strong jaw, and he leans in, kissing her on the mouth hard. She kisses him back, and he lifts her slight frame in his arms, gently placing her on the bed and lying beside her. They continue their kiss, exploring each other's mouths until Bobby's lips fall to her neck, and then her dress is being pulled down, and she helps him with her zipper.

They spend the night discovering one another. Cleo had the upper hand, having slept with Bobby in a future she'd burned. Bobby seemed grateful for her experience, and she for his. They slept entangled on the massive bed,

Cleo fearful of letting go of this connection. This was deeper than in her previous life. It felt more emotionally charged than sexual. She feels satisfied on so many levels that she can't put the sensation into words. Words would be insufficient.

Cleo looks at the sleeping Bobby, his expression so somber. Still, fear creeps into Cleo's heart. She could love Bobby. Maybe she does. Not in that friend zone or friends-with-benefits way, but in the classically beautiful way one person can love another. But will he want to remain friends, as he did in that other life, or could he love her back? Truly love her. Get married and have babies, love. Her mind is racing now, and she moves to get up to release her anxiety.

Bobby notices and slides his hand over her stomach to stop her. He lifts his head a few inches off his pillow, and Cleo is caught in his gaze. Bobby smiles, and she leans in to kiss him, testing him. He kisses her back, pulls away, and Cleo finds herself insnared in his honey-brown eyes.

"I love you, Cleo McCarthy," he says tenderly. Cleo feels an explosion in her chest that conducts heat to every extremity. She collapses into him, feeling a weight fall away, a weight of holding back, and tells him with absolute clarity, "I love you, Bobby Patel." They hug, pulling the other impossibly close, the heat of their bodies mingling. This is it, Cleo thinks; this is the life I was meant to live.

Game Changer

Rather than overanalyzing this new development, Cleo chooses to bask in it. She and Bobby enjoy moving through the tradeshow and attending the talks together. They return to their room to reenact the passion of the night before twice over the course of the day. They use their conference passes to buy reduced-rate tickets up the CN Tower, where they enjoy dinner in the revolving restaurant. They spend another emotionally charged night in their King-sized bed, then wake and repeat the day before. They forego the sites and institutions they'd planned to see, like the Hockey Hall of Fame, to spend every free moment in their hotel room.

On the conference's closing night, they sit at a table with Bobby's associates, whom they'd met at the reception party. Ernst, the oldest of the three, is from Zurich, Cleo thinks he'd said. A theoretical physicist. Marian is from Montreal, another theoretical physicist who teaches mathematics at the University of Toronto, and was a speaker at this event. Karl is from Sweden and identifies as an experimental physicist specializing in observing natural phenomena and developing and analyzing experiments. Cleo appreciates that she will be hard-pressed to understand their conversations on an intellectual level while trying to navigate their accents.

"Cleo has some interesting thoughts on time travel," Bobby offers up to the group as they are served their first course of the night. Cleo tries to wave off Bobby's attempt to include her, but Marian is intrigued.

"Tell us, Cleo," she says, her accent not as thick as Karl's and prettier than Ernst's. "I have spent some time on the mathematics of time travel."

"Uh, well," Cleo puts her salad fork down, mildly embarrassed by Bobby's announcement, "You probably know about the ring laser, uh, by a theoretical physicist interested in time travel." All three nod in unison. This could be good, she thinks.

"His math is on point," Ernst says, his Swiss-German accent thick. "Though, beyond the mathematics, it is an impossible feat."

"Yes, that's what I understand. Uh, not enough energy could be generated to spin it fast enough," Cleo replies, noticing Bobby proudly looking on. The butterflies beat against her sternum, but she does not let this stall her. If she can make more headway and get an explanation as to how she's traveling through time, all the better. She explains her concept of time travel as it is happening to her and how Franklin is there each time she returns to her initiation day. Then she sidetracks herself by questioning that if Franklin is experiencing his own life as a time traveler, how can he always be at her initiation day? Of course, she presents the concept as fiction for a book, referring to herself as Jane Doe.

"Fascinating, Cleo," Karl is the first to respond. "The first thing that comes to mind is superposition," he explains, "the ability of a quantum system to be in multiple states simultaneously until observed. Do you know this?"

Cleo looks to Bobby, who had explained a bit about the quantum realm when discussing the white noise communication angle. She nods, expecting Bobby to fill in the blanks later.

"Ya? I'm proposing this because, like everything, our brains are composed of atoms, which also work at the quantum level." He pauses as if gauging the others' reactions before continuing. "Now, this could put me in the realm of quantum mysticism and maybe get me kicked out of the community, but yours is an extraordinary scenario that hasn't been reproduced in a lab, so...."

"But Karl, traditionally only quantum states experience superposition. People and animals and other macro entities don't," Ernst chimes in.

Karl is undeterred. "I think the principle can be applied because we have free will; take a left turn or a right, be angry or happy, fight or flee, these options are all in superposition waiting to be realized. If you decide you will be happy, then BAM," Karl pounds the table with a flat hand, and the dishes and cutlery shudder. "That's being observed. That's being *measured* because it's happening. But before it happens, and infinite options are open to you, you are in superposition with your thoughts. Anything can happen, and that's what superposition is: infinite possibilities before one is observed."

"So how does that affect time travel?" Marian queries, her salad course finished.

"Superposition doesn't. Cleo, I can't claim to know exactly how your Jane Doe would travel back in time, but I'm proposing that superposition affects each version of them." Karl appears to collect himself, placing his fork down. "You see, if your Franklin were there once and that instance of him was observed, then as long as that instance of Franklin is observed again and again by someone, then there he is, prepping your Jane Doe on their initiation day."

"Okay, that makes sense. As much as any of this can, and I'm sorry if my novel idea is dumbing your conversation down." The table shakes their heads, and Cleo feels better about her offering. "So, to clarify, each time Jane Doe meets Franklin at her initiation day, she's the observer, and so a version of him pops into existence?"

"Right." Karl's fingers drum on the table.

"So, next question," Cleo is feeling more at ease now, "when Jane Doe leaves a future, and it disappears, it's because she's not there to observe it anymore?"

"Makes perfect sense to me!" Karl seems elated that Cleo understands, his head snapping left to right, smiling at his peers.

It seems that Franklin knew what he was talking about. He just didn't have the science to understand why.

"If superposition is the explanation behind Franklin turning up for your Jane Doe each time she jumps to her initiation day, then an instance of him must always be in that moment," Bobby surmises, the fingers of his left hand massaging his beard.

"Ya! Meaning, when Jane Doe observes him, he blinks into existence. It's a lot to process and too much to explain, but it is a novel, after all, and superposition ought to cover it." Karl points a delicate finger at Cleo.

Cleo feels seen. Her gift validated through science. She takes Bobby's right hand under the table and squeezes. "It's very Matrix," Bobby jokes. "But honestly, how can you know anyone outside this room exists when you're not observing them?"

"Right, Bobby," Ernst agrees. "There could be nothing outside of this room right now. It may only appear as we open the door and move through the space."

Cleo considers this and shakes her head. *Too much!* That she can accept superposition and the idea that observation makes Franklin exist in every instance of her initiation day and that each future disappears when she isn't observing it will have to do for tonight.

Marian looks from Bobby to Cleo and says, "Concerning your Jane Doe traveling back in time, Carlo Rovelli, a wonderful theoretical physicist who has written books on the subject, suggests that our perception of the flow of time depends on our perspective, and he states that it is better understood starting from the structure of our brain and emotions than from the physical universe. So perhaps you can use that angle when contemplating how Jane Doe is accomplishing time travel to the past."

This hits home, Cleo realizes. Recalling the memory and its associated emotions and senses makes it real. It's how she travels back to that moment at her desk, staring at her computer screen. The more these brilliant people engage in her reality, the more she feels permitted to experience it.

"There are very few options for time travel into the past," Karl adds. "So what Marian is suggesting has merit. It can't be explained, so it would work well for a science fiction novel." The table's plates are cleared, and new cutlery is placed for the second course. Then, plates of Cornish hens, Broccolini, and Parisian potatoes are slid in front of them.

"Ya, Marian's example is not unlike the Gateway Process," Ernst insists. "The CIA's attempt to discover time travel by syncing the brain's two hemispheres in the early 80s. It was proposed this would create a powerful stream of energy, like a laser." He moves two halved, tiny potatoes on his plate, joining them to illustrate his point. "That was McDonnell, a U.S. Army General or some high-ranking soldier who was put in charge of the Gateway Process. It was all declassified in the early 2000s." He looks directly at Cleo, his bushy, white eyebrows arching. "You could look it up."

Marian looks excitedly at Cleo, offering another option. "A further proposed method to travel to the past is through wormholes," she leans in, eyeing the others at the round table, then refocusing on Cleo. "A wormhole is a hypothetical tunnel that connects two distant points in space and time." She leans back in her chair. "Think of it as a shortcut that allows your Jane Doe to bypass the normal flow of time. If we could find or create a wormhole and control it, theoretically, we might be able to step through it and emerge at an earlier point in time." Maybe Marian intuits Cleo's mild confusion over the myriad potential options for time travel assaulting her, or perhaps she reads her expression correctly; either way, Marian defaults to Cleo's original thought.

"Of course, what you'd suggested earlier – the ring laser – created by manipulating and harnessing a powerful gravitational field that bends space-time, turning it back on itself to form a loop, is intriguing. If, as Einstein posited in his theory of general relativity, light can affect gravity, and gravity can influence time, then a ring laser, with enough energy behind it, ought to produce your timelike curve."

"I like this idea best, but that theory is also nearly impossible to prove because of the enormous energy proposed to run the machine," Bobby inserts. The four nod in agreeance.

"I'm so glad I joined Bobby at this conference," Cleo admits, smiling brightly. "Meeting all of you - I've been given priceless expert knowledge. So, thank you."

The remainder of dinner revolves around topical conversation relating to conference business, and Cleo is left to contemplate the science of her gift.

As Cleo and Bobby prepare for bed, Cleo feels a nagging urge to tell Bobby that the Jane Doe in her story is her, that Franklin is a real person, and that she can travel back in time. Would that ruin everything? Would he think her mad and question his feelings for her? Are they so fickle? Why chance it? Everything is perfect. Just don't jump!

Lying in bed after another lengthy show of mutual affection, Cleo and Bobby remain tangled up from the waist down. Cleo moves her legs first, sensing a cramp coming on.

"So, do you think you have enough real science to move forward with your plot?" Bobby takes a mouthful from the water glass at his bedside, swishing it around in his mouth and passing it to Cleo.

"Oh, yes, tonight was very useful; thank you so much for bringing me," Cleo says, then, after a pause, "Was this a plan all along? I mean, to get me here and ... the King-sized bed and everything?"

"Mmhm," Bobby mutters, swallowing his water. "My master plan!"

Cleo shifts to her side, facing Bobby. "Really? Did you *really* plan it all? How long have you been in love with me?" She feels like a giddy high schooler.

Bobby shifts his position to face Cleo. "Honestly? Since our senior year." Wow, she thinks, he's been holding back a long time. "How about you?"

"Ah, like, forever. I didn't know what it was, or I didn't want to admit it. I was worried we'd ruin the friendship." And that was the truth. She hated what happened in that other life. She playfully drags her nails down one side of his face, combing through his thickening beard. "I thought you weren't a relationship kind of guy."

"Me?" Bobby says defensively with a healthy dollop of his distinctive sarcasm. "Look, I know I've come off that way, but I was so relieved to hear you say it back. And yes, I planned for this to happen. I said to myself 'self, it's now or never. You can't go on like this. You need to tell her and make it count.'"

"You sure managed all that," Cleo purrs, leaning her forehead against his. "I'm so happy, Bobby. I could stay like this forever."

"Too bad we can't be like Jane Doe and Franklin in your story," he says, to Cleo's surprise. "Make this our initiation day and pop back whenever we want." God, she thinks, he's attentive. He's the best version of himself in this life.

"If only," she agrees, rolling onto her back. "I'm going to have a shower."

Bobby watches her rise, and she notices how his gaze fixates on her nakedness as she moves around the bed and enters the bathroom. She feels seen by Bobby too now. For the first time, really. All her flaws are on display, and he looks on lovingly. How could she ever jump from this life?

Cleo gets in the shower and lets the water fall over her body. She recalls Franklin's sad story of when he'd lived to a ripe old age with his wife, tried to bring them back to his initiation day, and lost her. Cleo had sensed a large part of him would have happily died with her in that life. But that wasn't his fate; now, he lives with the memory that haunts him.

That wouldn't be her. Even Parkinson's wouldn't force her to leave Bobby in this life. He will tend to her needs. He will be there for her.

Suddenly, Cleo feels guilty. It seems almost like a punishment to think Bobby would suffer her disease along with her. He doesn't deserve that. He deserves better than that. Better than her. Shit, she thinks. I'm self-sabotaging. Bobby knows the deal. He knows, and still, he loves her. That's real love. But the true test will come years from now when she is nearly paralyzed with tremors. She won't put him through that, she decides. How could she?

Only Fools Rush In

Cleo wakes up before Bobby to the soft sound of her phone dinging. She rolls over and retrieves it. It's a text from Franklin. He's wondering whether she's experienced the pull of a singularity in Toronto. She answers no, mercifully. That would have altered the last couple of days dramatically, she thinks.

She asks Franklin about growing old and whether she will pine for that experience if she never allows herself to embrace it.

Franklin reads between the lines. **You want to grow old with Bobby,** he types.

Yes, she replies.

You're in love, he types, and she can sense the melancholy in the statement.

Yes, she states. **But this has been a long time coming, Franklin. We've both admitted we'd been in love with each other for years. It's only now we**

dared to tell one another. She waits for dots to occupy a text bubble, but it's not immediate. She wonders whether he's disappointed in her. He'd warned her off love, after all.

It's no one's fault, Cleo, Franklin finally replies. **It was a pre-existing condition. You've heard my story. You know how I have suffered. Perhaps this is your destiny. This life.**

Thank you for understanding, Cleo writes. **I'm happy. Bobby's happy. I want to try.**

Then be happy, Cleo.

Thank you. I'll see you at home?

Yes.

That is the extent of the conversation. She doesn't feel judged by Franklin, and it's not like she has a choice. Love is love, and why shouldn't she be happy? Still, she wonders how long she'll allow this happiness. She can't let Bobby's life be about her disease. Can she?

The clock radio comes to life, playing a song Cleo remembers from high school. She reaches to turn it off before it wakes Bobby and receives another message, or part of the overall message, through the white noise.

"In another future ... In your future..." There is an intensity to the words, unlike the others. It sounds more urgent. She experiences goose flesh and the rising hairs on the back of her neck she's become accustomed to with each chilling message. Cleo picks up her phone and enters the new words into her Notes app. She silences the clock radio when the white noise returns to music. Bobby stirs beside her, and she turns to greet him.

"Sorry, I forgot I'd set the alarm. I wanted to go to the gym." She kisses his forehead, leaving her lips attached to his furrowed brow for a long moment. "You stay in bed. I'll be back in an hour."

Bobby mumbles, 'I love you,' and Cleo says it back, her mood elevating. She dresses in her gym clothes and leaves the room. After a half hour on the treadmill and a few minutes of stretching, she showers in the changeroom, dresses, and does her makeup.

Bobby is up and prepared to take on the day when she returns to their room. Today, they will be returning to Chicago via Pearson International to O'Hare. After a complementary breakfast, Bobby drives them to the airport, and they settle in for the short flight.

Cleo and Bobby part ways at O'Hare. Bobby heads to Michigan to tackle budget and tax issues, education policy, environmental protection, energy, health care policy, and other think-tank things. At the same time, Cleo takes the train home to her Chicago flat in the South Loop. They're both emotional. Cleo hugs him tightly. Bobby is the first to let go. This terrifies Cleo.

"Call me when you get back," she says. "I already miss you."

Bobby bends to kiss her. Cleo's fingers thread through his hair, pulling him close again. When the kiss ends, Cleo's tear-soaked cheek slides against his. Something hurts in their parting. Something deep and primal. It's like a survival instinct kicking in. She's afraid. Will he call her? Will he revert to the Bobby she thought she knew?

"I love you," he says, gazing into her eyes. "I'll be back on the weekend." He takes her trembling chin between his thumb and forefinger, kisses her petite nose, and squeezes her shoulder. "Promise."

"I know; I love you too," Cleo manages through her anxiety. "It can't come soon enough."

"I agree." Bobby turns and walks to the rental car station, and Cleo watches him go. She studies his gait, wishing he could move back to Chicago. Or maybe she could move to Midland, Michigan? She'll look up jobs when she gets home, she decides.

The train back allows Cleo to spend some time on the words and phrases she's collected from the white noise on her phone. She's never been good at puzzles or riddles or anything involving letters that need rearranging to spell a word. Perhaps she will present it to Bobby and use his intellect to piece the message together. But does she have all the words? She stares at her screen.

YOU... FIND... OTHERS LIKE US... BOBBY... MERGE... TIMELIKE CURVE... YES, BOBBY... HELP... DO IT AGAIN... IN ANOTHER FUTURE... IN YOUR FUTURE...

And then there are the numbers: 355711547. What are they? A date? No. A time? That wouldn't make any sense. An address? Maybe? She admits she won't make heads or tails out of this. Maybe Franklin will be able to put it together? She texts him an invite to her place for dinner and to review the message.

*   *   *   *

Cleo shares a hug with Franklin in her foyer. Then, she takes his coat, mittens, and fedora, and while he moves into the small living room, she hangs everything up.

Cleo offers Franklin a drink, and he accepts a red Zinfandel. Cleo joins him but can't shake the feeling that he's disappointed in her.

"So, you look good. You're glowing!" Franklin smiles and sips at his wine. Cleo gives him a sideways glance.

"Glowing?" She's never been described as glowing before and feels her cheeks redden. Franklin nods and leans back into the couch.

"Love will have that effect on a person," his smile collapses, and his head follows. "I'm sorry, Cleo, I meant that sincerely. I just ... I get attached too easily."

Cleo leans over the small coffee table from her seat and lands a hand on Franklin's knee. "I'm very fond of you, too," she tells him. "But please, just be happy for me. I'm a big girl. I understand the risks."

Franklin nods and lays a hand on top of Cleo's. "Yes, I've every confidence in you, Cleo. However, I worry that you'll decide to jump in fifty or seventy years and regret the life you chose."

"You can't regret the future you had with your wife – with Marla," Cleo says pleadingly.

"No, I don't suppose I do," Franklin agrees, "but it is a heavy burden, as I'd mentioned, jumping, and then a different Marla presents herself with each jump. Never again have I been able to make her love me."

"And that's why I want to stay in this life," Cleo explains, "for as long as I can, as it may never come again."

"You have a fair point," He admits, "and I won't mention it again for fear of being left off the guest list for your wedding." He laughs to himself quietly.

"Good," Cleo leans back in her chair. "Then it's settled. You'll be the ring bearer." She laughs, imagining a wedding, and the timer on her stove indicates dinner is ready.

She and Franklin sit to enjoy a pork loin with potatoes, peas, and broccoli. It always impresses for such a simple recipe, and Franklin has seconds.

Over dinner, Cleo raves about Toronto while Franklin nods, mindfully chewing his food and sipping his wine. After dinner, she leaves the dishes in the sink and lays out several scraps of paper with words written on them.

"Now, here are all the words I've heard so far from the phantoms," she explains. "This is my best guess at what sequence they go, and some words were said together without a pause, so I've put them together." There are eleven pieces of paper. Cleo watches as Franklin's eyes narrow.

"Do you have them in the order they were uttered?"

"Yes, and I've numbered them," Cleo points to the tiny numbers scratched on the bottom right corner of each. Franklin loosens his tie and removes his dinner jacket. He scratches at his receding grey, tight curls.

"Have you tried to add your own words in between these?" He asks. She is hoping he might be better at that and tells him so.

Franklin then requests paper of his own and sits to jot down Cleo's words. "Maybe the first line says, 'You MUST find others like us.' Which is what we've been doing. What I've been doing for centuries."

Cleo feels vindicated by that. They both do. The work they've been doing is likely one part of the message. "I think you're right about that," she says.

"Merge ... I wonder if they want us to unite as a group?" Franklin writes something on the paper. "It could say, 'you MUST find others like us TO merge IN A timelike curve,' and then, perhaps, 'Bobby CAN help.'?"

Cleo stands behind Franklin with her arms folded in front of her. "I mean, *yeah*, it could be." She pulls a kitchen chair next to him and sits. "When I asked what it meant when they said Bobby's name, I asked if they meant he could help, and it answered 'Yes.' So that tracks."

Franklin looks at her, and she looks at him. "Then this life makes the most sense to accomplish our task. Bobby loves you. He'll do whatever you ask."

"Sure, but I was hoping not to mention time travel to him this time," Cleo feels trapped. "I don't want him to think I'm nuts." She chews at her thumbnail.

Franklin's features pull into an austere expression. "You mustn't lie to the man you love, Cleo. It's a terrible weight to bear. My wife and I lived in peace because we were always open with each other. I told her before we were ever married. She knew who I was. What I was."

Cleo senses the weight he's put behind this latest warning and nods. She removes the thumb and clasps her hands together in front of her. "I'll tell him, I will."

"The phantoms have involved him. He can't be left out of the process, whatever that may be."

Cleo refocuses on the scrap papers and points to the numbers. "These were said in a line just like this. Any thoughts on what they might be?"

"These are interesting," he says, "Numbers could mean so many things. 355711547. Three hundred fifty-five million, seven hundred eleven thousand, five hundred forty-seven ... dollars?"

"That's a lot of money," Cleo feels slightly excited to think the phantoms might be planning a heist. "But ... unlikely?"

"Yes, I don't see any reason to talk in monetary terms through such an advanced form of communication."

"Is it advanced, though?" Cleo feels confrontational over this statement. "Isn't it just what we experience every day? It's just frequencies carrying messages."

"Yes, but they're coming through in multiple locations around the world and -" Franklin stops, a look of eureka stamped upon his face, and he asks Cleo to bring her laptop to the table. She does.

"Punch the numbers into your internet's address bar, Cleo," he tells her. "It could be a numbered business."

One page of nonsense content appears. Images of nothing cohesive, but then Franklin points to the maps tab. "Click on the maps icon," she does. He looks at Cleo and says, "It might be location coordinates."

"Like GPS?" Cleo feels like they just cracked the code and punches in 'GPS location.' She chooses from the first link, 'What's my location?' and sees the format numbers are broken into latitude and longitude. She and Franklin share a knowing grin.

Latitude: 41.86

Longitude: -87.62

"So," Franklin scribbles the numbers out with decimals, "if we take our numbers and break them up left to right, we'll have 35.57 Latitude and 115.47 Longitude." He looks to Cleo, directing her to punch the coordinates into the GPS finder with his eyes. She does. It returns a location in California. Cleo opens another tab and pulls up Google Maps, entering the longitude and latitude into the directions field.

"What's that? It's in the Mojave dessert?" Franklin asks, motioning at the screen to the dark, rectangular boxes scattered across the desert floor. "Can you pull out? I can't make out what that is."

Cleo is equally stumped by the visual. Her heart is thumping in anticipation. More nonsense? Then, as she pulls further back with the zoom function, they see what appears to be a massive tower and an entire facility situated in the middle of these rectangular blocks. "What the fuck is that?" Cleo feels she's stumbled upon an Area 51-style secret.

Franklin looks at her, an excited intensity playing across his face. "That, Cleo, is an excellent question."

She zooms out further and realizes there are two of these facilities, each surrounded by thousands of blocks. She zooms in on the lower facility and is offered the name. Ivanpah solar electric generating system. Franklin jolts back.

"A mirror array!" He nearly shouts. This causes Cleo to flinch. She looks at him crossly for scaring her, then returns her attention to the strange structures, zooming out again. Now, there are three in total, and what appears to be a massive solar farm that looks like an afterthought. "The energy that must put out," Franklin says, fingers running across his creased brow.

"A mirror array," Cleo says, "so those are all mirrors in those circles facing the towers?"

"Yes, they concentrate the sun's rays by focusing the mirrors on the central tower, creating an intense heat to run the turbines," Franklin answers. "It's a very sustainable way of producing energy."

"It must create a lot of it," Cleo recognizes, "it must be as hot as the sun in that tower." She types the facility's name in a separate tab, and they read about it.

"Occupying about five square miles of sun-drenched land in Southern California's Mojave Desert, the Ivanpah Solar Electric Generating System is a major accomplishment," Cleo reads aloud. "It was officially dedicated as the world's largest concentrating solar thermal power plant in operation." She turns to Franklin, who shrugs.

"Why would the phantoms direct us to a power plant?" He wonders.

"Maybe it's not the power plant itself; maybe it's just the location," Cleo theorizes. "But whatever the reason, we need to go there."

Franklin stands and paces a moment. "I don't want to rush into this, Cleo. We have time." He looks up and laughs at himself.

"I feel like we've just revealed a big piece of the puzzle," Cleo says, standing. "But you're right. We need to know why they're sending us."

"Yes, we need more of the message to materialize," Franklin states. "We'll have one chance at deciphering it in this life and carrying out whatever the message is asking of us."

Cleo understands. If they fail at their attempt and have to jump to try again, she will lose this life, Bobby, and the bond they've enjoyed. Lose love. "Then we wait," she agrees, "we wait for the full message."

FRANKLIN

With more information, the more mysterious Franklin's riddle becomes. Still, he is heartened to see that it is coming together. Now, they have a location where something substantial is to happen. There is no doubt that Cleo and Bobby will be involved in this. He will ensure that he is included in every aspect to ensure the completion of the riddle that has perplexed him for so long.

It has been nearly one hundred years since receiving the riddle. Whether it was meant to be presented as such or just another scattered message like Cleo's, he can't say. Perhaps he didn't receive the entire thing. But knowing Cleo's message's what, when, where, who, how, and why will no doubt assist in solving his own.

He had not enjoyed such exciting times since he'd lived a passionate and loving life with his wife. His goal is to make her love him again using his unlimited mulligans – as Cleo put it. One day, he's decided. One day, it will be as it once was, and he will be happy.

Las Vegas

A week after discussing waiting for the entire message to come through with Franklin, Cleo is in Las Vegas with Bobby for a weekend at another much larger conference. All courtesy of his work. Cleo reads through the marketing material as they settle into their accommodations at the Mandalay Bay Hotel and Resort. The APS Meeting welcomes a diverse international community of over 10,000 scholars to celebrate the frontiers of physics, pave pathways into new research, and nurture the next generation of scientists.

"I didn't get the sense that physicists and scientists love to party from the last conference," Cleo calls out from the bed to Bobby, who is brushing his teeth.

Bobby's head rounds the bathroom door, pausing his electric toothbrush. "What do you mean? We love to party!" Foam drips off his beard to the floor. Cleo throws the pamphlet at him, laughing.

"I can't believe I'm in Las Vegas," she admits. "I never thought I'd get here." Then she begins to seed her plan that took shape the moment Bobby mentioned this conference. "You know, I thought I'd rent a car and drive out to the Ivanpah solar power plant tomorrow while you're at the conference."

Bobby reappears at the bathroom threshold, wiping his face with a towel. "Oh? I thought you would lay by the wave pool with your toes in the sand, drinking buckets of Corona on ice."

"It's *February*, Bobby; the pools aren't open," she reminds him. "I need to amuse myself. But seriously, I'm drawn to this place. They have tours at 1 and 3 tomorrow, and I want to see it."

"Why the infatuation with power generation?" Bobby lays next to her and kisses her bare shoulder.

"Have you seen this place? It's like future world level stuff. Bunch of mirrors focused on a central tower to superheat it," she pulls the page up on Bobby's tablet.

"You know, McCarthy, most people go see the Hoover Dam, hike Red Rock Canyon, take in a show," he makes a face.

"Are you saying I'm 'most people' Bobby Patel?" She parodies offense.

"Cool! Can I come?" Bobby asks, avoiding the question. "I don't have to attend all the speakers, and I believe tomorrow from 2 to 6 is free."

Cleo considers this. She had hoped to get a feel for the facility. She considered even going off tour to wander, looking for some hint as to why the phantoms included this location in their message. But having Bobby there, too, couldn't hurt. After all, he must be brought into the loop at some point. He's part of the overall message.

"Sure, of course, you can come," she answers. "I didn't think you'd be able to. I'll sign us both up right now!" Cleo adds their names to the tour for 3 pm and manages to rent a car to get them there.

Tonight is another reception in their hotel that Bobby has opted out of attending, explaining he wants to see the sights and get dinner in the Eiffel Tower. That Cleo will have seen both the Paris and Las Vegas Eiffel Towers in the span of a couple of months excites her. Though she's slightly afraid of heights, this version is only half the size of the original, but an impressive sight all the same.

Walking the strip, they encounter all manner of Buskers along the way. They opt out of using the monorail, choosing to walk the strip. They get a beer on the street and walk with it. They pop into the New York, New York casino, lured in by the pings and melodies coming from within. Bobby bets a twenty on a slot and stops after he's made five dollars on his twenty-dollar gamble.

Once the Eiffel Tower is within view, she stops, overcome by the romantic ideation of what they're about to do, and hugs Bobby with her free arm, squeezing his hand with the other. Bobby looks kindly down at her, and they kiss. As night falls and electric light ignites the darkness, Cleo notices the air has cooled significantly. They came on this walk prepared, pulling light jackets from their backpacks.

They take the elevator up to the Eiffel Tower restaurant and are seated, glad Bobby had made reservations before ever taking the trip.

The menu is extensive, mouth-watering, and filled with classic French cuisine. The scent takes her back to the cafes of old Paris. The smell of rich sauces paired with each elaborate dish permeates the atmosphere, stimulating her appetite. It's incredible, she thinks, that she has retained the scent of a city from an alternate future she burned.

Bobby chooses a bottle of wine, and when it arrives, Cleo orders the filet of Mediterranean Seabass, knowing an appetizer would be too much. Besides, she would have the Eiffel Tower Soufflé if she had any room left.

Bobby orders the Creamy French Onion Soup, Broiled Beef Tenderloin Filet with a Classic Potato Gratin. Because it can take up to half an hour to prepare the soufflé, the server recommends he order it now so they can begin it midway through their mains. He does so, and Cleo feels weak in the knees.

Their view is of the strip with the Bellagio fountains directly across the street. The sidewalk in front of the fountains collects more and more spectators, and the show begins. It's a delight to watch from this vantage point. Cleo feels Bobby's hand land gently on hers, and she smiles, a tear teetering on her lower eyelid. She wipes it away, and Bobby's soup arrives. She manages a couple of spoonfuls to try it and decides it is an exceptional soup. Soon after, their mains arrive, and Cleo can hardly contain her reaction to each bite, eyelids fluttering.

They end their dining experience with the chocolate soufflé and are not disappointed. Bobby feeds Cleo the last peace with his fork and pays for the experience. To say it was dinner isn't saying enough. It was an event. Cleo feels satisfied to her core.

They take the monorail back to their hotel, where Bobby surprises her with a show. Michael Jackson's ONE. Cleo can hardly believe the life she's suddenly living. Shouldn't everyone have the option to experience their ideal life by jumping from one to another until they find it?

After the show, Bobby leads her to the hotel bar that sits like an island surrounded by slot machines. The melodies of the machines are surprisingly unintrusive, seated at a table where Bobby has ordered two gin and tonics. They sit together on the padded bench seat where Bobby's hand strokes her leg under the table.

Returning to their room, they roll onto the bed and undress frantically. They tear the covers off and hungrily satisfy each other's every whim. It's a night she'll never forget and one she hopes will be repeated in this life. This life is the one - until it isn't.

Cleo and Bobby spend an hour in the hotel gym the following day, and Bobby races off to hear two speakers before lunch. Cleo wanders the hotel, admiring the Shark Reef Aquarium, and puts a few dollars into a slot machine. Of course, she loses the money, but how could she come to Vegas and not try?

She enjoys breakfast at the hotel's Seabreeze Café and returns to her room. It has been made up, so she sits on the loveseat provided. She checks her email for the tour tickets for Ivanpah power station, placing them in her phone's photo folder for easy access. She feels like a secret agent preparing for a mission and shudders at the thought. She's more than a secret agent, she muses. She's a time traveler! But that part is over, she thinks. She wouldn't jump again unless the Parkinson's got bad. She won't have Bobby living in those conditions. She won't. But then, that's years from now, she asserts.

Bobby meets Cleo at the KUMI Japanese restaurant on the premises for lunch. "So far, so good," Bobby tells her of the speakers. "Heady stuff," he picks up a piece of the Dragon roll, places it in his mouth, and chews. Cleo loves to watch him eat. There's not much she doesn't love about him, though.

"Anyone I know there?" She says jokingly. Bobby smiles sympathetically, and Cleo clears her throat. "You'll be good to go at two today?" Cleo stirs her miso soup with chopsticks, picking out the tofu and popping them in her mouth.

"No problem. I'll meet you in the room?" he asks. "I'm going to want to change." Cleo nods, and they cheer with an authentic Japanese Sake.

"I'll pick up the car after lunch and park it across the road at the grocery store," Cleo explains, "it's a forty-five-minute drive on I-15."

"I have to say, I'm pretty excited about it," Bobby admits. "I told a guy I met at the second presentation from Winnipeg about it, and he's jelly."

"Jealous? *Of us?* Imagine that!" Cleo laughs and then lifts her bowl, draining the miso.

Picking up the car was easy. At the Green Valley Grocery Store, Cleo grabs a few snacks for the road and takes them back to the hotel, a short walk away, crossing over Las Vegas Blvd.

In her room, she meets Bobby, who quickly changes clothes to something more appropriate for the outdoors, and they're off.

Bobby offers to take the wheel, and Cleo does not put up a fight. The drive is only interesting because the landscape is so foreign to Cleo and Bobby. There is beauty in the desert, however. The solitude is strangely attractive to Cleo. Las Vegas has been a lot of people all at once. They pass a satellite casino resort named Buffalo Bills and a massive array of solar panels before they arrive at their destination, where a golf course looks painfully out of place in this barren wasteland. It's an oasis amid nothingness. Cleo supposes that was the idea.

The sky is a clear blue above the rustic mountains, as a backdrop to the three towers glowing blindingly bright at their peaks. They have passed into California, where the solar array sits at the base of Clark Mountain.

They drive through the open gate, where an official-looking woman stands to greet them. After they present their tour QR codes via Cleo's phone, they are directed to the parking lot, where they notice a few other vehicles and two tour buses offloading people. One is a Chinese tour company; the other resembles a local company full of Las Vegas tourists. Five or six other cars pepper the visitor parking.

As they move toward the mob of activity, Cleo and Bobby navigate the disoriented crowds to find an Ivanpah representative. He is armed and looks disgruntled over the influx of pedestrians descending on his protected space. He uses a wand, like those at the airport, on them and asks that they empty their pockets. He inspects their bobbles and directs them to the double glass doors where the Chinese tour group is currently assembling. They hurry over and let themselves in before the tour group. It's hot today. Hot for February, and they are grateful for the air conditioning inside. They present their QR codes again and are handed headphones to avoid missing anything the tour guide says. Next, they are asked to stand aside as the Vegas tour bus empties into the building, and its tourists excitedly assemble in a crooked line.

"Looks like we'll be merging with this group," Bobby tells her. Merging - the word takes Cleo back to the fragmented message from her phantoms. Would she experience any more of the message in this place? She ought to expect something to happen if it's such an integral location, as she suspects. This gives her a chill that Bobby notices.

"Too cold?" He asks, his right hand enveloping her, rubbing her upper arm. The friction produces a warming effect, and she realizes she is a bit cold. "I think they're being too generous with the AC," she suggests.

"Probably need it, though," Bobby ponders, "what with the amount of heat being created." A good point, Cleo concedes.

In minutes, they are asked to don their headphones and follow a short, thin woman through another door that takes them back outside, gathering around the base of one of the towers where two more armed guards watch over them. "At the tops of these towers," the guide says when everyone has resurfaced from the AC, "the energy is concentrated, and surface temperatures can soar above 900 degrees Fahrenheit." Bobby looks wide-eyed at Cleo, and she smiles. They walk toward another building as the guide continues to deliver facts.

"The Ivanpah solar plant covers a massive 3,500 acres of desert with a series of robotically-controlled mirrors that reflect sunlight and concentrate it on the sixty-nine-story high steam-generating towers." She stops and turns to face the group, and the many shuffling feet release a cloud of dust from the desert floor. Cleo's waving hand works to clear it from her face.

"It cost two-point-two billion dollars to build this facility employing one thousand people from 2010 to 2014." She turns to walk again and stops at what she calls a Heliostat assembly and Pad Bonding building. Then, after a quick tour inside with more information about the manufacturing and maintenance of a heliostat than Cleo cared to know, they are back outdoors and moving through the solar fields.

Bobby is holding her hand when she realizes her headphones have cut out. She is about to ask Bobby if his are working when white noise pierces the silence. She releases Bobby's hand and pulls the headphones off. She then realizes her mistake and mouths, 'Something in my ear,' to Bobby, places her pinky finger in her ear canal, and pretends to remove something.

She quickly places the headphones back on and waits for more of the message from the white noise to reveal itself.

"You must find ... like us..." it says, then a long pause of static. "Timelike curve at these coordinates... " More dead airspace. "Do it ... Merge everyone..." Next, the trained voice of the guide cuts back to describing the eight landmarks they are visiting this afternoon.

Cleo pulls out her phone and enters the words and sentences she just heard into her Notes app. They were right about the coordinates. That's heartening, she thinks. Some other words fill the empty spaces, which she discovers she and Franklin had guessed correctly. She experiences a sense of gratification. They are on the right track. Bobby looks over at her and shrugs. 'Sorry, it's Mom,' she mouths, pointing at her phone.

The group continues through the field, where the mirrors do not reflect the sunlight. Each is very large, Cleo observes. She can understand why it cost so much to build and place 170,000 of them. Finally, the group stops at a water distribution point where people can fill their bottles or drink directly from the fountains.

They return to the main attraction, the tower, and its boiler that heats the water, creating high-pressure steam, which drives turbines that send the resulting energy to the Californian power grid. Within this building, the group is placed in a conference room with folding chairs aligned to face a central screen. This will be the half-hour presentation that will take them from concept to construction to working power plant.

Cleo is happy she's received more of the message but doesn't feel it's enough to warrant visiting these coordinates. Surely, more will reveal itself than a few words. That's when the sick feeling tightens her abdomen, forcing her to stoop over from the discomfort.

"I need a bathroom," she tells Bobby in a whisper. She's embarrassed to admit it but wouldn't want to throw up in a group setting. Bobby takes her arm and leads her back the way they came. "I saw a facility just outside this room," he tells her. The guide stands at the door checking her phone but allows them passage when she sees Cleo's sickly white complexion. Bobby thanks her, and they reach the washroom in quick, purposeful steps.

Cleo thanks Bobby and closes the door behind her. The sick feeling is lessening, but the gravity is just beginning to weigh her down. Jesus, someone is about to jump, she knows. Here, at Ivanpah. That's timely, she thinks. But, of course, someone is about to jump. It must be why she's here. The weight of the event is bearing down on her, and she's finding it difficult to remain standing on her quivering legs.

"Everything okay, Cleo?" Bobby is concerned. She answers yes but in a shaky voice, not her own. He knocks. "Come on, McCarthy. I know that tone. You're not okay. Let me in."

She wants to let him in. She desperately wants that. She wants to lean on him and tell him what's happening to her. To tell him what's happening at this very moment at Ivanpah. Then, a bang comes down on the door, and Cleo is angry that Bobby would be so intrusive.

"Uh, Cleo, we have a woman out here that needs in there," Bobby says through the steel door. He sounds uncertain, which is weird for Bobby. He's always so confident. She snaps the lock back, trying to straighten up, and the woman falls into her with Bobby trailing. "Sorry, she has a grip on my wrist," Bobby apologizes for the intrusion.

Cleo is flat on her ass against the washroom wall. The woman, older, maybe five foot four, and heavy set, is on her knees facing her with Bobby's wrist firmly in her grasp. Cleo meets the woman's gaze and orders Bobby to close and lock the door. He does so, wearing a look of deep confusion.

Cleo's attention returns to the older woman. She recognizes the fear in her expression. The terrified, glazed-over look in her eyes, unable to grasp her current whereabouts. "You've just traveled through time," Cleo explains to her, the weight of the singularity now gone. The woman nods without understanding, her tight, long black curls bouncing.

"Bobby, please, seat her on the toilet," Cleo asks, and Bobby lifts the woman under her arms and places her as directed. Cleo can see the wheels spinning behind Bobby's eyes, having heard what she told this frantic woman. Cleo gets up and straightens herself out. She wants to focus on the woman first. She kneels to address her.

"My name is Cleo. What's yours?"

"M – my name? Uh, it's uh, Carri. I'm Carri, but -" she looks around her, "I'm not supposed to be here."

"No, but you've been here before," Cleo says, slowly nodding at Carri. Carri slowly nods back.

"It's just that I left for the weekend," she says, sitting up and releasing Bobby's arm. "I – I'm sorry, mister,"

"It's Bobby, I'm Bobby," he tells her like he's Tarzan and she's Carri.

"Bobby is with me. He's safe. You work here?" Cleo notices the Ivanpah patch on Carri's shirt. "In what capacity do you work here, Carri?"

"I'm the, uh," she shakes her head, "the GM. I run Ivanpah." This stamps a smile on Cleo's lips. There it is, she thinks. This is why she was summoned to Ivanpah. To meet Carri.

"There is a lot to cover, Carri," Cleo tells her, "Do you have an office where we can talk in private?"

Carri nods and stands unsteadily. "I – I was at home. It's my birthday," It's your initiation day, Cleo thinks. "There was a sudden burst of excitement. A surprise party ... maybe,"

They follow Carri one floor up, and she opens her office door, waving them both in. "I'm sure it was a surprise party. It shocked the hell out of me."

"That was your trigger, Carri," Cleo sits in one of the two guest chairs across from Carri, who cautiously rounds her desk. Bobby sits in the other, and Cleo lays a hand on his. "You've traveled back in time." She glances at Bobby, who looks Gobsmacked.

"Traveled through -" Carri sits heavily in her chair. "No, no, I was in one place, and now I'm here."

"You said you'd left for the weekend. When is your birthday?" Cleo asks calmly.

"It's today, Sunday," Carri says. Cleo looks at Bobby, and he looks scared.

"Today is Saturday," Bobby says in amazement, checking his phone to be certain. Cleo and Carri both look at Bobby. Cleo turns back to Carri and explains.

"You're a time traveler, Carri. This isn't up for debate. This is the day; you realize that." Cleo wheels her chair over to Carri's and takes her hands in hers. "The memory of this moment sent you back to it when you were startled by the surprise. It's not an uncommon trigger for people like us. People with this gift." Cleo explains, digging one of Franklin's cards out of her purse.

With her hands returning to Carri's, placing the card in her fingers, Cleo looks tentatively at Bobby, whose lips remain parted, and eyes carry a sense of wonder and betrayal. She perceives a long drive back to the resort.

"How is this possible?" Carri asks, studying Cleo's hands on hers.

"You're unique, Carri," Cleo continues, "you have something a scarce few enjoy. It's a gift that lets us relive our lives with a thought. To return to the moment we first realize we have this gift." Cleo is focused on Carri but feels the weight of Bobby's gaze on her. "There's no easy way to explain it. You must experience it. And you have."

"What you're saying is crazy," Carri manages in a whisper, eyes still fixed on their linked hands.

"It seems so now, yes, and that's the same for everyone experiencing their initiation day."

Carri looks up to meet Cleo's stare. "Is that what this is, then? My initiation into time travel?" Cleo nods. "I can go back to the age of the dinosaurs? Watch the pyramids being built. Witness Christ's birth?" Cleo shakes her head.

"No, Carri. You can only return to this moment -"

"It's a closed time-like curve," Bobby interrupts. He's leaning forward, frowning, and staring at Cleo, his eyebrows raised and pupils darting from Carri to her and back again. Cleo nods at Bobby apologetically. "Is this real?"

"It's real," Cleo replies, a lump forming in her throat, fearful this event has spoiled her for Bobby. She feels heartsick but has a job to do. There is a reason they were directed to the Ivanpah solar array, and she must discover it. Unfortunately, her feelings will have to take a backseat for now. As difficult as it is, she must swallow her sadness to understand why she's here and meeting Carri.

"Carri, we're meeting for a reason," she glances at Bobby again, who seems glued to his seat. "I've been doing this now for months. I've experienced several futures and jumped back each time. In each of my futures, I have received messages through white noise from someone somewhere in time." She squeezes Carri's hands to bring her out of her head.

"Carri, they told me to come here. That you've made your first jump can't be a coincidence. I believe they wanted us to meet." Then she looks at Bobby again to include him in the message. "Bobby, you're also a part of this," she explains, acknowledging that it's now or never.

Bobby snaps out of his trance-like state and straightens up in his chair. "I – I can time travel too?"

Cleo hates that he's come to that conclusion and worries that he will be disappointed. "No, Bobby, but you have been requested, by name, to help us achieve whatever we're being asked to accomplish."

"You don't know." Bobby surmises. "That's why you've been asking about the science of white noise. About how someone might communicate through it from different times." He runs his hands through his wavey, tangled hair and sighs heavily. "McCarthy..." it's a whisper, "What the fuck?"

"I know it's a lot to process, trust me," Cleo defends, her mouth drying up. She turns her attention back to Carri, whose dark skin looks a little paler than earlier, and is staring at Bobby. "But we three are destined for something, and we're close to discovering what."

Carri has tears streaming down the ebony skin of her cheeks. She sniffles and wipes them away, taking a deep, cleansing breath. "I need to get back home. They ... my family and friends will be worried."

"That future has passed, Carri," she tells her. "It's gone. It's like it never happened. Each future we jump from disappears, and a new one takes its place." She recounts Franklin's description of the candle being lit as the last one goes out.

"I can't just accept this," Carri says, her brows knitting together and intelligent eyes studying Cleo's. "You must understand that."

"I do. I've met a few people like us from different parts of the world, and it's usually the same. Time travel: it's a difficult concept to believe, I know. But you must. You're *proof.* It's your reality now. It's something you can do. Don't fear it. Control it."

"And if I end up here again?"

"I'll be here, or, at least, an instance of me will be here to talk you through whatever concerns you have."

"You just exist here? In this time?"

"No, it's more complex than that," Cleo looks pleadingly to Bobby.

Bobby clears his throat. "It's superposition. What you observe is your reality. Because Cleo is here now, an instance of her will always be here for you."

"And you?" Carri tilts her head slightly.

"Me, uh, I can't answer that," Bobby looks disappointed in himself. "This is *your* past. I'm not sure how I fit into it. I was your first point of contact when you returned, however. I brought you to Cleo," he's working through the equations, and Cleo feels that familiar flutter in her chest. "I guess I would have to be, so long as nothing on our end changes. If Cleo jumps again, our futures will be altered. The minor details will become blurred because no future can be the same. No outcome would share an identical conclusion." He looks at Cleo, and she shrugs, encouragingly nodding at him.

"Time is like an hourglass," Bobby looks reflective. "When sand fills the bottom, the bottom becomes the top and begins anew. No two grains of sand will fall in the same sequence as in past turnings. Like in chaos theory, each grain of sand's timing cannot be predicted, nor can the minutia of events in each future."

Cleo knows she is full doe eyes on him right now, but he'd put it so poetically. Imagine, Bobby, waxing philosophical like this. But, then, she snaps out of her reverie. "The thing is," Cleo returns her focus to Carri, "you want to be careful about jumping back to this memory because once you do, you erase the life you were living past this point."

"I think I get it," Carri says, rubbing her eyes. "What happened tomorrow never really happened. It might happen again, but this time, I'll be ready for the surprise and not remember myself back to this moment when I have a stack of files that need processing."

"Right, your futures remain only in *your* memory," Cleo clarifies.

"Then why is this happening?" Carri asks, her anxiety falling to manageable levels.

"Yes, that's the question." Cleo leans back, releasing Carri's hands. "But whatever it is, it will involve you, Carri. Maybe it will involve this place. I don't know yet. But if you can visit the QR code on the card I gave you," Carri opens her fist to reveal Franklin's business card. "You'll discover a lot more and will be contacted by a man named Franklin." Cleo feels Bobby's gaze on her again.

"Franklin? He's real." He leans back in his chair now. Cleo nods at him.

"We have a lot to cover, Bobby," Cleo tells him. "A lot." Bobby nods, and Cleo turns back to Carri. "Visit the site, Carri. Please read the FAQs, and Franklin, who was my first contact when I jumped, will be in touch. I'm going to fill him in on the details of today so he will have a better idea of the significance of our meeting here when you talk."

"Okay," Carri's gaze transmits understanding. "So, I'll go home and go to bed, and when I wake up, this will all still be real?"

"Yes," Cleo assures her. "Visit the website. Wait for Franklin to connect." Cleo takes a pad from Carri's desk, writes her phone number and email address, and slides it to her. "I'm here too. Call me if you need me. Do you have a card I can have?"

Carri writes her number on the pad, tears the paper free, and hands it to Cleo. "This is my personal cell number. You can always reach me on this."

The women share a look of conviction between them, and Cleo stands. Bobby stands next while Carri remains seated. "It's been a pleasure, Carri," Cleo tells her, opening the office door.

"The pleasure is all mine, thank you," Carrie returns, holding up Franklin's card.

Bobby and Cleo return to the group, who are enjoying refreshments after the film. "Can we get out of here and talk?" Bobby asks, his tone revealing nothing of his feelings, holding Cleo's upper arm. Cleo nods, and they leave the facility, get in the rental car, and Bobby drives them back onto the I-15 headed to Las Vegas.

Coming Clean

On the drive back to the Mandalay, Cleo types her text to Franklin as quickly as possible so she can address the elephant in the car. Bobby is silent, allowing her to update a man he thought was fictional until a few minutes ago. She's wary of having this conversation. She knew it was inevitable, but she hadn't expected to blindside him the way she had.

She places her phone down on the center console and takes a deep breath. She doesn't look at Bobby for fear of chickening out. "You probably feel used," she begins. "Please know that's not why we're on this trip together." She can feel her heart hammering, the blood thumping in her temples. She finds it difficult now to take a full breath.

"Bobby, I love you," she turns to study his expression, "I've always loved you; I'm not with you because I need you - I mean, I *do* need you, I understand that now, but I'm not with you to use you for this fucked up project." Her throat seizes painfully, and she breaks into a sob. Her hands cover her face, and she bawls like a child. She's overwhelmed and terrified over how he must see her now, the callous woman pretending to be interested when all she needs are his brains and peers.

She pulls a box of tissues from the glove compartment and blows her nose. Bobby looks stoic at the wheel. She's ruined everything, she thinks. Next, she watches a single tear trace down his cheek, mingling with his beard. This crushes her. She's never seen Bobby cry, and she's the reason. It's too much. "Oh, Bobby," she cries, "I'm so sorry this is happening," her hands reach for his at the wheel. He turns, her hands landing on the leather steering wheel, and he stops the car with a jolt on the shoulder of the highway.

She retreats as he turns to face her. A tear falls from the other side of his face. "Cleo, shut up," he tells her, removes his seat belt, and then leans in to kiss her. She places both hands on either side of his face, pulling at his short beard. The kiss lingers, and he looks sympathetically into her eyes when he moves away.

"Don't you dare jump from this reality, McCarthy," he commands, voice cracking. "I can't lose you." His chin trembles, and Cleo smiles an ugly, bittersweet smile, shutting her eyes tightly as tears build and fall like rain into her hands that have returned to shield her face. She weeps. The intensity of meeting Carri, holding that conversation with Bobby in the room, and the sense of relief over Bobby, her confidant, finally knowing the truth incapacitates her.

Bobby lets her cry as he rubs her shoulders through it. "Have you met other instances of me? Are we always like this?" His voice is low and calming. Cleo shakes her head.

"We were never ... like this," she replies through shallow breaths, pulling more tissues to her face. Again, she feels raw with emotion. "I can't ... lose you either," she manages before jerking into another sobbing spell.

"Then we make whatever this is work. Whatever you're struggling to uncover, whatever mystery you're out to solve, we do it now. We do it together." His tone reminds her of a schoolteacher explaining precisely what the day will entail. She nods emphatically, drops her hands, and lays her face on his chest.

"Thank you, Bobby," she mumbles into his shirt, her free hand pulling at his collar like a cat kneading at its blanket. Bobby stays with her like that until she collapses into sleep. He then restarts the car, pulls back onto I-15, and drives slowly back to their resort.

Cleo and Bobby sleep for two hours in their room, recovering from the day's events. Bobby is up first and making coffee when Cleo rises on her elbows. The smell of coffee envelops the room. "It's seven-thirty," she says, amazed to have slept into the evening, studying the clock on her bedside table. "I'm hungry."

"I thought I'd make us some coffee," he says, stirring a cup.

"Here's something that feels like a paradox, Bobby," Cleo says, sitting up to accept her coffee. "How did I originally go back in time to my initiation day if traveling back is such a problem?"

"That's been bothering me too," Bobby admits, sitting at the foot of the bed. "I don't know if you really traveled back," his brows raise as if he's said something outlandish. Has he? "I think because your closed timelike curve or loop seems to destroy futures when you are not present in them, you merely dropped one future to begin another from a point that you're tethered to." He gives her a moment to absorb that. "What I mean to say is we all have that moment, or several, defining life events and experiences, including all the moment's minutia, that helps form our personalities. And perhaps that moment is there to be revisited by those with the capacity to start again." He pauses. "Or maybe it's that none of those futures really happened, and you're trapped at that moment, existing in superposition, experiencing these futures until one is observed, and here you are."

"In that scenario, I'm not traveling in time at all," Cleo feels deflated.

"Look, either scenario is completely amazing," Bobby says, caressing her foot, "being locked in a superposition state experiencing endless alternate futures would be equally improbable to traveling backward in time."

"I'm not fighting you on your theories; it's just that I remember those futures like they were yesterday." Cleo is pleased to think that maybe she's tethered to a moment when she decided to take a chance rather than when she was diagnosed with Parkinson's. She would hate to think that was her defining moment; instead, knowing that taking a chance to live her best life was her moment.

"We're in strange territory, Cleo. There's no question about that."

"No, none, but whatever the scenario, I believe we need the rest of the message to move forward."

"Agreed," Bobby stands and sips his coffee. Cleo loves how invested he is in the outcome. How invested he is in her, in them. He will make this happen just like the phantoms said: *Bobby ... Help.* "I'm going to have a shower," Bobby announces.

Cleo picks up her phone and checks her texts. One from Mom and Dad is wondering how she's enjoying Vegas. One from Trish is wondering the same. They've all known Bobby as long as she has and love him. Mom was overjoyed when Cleo told her what had transpired in Toronto. Trish is still in the dark, and she's not about to get into that conversation right now. She quickly answers both messages and moves down to Franklin's newest text in response to hers.

It's fascinating what's happening, Cleo. You are making more headway in your short time than in all my four hundred years.

We need to understand *why* the solar array and how your Carri can help us. I've spoken to her briefly, but I want to meet with you and Bobby now that he's involved when you return.

Cleo texts him their flight details and promises to see him on Sunday evening. Then Cleo rises from the warm bed and slips into the shower next to Bobby. They wash up and get dressed for dinner. Bobby has expressed no interest in the remainder of his conference, and they slip out of the Mandalay to have dinner at the Hofbrauhaus, which is off the strip.

The Hofbrauhaus restaurant in Las Vegas is the only replica of the original found in Munich. It boasts excellent beer, a love of Cleo and Bobby's, and traditional meals like schnitzels and sausage and sauerkraut and spaetzle and pretzels. This visit was discussed at length before they embarked on their trip.

They take the rental car and stand in the reservation line just ten minutes before they are admitted. The music is Oompapa, appropriately, and the tables are long wooden planks shared by strangers and families alike.

Cleo and Bobby enjoy a liter of beer each, even as Cleo struggles to lift the giant glass stein. "I love my beer, Bobby, but this feels like too much," she giggles at herself, one hand pushing up at the bottom of the mug and the other tilting the handle to drink. Finally, she manages a gulp, and the stein slams down on the table, beer leaping out of the vessel.

"You got this, McCarthy," Bobby encourages her, winking. "I'm getting the schnitzel for sure," he says, eyeing another table's plates.

Cleo turns back to Bobby after following his gaze. "That's way too much food!" She attempts another sip of beer by lowering her mouth to the rim and tipping the stein.

"This is a treat," Bobby admits, his attention occupied by every corner of the place. He points out a man being bent over a table by the server dressed in a German dirndl with a large paddle in her hand.

"What the -" Cleo gets out before the paddle comes down hard on the man's ass. She and Bobby cringe at the sound echoing throughout the beer hall. "Jesus," Cleo reacts with a hand at her mouth.

Bobby turns to her, wide-eyed, "How do I get one of those?!" He laughs. The assaulted man rubs gently at his behind while his friends immortalize the moment with their phones.

"You want one of *those?*" Cleo asks, eyes bulging, finger pointing. "Does that look *fun* to you?"

Bobby is nodding, a grin growing across his handsome face. "Uh, yeah!"

"Uh, *why?* He was just spanked! You want that pretty little thing to spank ... oh, of course, you do." She rolls her eyes and puts her hands up in the air. Men! "You do you, honey."

They order their dinners and manage to empty their liter beers when their waitress offers them schnapps. They agree to a shot, and Bobby is asked to stand. He looks excitedly at Cleo, who can't help but laugh at what she sees – A large, wooden paddle appears from behind the server's apron.

"Drink your schnapps," the server orders, her braided, blonde pigtails bobbing as she watches him push back the bitter-sweet Jager. Cleo sips at hers and decides to pull out her phone and capture this moment as Bobby leans over the table. The server counts down from three, two, one, swinging the paddle with false starts, and then WHACK! Bobby's eyes seal as he grimaces from the sting in his pants. Why on earth would anyone want that? Cleo asks herself, shaking her head.

"I got it all on video!" She shouts over the noise of the hall. Then, the server invites her to experience this painful and humiliating process. She smiles brightly but shakes her head, "I'm not finished with my shot yet." Cleo winks at her, and the server winks back.

Bobby delicately lowers himself back onto the bench. Cleo shakes her head, still smiling. She took a video. She hadn't bothered to take a photo in some time, knowing she would likely jump to her initiation day and lose whatever content she'd captured. But that can be put to rest for now. This life is the one - until it isn't.

They drop the rental car off and walk back to their resort. It's late, and Cleo is exhausted. Bobby could go all night but yields to Cleo's needs. Besides, they have a plane to catch at eight in the morning.

Catch Up

On the flight home, Cleo wonders whether the terrifying experience of her plane falling apart over the Indian Ocean might play out again in this life. It's a dark thought that creeps in each time she boards another plane. However, she's managed quite a few flights since, without incident, she reminds herself and feels safe with Bobby beside her. She misses the first-class pods from her European vacations with their warmed nuts and champagne but won't overspend in this life since she isn't planning to jump from it any time soon. She smiles, lays her head on Bobby's shoulder, sighs, and falls asleep.

Bobby joins her on the trip from O'Hare to her apartment. He will stay for dinner. Franklin will arrive in a few short hours, and Cleo decides to order in, too tired to put something together.

Franklin arrives precisely when planned. "A time traveler is never late for anything," he jokes, removing his hat, gloves, and jacket. Cleo hangs them in the closet and ushers him in. "Bobby, I presume," he introduces himself, and the men shake hands.

"Happy to have you in the fold," Franklin says, sitting on the chair adjacent to the couch.

"It's been quite a weekend," Bobby says, smiling at Cleo, who joins him on the couch. "Cleo has briefed me on everything. But, we think she needs some time alone with the white noise to pull the remainder of the message so we can act on it purposefully."

Franklin's brows raise, his hands pressing firmly into his knees. "I'm impressed," he looks to Cleo, then back to Bobby. "I think that's a splendid idea."

"Cleo tells me you've been at this for four hundred years," Bobby's head shakes. "I don't know what I'd do with so much time."

"When I first began to recognize the singularities and followed them to their conclusion, it was an eye-opener," Franklin answers, laughing.

"Like what happened with Cleo finding Carri on Saturday." Bobby relates.

Franklin nods. "Exactly like that. It's world-changing. I fear I didn't handle the first one very well. I expected them to answer my questions, which confused them more." Cleo rises to pour some water and hands them off to the men.

"It's utterly fascinating what's happening to you both. I'm honestly just getting past stunned to understanding the possible science driving it." Bobby takes a long drink.

"Yes, Cleo filled me in on your thoughts. Superposition. That we have never left our initiation day and simply watch possible futures unfold is fascinating." Franklin sets his glass on the coffee table.

"It's astounding," Bobby adds. "The idea that in this life, Cleo observing us makes it real," Bobby leans back, releasing a breath.

"I still feel the closed timelike curve best describes our gift," Franklin posits. "Though near impossible to explain, our memories are too tactile to think we didn't experience them with all our faculties."

"Experience trumps theory every day of the week," Bobby admits, and Cleo looks at him quizzically, sure he's said that before. Perhaps in a past future. "I defer to your centuries of practical familiarity with your ... gift."

"And we will defer to your scientific background to understand why Cleo was drawn to the solar array and Carri," Franklin states.

"I have some thoughts on that as well." Bobby leans in, elbows resting on his thighs, hands clasped together. "I agree with your closed timelike curve theory. I know the math works; light can distort space, and because space and time are forever linked, light can affect time if it is powerful enough to create a gravity well."

"Like a Blackhole," Cleo adds. "Isn't that what they say Blackholes do?"

"Yes, just like that," Bobby replies. "Blackholes spin at tremendous speeds, warping spacetime. We don't really know to what end, though."

"What are you suggesting?" Franklin leans forward, the gravity of the conversation drawing him in.

"In other futures, Cleo tells me we also discussed the ring laser hypothesis. So, it's been a recurring theme. It lends itself beautifully to the timelike curve." Bobby pulls his ever-present pad from his shirt pocket and lays it on the coffee table. He draws a circle.

"The idea is to fire two beams of laser light traveling at opposing directions that reflect off mirrors to create a closed loop." He draws one circle rotating one way and another the other. "Now, a ring laser isn't anything new; they're used in gyroscopes on planes and ships to measure the interference pattern between the beams, which explains speed and direction.

"The solar array has mirrors already set up in a circle. It also has a massive power source," Bobby continues. "And now we've met the one person who could give us access to these facilities."

"Then, the message is asking us to create this ring laser," Franklin surmises. "But to what end?"

"We know there's more to the message than what I've written down," Cleo answers. "So, it must be waiting to be heard. That's why we think it's a good idea I spend some time with my radio or your EVP and just wait it out."

The landline rings, and Cleo jumps up to answer it. She buzzes the delivery person up and collects their dinner. She places the Thai food on the kitchen table and waves Franklin and Bobby over to fix themselves a plate.

"I can't imagine the power plant has enough output to truly warp spacetime, but that's where the message is heading. The why of it is still a head-scratcher." Bobby says, loading the Pad Thai and coconut shrimp onto his plate.

"The ring laser is supposed to be a catalyst for time travel," he continues, "so if you guys are already time travelers, I don't get the why."

Cleo reads from her Notes app the words she has gathered. "You must find others like us. Bobby. Timelike curve. At these Coordinates 35.57115.47. Yes, Bobby help. In another future. Do it again. In your future. Merge everyone."

"That could be in the correct arrangement or not, right?" Franklin asks.

"These are as close to the order they came to me as I can put them. Then some were repeated with new words, so I just inserted them," Cleo explains, covering her mouth as she speaks. "The coordinates are confirmed. Bobby's inclusion is confirmed. A timelike curve is confirmed. But the whole 'in another future. Do it again. In your future.' Is unclear."

Let's give you the time to connect again for an extended period," Bobby reiterates. "Without the whole message, it's not enough to act on. If your phantoms want us to create a ring laser at the Ivanpah array, they need to say as much."

Franklin nods his head. "I would feel much better about it if we had fewer doubts." He stands and places his plate in the sink. Then he turns to address both Bobby and Cleo. "We're dealing with some exceptional circumstances. There really is no room for conjecture."

Bobby grunts agreeance, and Cleo nods, her mouth full. "Are you leaving?" She asks, hand over mouth again.

"I am," he replies, performing a half-bow. "Thank you for dinner, and thank you, Bobby, for being a part of this."

"I wouldn't miss it!" Bobby replies emphatically. Then Cleo says, "I'll let you know the moment I have more to tell."

"Good. Leave your radio on overnight, and perhaps that will encourage the white noise to return." Franklin tips his fedora and leaves Cleo's apartment.

At eight o'clock, after he's helped clean up, Bobby kisses Cleo goodbye and makes his way back to Michigan. Cleo suddenly feels vulnerable in the dark.

Her right hand trembles as she lies in bed, reading and contemplating work the following day. She reacts by gripping her wrist with her other hand. This is a constant reminder of the one reason she might jump. This disease. This plague that holds such a terrible influence over the rest of her life. As the tremor increases, she cries softly, wishing Bobby were here to comfort her. Wishing away the tremor. After a time, it passes, and she massages the muscle of her forearm with her thumb.

*   *   *   *

Following a difficult night that gave up no more information via the radio, Cleo's phone reminds her that she will see her specialist, Dr. Ross, later today. Time to get serious about her disease, she thinks. Unfortunately, this isn't going to miraculously go away, so she'd better be a little more forward with the doctor and demand treatment rather than just monitoring its relentless progress.

At work, she passes Barbara standing at the threshold of the lunchroom, as always, and smiles at her, the memory of their confrontation playing itself out again. She feels like she has one up on her now. Her guilty pleasure that no one can undo.

Bobby had sent a Good Morning text, which lifted her spirits. She replied with an I love you and received it back. Cloe's projects demand all her attention throughout her workday, and when four o'clock rolls around, she busses to her doctor's office.

"Tremors and rigidity are to be expected," Dr. Ross tells her, brows furrowed as he watches her hands, on display in front of Cleo, palms down.

"It's happening more frequently," Cleo insists, "so I'd really like to avoid any more if possible."

"You want me to start you on the medication," the doctor raises his gaze to Cleo's. She knows he'll fight her on it, but she wants to live a normal life as long as possible. She nods. "Yes."

"It's still early days, Cleo. I'm really not comfortable starting you on the monoamine oxidase type inhibitors to stop a tremor here and there that lasts less than five minutes." His expression is dire, the corners of his mouth turned down. "The possible side effects could be worse than the tremors, believe me."

"But I may not suffer the side effects," she defends.

"You're just not there yet, Cleo." He motions for her to lower her hands. "All medications take a toll on the body. I want you to wait." His frown morphs into a sympathetic smile. "You're otherwise a healthy twenty-four-year-old woman. Take comfort in that."

Cleo is disappointed but needed the reminder that medications aren't the be-all and end-all. That they, too, carry risks. She passes the front desk and waves weakly at the receptionist.

At home, she boils some noodles and fries tofu for dinner. She takes a call from Bobby and feels momentarily weak, taking a seat. Bobby isn't talking about time travel or closed timelike curves; he's just telling her about his day, listening to her talk about hers.

As much as Bobby has become a part of the process of understanding the message and performing the task as laid out, he has become so much more to Cleo. He is her everything.

"So, because we're having this conversation, that means you haven't jumped, right?" Bobby asks.

"What do you mean?" Cleo asks back in her best deadpan. "Jumped?"

A long pause on Bobby's end, and, "Fuck off, McCarthy," he says jokingly. Cleo can't help but laugh.

"You're coming Friday?"

"I am," Bobby replies. "I'm working on constructing the two lasers through one of our partner companies here. I'll hopefully bring the specs to you Friday."

"A bit above my pay grade, but thank you for doing that," Cleo says. "I got nowhere with the message last night. Hoping for something more tonight."

"Probably isn't something you can force," Bobby suggests. "But keep at it. I gotta go. Love you."

Cleo responds in kind and hangs up. Bobby is taking this very seriously, and that's a relief. After all, he's the only one she knows who could develop an honest-to-goodness laser. She laughs lightly at the thought.

When Cleo lies down, and the radio is set on a station somewhere between 107 and 108 FM, she tries to relax and focus. What may come will come in its own time.

FRANKLIN

At home, Franklin paces the marble floors that run the length of his foyer. This leads to a lengthier hallway adorned with medieval armor, elaborately framed oil paintings, statues in a state of undress, and thirty-foot ceilings with walnut walls featuring half a dozen doors that lead to a dining room, study, library, kitchen, sitting room, and a four-car garage. Each room is larger than the last, and as he moves into the kitchen, he stands at his picture windows, hands linked behind his back, welcoming his view.

Rolling gardens surround the large, in-ground pool with stately pyramidal cedars trimmed to resemble cypress trees on either side of the estate. Lake Michigan butts up against his property, where a boathouse and dock complete the lakeshore lifestyle. The lake is frozen along the shoreline, but beyond it, Franklin watches the icy waves roll in, experiencing a deep chill that runs up his spine.

Franklin picks up a framed photo of himself from the eighties, where his afro had reached a circumference of twelve inches. In the picture, his graduation gown falls over his slender shoulders. His smile is bright, imagining a future in wealth management. This was also the year he realized he was a time traveler. 1982. Newly graduated and placed at an up-and-coming firm, Franklin worked hard to prove himself. He's run the firm in eight of his lifetimes, including this one.

His first jump came after he'd felt deep compassion for another person. A deep empathy for their suffering. It happened five years after graduation while Franklin was well-established at the firm. The memory delivered him to his early twenties, a month before he was to graduate. It was the year he'd witnessed a terrible accident outside the university grounds. A young man on a bicycle was struck down by a car. The boy was muttering nonsense when Franklin reached him, taking Franklin's hand and squeezing as if transmitting his will. It's not a fond memory, but it is his initiation day.

That initial jump had robbed him of his first five years at the company. After a considerable time trying to understand what had happened and why, he jumped repeatedly, month after month, learning how the company worked. Then he spent another five years there, and when he wasn't promoted, he jumped back to try again. This was when he began living longer - decades, enjoying the fruits of his labor.

When he met Marla in year six, he stayed and thrived with her into old age. When she was at the end of her life, he decided to return to 1982 with her. Why couldn't she come with him and they relive their lives together? It was a gamble, but she would soon be gone. Of course, she could not come with him, and he started over. Alone, never to enjoy that connection again. Repeating the same successes, but never again with her.

He puts the photo frame down, wishing he had a picture of his wife to hold. A confirmed bachelor the last few lives has given him time to discover the others. To find those like him in search of answers. Franklin has found someone who can answer his questions when Cleo came into his life. She is special.

Tea is served, and he takes it in the sunroom, where he can continue his contemplation while enjoying his view. Retirement is fine but can be dull from time to time. Ten separate times, he's pursued the same career to end up here in eight of them. Each time, he has no regrets. He remembers how full of light this house was when Marla, his wife, resided in it. He remembers their last night together as he held her in his arms, reminding her of his secrets - asking her to join him as he jumped.

The tea is hot, and he sears his tongue. Silly, he thinks. Pay attention, man. You can have that life again. Though he's feeling long in the tooth to say he would have it in this timeline. Once Cleo's message is resolved, and with it, his riddle, he will jump and try again. The decision to jump that night was a selfish one. She was dying. He didn't want to be alone.

Franklin wipes a tear from his gaunt cheek with a cloth napkin, remembering the panic that ensued upon returning to his initiation day. Marla was gone. His life with her ... gone. It was an insult to her memory that she had never existed in that future past, and he'd never forgiven himself for it. Nor would he. So, he will try again.

Loose Ends

Tuesday night is filled with activity from the phantoms. The singular voice trapped in the white noise releases a myriad of words that Cleo adds to her Notes app. Some overlap existing words, piecing together complete sentences. Cleo's excitement builds, and the radio returns to its incessant static when the last word is added. Cleo reaches over and turns the clock radio off.

She leaps out of bed and snaps on the light, gathering up the pad of paper where she has arranged the words. She inserts what she's heard tonight. It reads as follows:

You must find as many of the others like us as possible. Use Bobby to create a timelike curve at these coordinates 35.57115.47 Yes Bobby will help. We have done it before. In another future. We need to do it again in your future and merge everyone.

Cleo leans back on her headboard, fills her cheeks with air, and blows it out dramatically. She wishes she knew who this person was who sent her this message. She wants to ask them questions. For example, why? What is the purpose behind all of it? Why are they contacting her and not someone else? She's pleased to say she has the whole message now, but it's only telling her what to do, not why or even how.

If she's reading it right, it is asking her to locate and bring everyone who shares her gift to the Ivanpah solar array, where they will create a closed timelike curve with Bobby's help. Also, it tells her that they have accomplished this feat in another future. That's curious, and she won't pretend she can appreciate what that must mean. Okay, but *why?* Why did they do it once and want her to do it again? The how may lie with Carri, the power station's manager. If she can arrange for them to set up Bobby's lasers and Franklin can afford to bring a bunch of people from all over the world there, that's a start.

She won't sleep tonight, she fears, sending Franklin a text. She admits she is fatigued, though, and when she doesn't hear back from Franklin immediately, she tries to settle in bed. Her mind is racing. Perhaps this limited message was the best they could hope for when communicating through time. Make it short and sweet. But Cleo doesn't have any reason to trust the eerie voice that's coming through the static. Who would? Yet Franklin is committed, so Cleo feels justified in their mission, and Bobby is running on his trust in her.

Cleo throws the sheets off herself. "Fuck," she utters. "I'm not sleeping tonight." She rises and makes a decaf coffee, the possibility of sleep not wholly lost. Still, she's full of adrenaline. So wired. This will make for a challenging day tomorrow. She shakes her arms and runs on the spot momentarily, alleviating the rush. Why can't these thoughts occur in the morning?

Cleo sits on the couch, the pad of paper with the completed message now staring back at her from the coffee table. Is there an urgency to it? Of course, time travel should negate any urgency to anything, but if she's going to complete this task in this life, then maybe there is a countdown on.

Cleo drinks from her cup, and the decaf warms her chest and belly. She lays on her side and pulls the throw blanket over her. Too many thoughts fight for leverage, and she puts the coffee on the table, opting to perform deep breathing. She closes her eyes and drifts off to sleep with an exhausted sigh.

Morning is announced by her phone and clock radio blaring opposing sounds. One is a song she recalls from her childhood, by Jim Croce, something her parents played on repeat, and the other is a nagging beeping meant to ensure she gets up. She rolls out of the couch and lands with her knees on the hardwood. She stops the phone and sees Franklin's reply to her late-night text.

This is exciting, Cleo, he writes. With the message completed, we can act.

We need the lasers and to discuss a plan with Carri. Cleo writes back. And I don't know how far along Bobby is with the lasers. She can't believe she's used 'lasers' in two consecutive sentences. He said he would be bringing the specifications this weekend.

If he's managed to have specifications drawn up, we're close.

They would need to be built, Cleo fires back.

Yes, ask Bobby how long until they are built.

Cleo says she will and signs off. **Bobby,** she writes, **How long until we have working lasers?** God, she thinks, I hope no one is listening to these conversations. She pulls back the curtain to her street-facing window and peeks out. For whatever reason, she studies the street below for black cars circa 1960. Because that's what she suspects the FBI, CIA, and Men in Black would drive, Cleo reminds herself. "You watch too many movies."

Morning, Cleo, Bobby writes back. **You sound like a Bond villain or, better yet, an Austin Powers villain. LOL**

LOL, sorry. But I've received the rest of the message, and Franklin wondered how long. Her thumbs type madly at her screen. **I feel a sense of urgency and think the sooner we move on this, the better.**

I just received the specs this morning, with the complete list of parts for procurement. I'll put it through right away, and maybe we'll have a working system in a month.

A month is too long, Cleo insists, pacing her floors and chewing on several strands of her hair.

I'll put a rush on the orders. I'm working with a huge company on these and might be able to dip into existing stock. I'm also working with a software company to design the code to run the lasers. It's a good thing I have buy-in on the project from my peers here. They're every bit as interested in the effects of laser tech in an existing solar power array's battery regeneration. LOL. Carri was great. She explained the potential of including battery storage at Ivanpah. But I'll let you know. Love you

Thx. Love you back. See you Friday night. She hadn't realized Bobby had conceived such a diabolical lie to encourage buy-in for their project. And that he's included Carri is brilliant.

XOXO.

Cleo explains the timeline as Bobby has laid it out to Franklin. He is okay with the time it will take and tells her he will approach the others via email, ask them not to jump again, and prepare them for a trip to Nevada.

Cleo showers and senses a tremor building in her right hand. It persists through breakfast, the bus ride to work, and half an hour after she's arrived. Barbara notices the tremor and pulls up the empty seat beside Cleo's desk.

"Is everything all right, Cleo?" She whispers, genuine concern pulling down her expression. "Has something happened?"

Wow, Cleo can't quite believe how affectionate Barbara is being. "Uh, nothing that hasn't been building for a while," Cleo answers sheepishly.

"Is it something you'd like to talk about?"

"Uh," Cleo is caught off-guard by the warmth she's experiencing from a woman she has always disliked. "I ... HR knows all about it."

Barbara blinks and nods, her smile sympathetic. It's all very surreal to Cleo. "I understand. Well, if you ever want to talk about it with me, I'm here." Barbara stands and silently exits Cleo's cubicle.

Cleo wants to thank her, but the words are caught in her throat. This Barbara is *nice*. She hasn't had any interaction with her since her last jump. Just a nod here and there to acknowledge the other's existence. "Oh, there's no way I'm jumping from this life. Nope." She wheels around in her chair, returning to the design on her screen.

The following two days are much the same, minus the tremor, and before she knows it, Bobby is knocking at her apartment door.

They embrace, mouths locking in an eager kiss. Cleo guides him to the bedroom, where they spend their energies making up for four days apart. They lie in exhausted bliss atop the covers. "That's a welcome I can get used to," Bobby says breathlessly.

A satisfied hum is Cleo's reply. She stretches and rolls to her side to look at Bobby. His amber skin glistens in the light. It was exciting to have left the lights on. Bobby has a lean, muscled physique and is a joy to watch. She feels confident in her skin with him, so leaving the lights on made the last hour more intimate.

"I'm starving," Bobby admits. "Do you have anything here or want to go out?"

"I let Trish know you'd be here tonight. Do you mind if we invite her out?"

"Does she know?" Bobby's question is direct. Cleo hasn't told Trish in this life that they are an item. She's a little nervous over it if she's being honest.

"No, but I thought it was time," Cleo admits. "And going out for a few drinks will make it easier."

"She's not going to be upset, is she?"

"Well, we did have a pact back in high school," Cleo offers. "Not to go there ... with you."

Bobby doesn't look surprised. That's his confidence peaking. "She's married with children."

"Oh, so you'd have hooked up with Trish otherwise?" Cleo feigns jealousy.

Bobby smiles and shakes his head. "It was always you for me, McCarthy." He leans in and kisses her hard on the mouth.

"Okay, then we'll tell her tonight." It's almost comical to Cleo that something this trivial could occupy space in her brain. But Trish is her best friend, and there is a broken promise in this confession. Still, Trish seemed to take it all right in the other future when she witnessed Bobby kiss her forehead at the pub. So, how bad could it be?

As Cleo and Bobby arrive, Trish and her husband, Dave, are seated in the booth. Cleo is thrilled to see Dave here. Trish can't get upset if her husband is right here beside her. They stand to greet them, and Cleo hugs them both while Bobby hugs Trish and shakes Dave's hand.

They enjoy a couple of drinks each and share a half dozen appetizers. The conversation is easy, and so Cleo makes the announcement.

"So, we have news too," Cleo raises her hand from under the table with Bobby's attached. She studies Trish's expression. It's hard to read. She's stunned, but is that a smile sliding up the right side of her face or a frown dipping to the left?

She looks at Dave, whose shocked expression quickly turns into a smile. Next, she looks at Bobby, who looks at her with a sheepish grin, likely to avoid Trish's burning gaze. His grip tightens in hers.

Trish is holding her breath, caught off-guard, processing how to react. She blinks and breathes again. Cleo realizes she's been holding her breath, too, and inhales, her lungs aching.

"I *fucking* knew it," Dave nearly shouts, elbowing his wife in the arm. This alters Trish's expression again, leaving Cleo at a loss. "You *can't* just stay friends forever."

Trish smiles, baring her teeth, and Cleo winces. Then, her heart drops to her stomach, and the deep-fried cheese sticks no longer seem like the right decision.

"You guys," Trish says animatedly, her hands reaching across the table, landing on their entangled fingers. "This makes me so happy!" She turns to Dave. "We're on a double date!" She laughs.

Cleo and Bobby laugh along, looking at each other, trying to decipher whether Trish's joy is manufactured.

"It just happened, you know?" Says Bobby, and Cleo notices the lack of confidence in Bobby's explanation, feeling slightly betrayed. How it occurred certainly did not *just* happen. But she assumes this is for Trish's benefit.

"Honestly," Cleo joins the ruse. "We were in Toronto together, and BAM! You know?" She looks down at the chicken wing remaining on her side plate.

"So, you're in a relationship." Trish leans back, her palms up, pointing accusingly. "How long?"

"Uh, you know, when we were in Toronto. Like what, a couple of weeks ago?" Cleo looks to Bobby for support. He nods.

"Wait, so, Las Vegas, you two went to Las Vegas as a couple!" Trish is piecing it together.

"Yeah, Cleo was my plus one at the conference," Bobby leans in, back straight, exuding more confidence now. And why shouldn't he, Cleo thinks?

"A long-distance relationship, though," Trish questions its validity. "Are you moving to Michigan, Cleo?"

"Oh, well, it's not out of the question," Cleo replies, her back up. "Anything's possible." Bobby nods next to her, hearing this for the first time.

"My placement with the think-tank isn't forever either," he adds quickly. "We've got time to consider the future." Bobby looks at Cleo, and they share a knowing smirk.

With that, Trish seems satisfied, and Dave orders another round for the table. "You don't need to *grill* them, babe," he tells Trish.

"I wasn't *grilling* them," she replies sharply. "I'm just ... getting the story. I had no idea." She wears a wounded expression.

"It's been a bit of a whirlwind romance for us too," Cleo admits, "but we're very much committed." She nods at Bobby, who returns the gesture.

The fresh round of drinks arrives, and each takes a sip. An awkward silence follows. Dave recovers first, asking about Las Vegas and explaining his recent trip there on business. Trish and Cleo share a look that makes Cleo feel unfaithful to her friend. But then Trish erases that sensation by placing both hands on Cleo's.

She leans in, and Cleo follows her lead. "I'm happy for you," she says, squeezing Cleo's hand. Cleo places her free hand on top of Trish's. "It's been a long time coming."

"Why do you say that?"

Trish's expression twists. "*Come on,* Cleo. You've been in love with Bobby forever. It was unfair of me to make that pact with you."

"You *knew?*"

"I'm a bad friend for having asked that of you. Fuck the Three Musketeers," she says with a jolt of her head. "Now we're the *Four.* You deserve happiness. I hope Bobby can give you what you need."

"He can ... he does," Cleo's throat is closing with emotion. "So, you don't hate me?"

"Oh, Cleo, I *love* you!" She bends further over the table and kisses Cleo on the forehead. Tears fall, and the boys know well enough to leave them alone.

Saturday morning sees Bobby and Cleo rising with the sun, unable to sleep from the promise of lasers. Bobby pulls the specifications up on his tablet for Cleo to review.

"All Greek to me, Bobby," she says, impressed by the schematics before her. She's always appreciated technical diagrams and has included many in past graphic design projects. "How big are these things?"

"Not very big at all. I know you're hoping for Dr. Evil's Moon laser, but that would be cumbersome. The laser apparatus is roughly your size and weighs less."

"So, they'll be on a tripod or what?"

"Right, they'll need to be horizontal, firing on the mirror, and each mirror in the array will have to be repositioned to form a circle the laser light can bounce off until it creates a closed, continuous loop. The other laser will perform likewise but in the opposite direction."

"And that should warp space-time," Cleo says, "creating a timelike curve."

"Well, I don't imagine the solar array will offer nearly enough energy to cause that effect, but we're going on faith here. With a little science to back it up."

"But it must offer enough power if this is the plan," Cleo rationalizes.

"There are still unknowns to factor in. Unknowns, as yet unknown to us."

"That's a mouthful," Cleo says, clearing her throat. "This is something we should share with Carri?"

"Soon, I'll need the software to run the lasers first."

"But Carri should be brought up to date. We can't have her jumping when we need her to facilitate all this." Cleo worries.

"Okay, let's bring her into the fold this aft to prep for the event. Has Franklin started to inform the others of their role in this?"

"He's on it," Cleo stands to pour coffees. "We have ninety-nine souls like me to bring to Ivanpah. It will be a monumental task."

"Franklin seems like the guy to manage it," Bobby sounds confident. Cleo shares his certainty in Franklin's ability. However, it feels like everything is coming to a head, and though Cleo will be happy to have it all in the past, she wonders if she will miss it.

*   *   *   *

Carri answers their video call after lunch. She seems uneasy over the plan as they lay it out. Cleo can sense her distress. This is her career they're potentially sabotaging. Who knows what effect the lasers will have on the mirrors? Or how creating a closed timelike curve will affect the physical structure of the power plant. It could collapse, explode, or vanish for all they knew.

"I'm concerned for the safety of everyone involved," Carri says adamantly. "Bobby, I have gone along with your plan and discussed the battery regeneration concept with your suppliers and peers, but I have staff here that I'll have to ask to leave. It will seem very odd to everyone. I don't know how I'll pull that off."

"I completely understand your apprehension," Cleo starts. "The thing is, Carri, we've accomplished this in an alternate future. Possibly several other futures. So, it *can* be done. You've done it before."

"I've done it before ... in another future or futures," Carri repeats, seemingly to make it more real. She sighs and rubs her eyes. "It's hard to get my head around."

"All I'm telling you is that you've managed to pull it off before," Cleo reminds her. "That's got to mean you can do it again. We all have our marching orders. Franklin's bringing the others like us to you. Bobby's building the lasers and the software and delivering them. You have to secure the facility for us, and I am apparently the liaison between times."

Carri shakes her head and sighs again. Her office is dark, and she whispers most of what she says. It's just ten o'clock in the morning there, but she seems to have dimmed her office lighting and drawn the blinds to make it seem like she's left for the day.

"If I've done it before, I can do it again," She states confidently. "I'll figure it out. When will you know when you're arriving?"

"I'm trying to fast-track the tech and simultaneously creating the software to run it," Bobby answers. "I think we could be there in two weeks. Maybe three."

"Okay, that gives me time. If it were to fall on a holiday, that would be ideal." Carri flips a paper calendar on her desk. "The third Monday in February is President's Day."

"That's days from now." Cleo looks at Bobby, her face twisted in angst.

"It will just be a skeleton crew of security here with me," Carri explains, and it sounds very appealing.

"That's a tight timeline," Bobby sounds unsure of himself. "What about March? Spring break?"

"Many people take vacations then," Carri reviews a folder she pulls from a drawer. "But it's not going to be empty here like President's Day. The less personnel, the better. Who knows what damaging effect this experiment might have on the complex."

Cleo and Bobby share a look of concern. "That's seven days away," she says. "Can you get what you need before then?"

Bobby scratches his beard while his gaze employs an intensity that cools the blood in Cleo's veins. Then, finally, after a long moment, Bobby answers. "Nothing's impossible. I'll push harder."

"If we can't agree on President's Day, Cesar Chavez Day is March 31."

"That's too late," Cleo replies hastily. She feels it in her bones. "I'm sure we need to do it before that."

"Then let's say President's Day for right now. I'll arrange a distraction to take my security team to the west array while we bring in our people and set up the equipment."

Bobby rubs his palms together and nods. "Let's pencil in that date, and we'll get back to you in a couple of days. I should have a better idea if I can have everything ready by then and what, if any, damage might occur if we achieve the gravity well."

Carri agrees to wait for their call two days from now before she begins to implement a plan and signs off.

Cleo looks at Bobby anxiously. "Do you think we might blow up the whole array?"

"I hadn't honestly considered it until Carri brought it up," he replies. "But it's a valid point. If we somehow create a closed timelike loop on the property, we might find ourselves on the event horizon of a spacetime scenario none of us could have predicted."

"Jesus, that's just a little terrifying," Cleo stands, moving away from her desk where they sat to converse with Carri.

"Look, if we don't at least try, we're failing whoever is on the other side of your white noise." Bobby joins Cleo in the bedroom, where she is pacing.

"That's the thing though, Bobby, I can't even be sure *who* we're listening to. It could be some time witch luring us into a trap or something."

"Again, too many movies, McCarthy," he lays a hand on her shoulder and squeezes. Cleo's head falls back, and she moans as Bobby manipulates her tense muscles. "But if you're really worried about it, maybe there's another message waiting to be heard?"

Cleo's head shakes slowly. "No, I'd know if there were more to it or another waiting in the wings. I don't feel bad about the plan, but what could a timelike curve do to a place or people?"

"That's up for debate since we'll be the first to attempt it at this scale." Bobby gently pushes the balls of his palms down on Cleo's shoulders, continuing the massage. "We could all be pulled into another time, or maybe other times will appear in ours. But, without vastly more energy to put into it, I can't see how we'll achieve what we're setting out to do."

Cleo turns her head, careful not to interrupt her massage. "You think we're destined to fail?"

"No, I don't know what to expect. Just theorizing. But the math is clear: to twist space into a time portal, we would require the power of the sun or more, not mere megawatts." Bobby says this very matter-of-factly. Because it's a fact, Cleo supposes.

"After all the effort we're putting into this, I hope it's not for nothing."

FRANKLIN

Franklin paces his estate while on the phone with his travel agent. The logistics of bringing so many people from all over the world to Las Vegas on a dedicated date have become complicated. For one, nearly ten are unaccounted for. If they are missing individuals, will the attempt be a failure? He can not allow things to become unhinged. He sends his agent's affiliates to the missing individual's homes. They have one shot at this. This lifetime has been far too favorable to think another might mirror it. No, this is the time to act.

The news of Cleo's message having been deciphered is promising, and because of this, Franklin's riddle now makes sense. With this new knowledge secured, he can set his plans in motion.

He will play his cards close to his chest. He will be the man Cleo and Bobby need. Until it no longer serves him.

Damage Control

Bobby spends the remainder of his Saturday communicating with his think-tank sponsors, who have agreed to back his project. But, of course, they don't know the true purpose behind the lasers, so he is careful with what information he relays.

"It's not like it's super-heated," he tells Cleo, straight-backed, seated at the small dining table. "They don't have to worry about my supervillain status. My lasers won't even melt the mirror arrays in the time I expect to run them."

"No?" She's always pictured Star Wars blasters and industry lasers for cutting steel.

"Nope," Bobby pulls up a schematic of one of Carrie's heliostats. "And the heliostat's reflective components utilize a second surface mirror. Like a sandwich. These mirrors generally consist of a steel structural support, an adhesive layer, a protective copper layer, a layer of reflective silver, and a top protective layer of thick glass," he explains, typing something while continuing his explanation. "Creating a gravity well inside the loop will mean the lasers' light needs some serious power. This is where the energy from Ivanpah will come in handy. Not to bolster the heat energy of the lasers, but to maintain the six-hundred-seventy-million miles per hour for as long as needed."

"Light speed, I guess?" Cleo laughs as she busies herself in the kitchen. Bobby looks up momentarily.

Cleo notices the crease on Bobby's forehead. "My problem is that there isn't enough dedicated energy to create the gravity well merely by tapping into Ivanpah. Not even a nuclear reactor would have the resources. Conservation of energy is the first hurdle," Bobby seems to be talking the problem out rather than merely explaining it to Cleo. "The kinetic energy that is created must be maintained. But there is plenty of room for supposition since we're following limited instruction, supposedly originating from another time, and that's got to mean something."

Bobby is applying hard science; Cleo knows and seems convinced that something more will fill in the blanks to achieve the desired effect. "My lasers will draw their energy directly from the Ivanpah array and are designed to throw a six-foot-wide beam of laser light from their elevated positions, bouncing off the heliostat mirrors, which Carri will have altered, repositioning them to reflect a perfect circle, creating the closed loop."

"And what about the software to run them?"

"The software is simple," he waves off the question, "and the diodes will allow for peak optical amplification." As he explains this to Cleo, she knows the immediate concern for Bobby is that his supplier company is missing the diodes he requires from their stock.

"So, is President's Day not feasible?" Cleo senses Bobby's angst. "If we have to wait, we have to wait, Bobby; it's going to happen eventually."

"But you said you didn't think we should wait," Bobby replies, and he's right. Cleo feels the burden of the project weighing on her. She doesn't want to stress Bobby out.

"Yes, but I mean, I don't have any empirical proof that the sooner, the better. It's just a feeling," Cleo admits.

"Listen, you're the closest one to this thing. If you have a feeling, I'm willing to bet on it." Bobby reaches for her hand, and she places it in his. "I'm pushing for this to happen on your schedule. I may be a man of science, but I believe in a sixth sense and think you have a mastery of it." He squeezes her hand, releases it, and turns in his seat to face his computer. "I'm going to make this happen, McCarthy."

Cleo smiles and massages his neck muscles, leaning in and kissing the top of his wavy locks. "Then I'm going to have Franklin fly everyone into that casino resort just outside of Vegas – what was it called?"

"Buffalo Bills," Bobby says distractedly.

"Right, the closer, the better. I'll have Franklin book a couple of buses as well," Cleo pushes off Bobby's shoulders. He groans.

Cleo meets Franklin nearby for a coffee to discuss the particulars and update him on their progress.

Franklin adds four spoons of sugar to his black coffee.

Cleo sips at hers and returns it to the table. She looks out the shop's window, watching people move along the sidewalk, avoiding the ice and dirty snow piled along the curb. "Is it weird that I haven't experienced another singularity since Carri?" she asks, absently studying the scene outside.

"Nor have I," Franklin adds. "Still, it's more common not to encounter others like us. But, then again, perhaps we've discovered all we will in this city."

"Maybe there's no one left to discover," Cleo wonders. "We're at the precipice of this journey. The message has been revealed. We visited Ivanpah and met Carri. We're working on the plan."

"And the plan," Franklin says, "it's achievable?"

Cleo nods, "Bobby is very invested and seems convinced that what we're doing will give us results."

"It's the results we're not clear on," Franklin focuses on Cleo. It makes her slightly uncomfortable, the look he's giving her.

"We have what we have," Cleo admits with a shrug.

"And you haven't received any more of the message? Or an additional message?" Franklin sounds as though he's trying to catch her in a lie.

"Why wouldn't I tell you if I'd heard more from the phantoms?" Cleo says defensively.

Franklin relaxes and leans back into the booth, the vinyl bench cover squeaking behind him. "I'm sorry, Cleo;

I don't mean to sound accusing. I just wish there were a little more to go on."

"Are you doubting the plan?"

"Not in its entirety. No. I'd just hoped for an explanation of what the phantoms hope to accomplish."

"Isn't that much obvious? They want us to create the closed timelike curve."

"But to what end?" Franklin slowly turns his cup on the table. His dark face pulled down, making him seem much older than his sixty-odd years. "We already have the power to travel back in time. So what benefit is this to us?"

Cleo considers the question. "Maybe it's not about us. Maybe we're beholden to this task because we're the only ones who can achieve it." Franklin looks unconvinced, and Cleo senses he's having second thoughts.

"I will, of course, do my part to complete the plan," he assures her. "I'm sure the phantoms aren't asking us to do something arbitrary or evil. I must trust in that."

"I agree," Cleo says, placing her cup on the table and pushing strands of black hair behind her ear. "Bobby is also looking into the possible effects of creating the timelike curve to prepare for any dangers."

"Good. That's good he's being proactive."

"Yeah," Cleo feels Franklin has sucked some of the excitement out of the project. "Are you okay?"

"Ah, well, no, not really," he continues to spin his cup on the chipped tabletop. "I saw Marla last night, my wife." He looks down at the table again, distracted.

"It didn't go as you'd hoped," Cleo acknowledges his pain. "But you can keep trying."

Franklin shakes his head. "She didn't even remember me from a week ago when I introduced myself in the grocery store, and we talked for twenty minutes." He looks distraught. "She has dementia, I think. That means this life can't grant me the wife I'd once loved. Still love."

Cleo reaches across the table and lays a hand on his forearm. "I'm so sorry, Franklin. You have time yet. You know you have all the time in the world."

"When we've completed our little project, I will jump," he's nodding through the explanation. "Once this is done, I will try again."

"I know you will," Cleo says, squeezing his forearm. "And it will happen again." She sounds encouraging but knows how little chance there is in the future repeating like that. This is why she's so hesitant to jump from this life. She will never experience another like it. "We've come so far, Franklin. We need to see this through."

He nods emphatically. This serves to settle Cleo's concerns. "If you need me to help arrange flights and rooms for the others, let me know."

"I have it all arranged through my travel agent now," he places a hand atop hers. "I only need to make the call, with the addition of the resort and a means to get them all to the solar array. Everyone will receive an email from the agent – you and Bobby included, and I'll be CC'd."

"We're in good shape then," Cleo breathes easier. "We're just waiting on parts."

Cleo finds Bobby still on his computer at the kitchen table in her apartment. He waves her over to view the simulations he's created. She watches his screen as he presses play.

"This shows the potential energy released from the closed loop we will create with the lasers." Cleo nods. "All the bits flying around have been given weight values. From sand granules to people, to cars to buildings."

Cleo leans over to watch as some of these values are being whipped around from the force of the spinning like coffee grinds in a stirred cup. "I-Is that a cat?"

Bobby laughs. "No, it's just a value that maybe looks like a cat." Bobby runs another simulation. "In this one, you can see the force of the spin funneling out a hole in the ground." He pulls another up. "This one shows the first tier of heliostats and buildings trembling inside the ring laser. And so on."

Cleo straightens up from her bent position and experiences a moment of intense dizziness. Bobby notices and catches her as she begins to sway. "Whoa!" he says.

Cleo regains her balance. "Shit, I nearly blacked out." She is lowered onto the couch gingerly by Bobby. "Too much spinning. I don't know how I'll manage the real thing."

Bobby crouches in front of her. "That's the thing, Cleo, we don't know what to expect. I had the quantum computer at the think-tank create dozens of possible outcomes. They're all very different, with one shared issue. None have the energy to create the gravity well proposed to time travel."

"Then why are we attempting it?" Cleo feels defeated for the second time today.

Bobby puts his hands on Cleo's knees. "I see it as a kind of partial recipe now. We can only play our part - do what the message asks and expect your phantoms to play theirs."

"You think it's a collaboration?"

Bobby points to his tablet and sits next to her. "If we can't reach the energy needed to create a timelike curve, then they must have something to offer into the mix. We do our part -"

"And expect them to do theirs," Cleo finishes his sentence. This inserts a calm into her growing angst. If it's not entirely up to them, their work ends once the ring laser is set in motion. "I can live with that."

Their hug is interrupted by Bobby's phone ringing in his pocket. He kisses her and pulls the phone out. Cleo notices on the screen that it is a company she is familiar with—one of Bobby's sponsors.

Bobby puts it on speaker when he answers. "Hello, Bobby Patel."

"Mr. Patel, it's Jim Herringer."

"Yes, Jim; you've good news for me?" Bobby sits up straighter, looks at Cleo, and winks.

"It is, I hope," Jim continues. "We've procured the diodes you asked for and have everything here. Our college Co-op students are looking for a project, and since they're here Monday, I thought I'd put them to work on your high-density lasers."

"Have them assemble them?"

"Yes, unless you have a conflict with that," Jim sounds like a nice man, Cleo thinks. "It's my understanding that your project is under some time constraints, and if you could pick up the finished product, that might work for you."

Bobby is still looking at Cleo, and his face scrunches up with a smile and a thumbs up. He collects himself. "Yes, Jim, I'd be very appreciative of that. Thank you for the suggestion. I can be there Monday afternoon to review the student's work and take the equipment with me." Bobby sashays with his upper body. It's his happy dance, and Cleo nearly laughs out loud.

"That would be perfect, Mr. Patel. We'll see you tomorrow then."

"Yes, see you then, and thanks again," Bobby hangs up and lifts both hands for Cleo to connect with. She does, of course, the adrenaline pulsing freely.

"It's happening!" Cleo says it as if reality is just now settling in. Their fingers lock together in the high-ten, and neither releases the others. Bobby pulls her into him and kisses her hard. When they part, Cleo's lips feel bruised. But she appreciates the passion behind it.

"We should celebrate," Bobby insists. "I'm taking you out to a fancy dinner."

Bobby's excitement is all-encompassing, and Cleo leaps off the couch to meet his enthusiasm. Darkness creeps into her vision then. It's like the vignette effect in her photo program; the shadows start at the edges of her vision until she's in a tunnel, then the light at the end goes out, and she faints.

Bobby is bent over her when she comes to. She feels disoriented. He's placed her on the bed. She's in her bedroom. She looks left and then right to regain focus, instinctively raising a hand to her head.

"What happened?"

"Low blood pressure. Orthostatic hypotension, probably," Bobby's expression is filled with fear. Cleo places her hand on his cheek.

"I'm sorry, Bobby," her voice is a whisper. She feels exhausted. Bobby takes her hand from his face and kisses her palm.

"You've nothing to be sorry about, Cleo. It's just a symptom." Cleo remembers how dedicated to learning about Parkinson's Bobby was upon her prognosis.

"Just a symptom," she repeats. The word carries a foul taste. *Symptom.* She turns her face away, sorry for him having landed squarely in her path.

"Hey," he says softly, turning her face back to his gently, "It's going to be okay, Cleo. You're going to be okay."

"Am I?" She feels a bout of depression coming on. She's been so preoccupied with time travel, fragmented messages, and her new relationship that she realizes she hasn't had time to experience the grief she's still processing over her disease.

"Of course you are," Bobby is putting on a strong front, but she knows her disease plays on his mind too.

"I never wanted this for you, Bobby," she tells him, her voice still a whisper. Tears track down her cheekbones and pool in her hair. Bobby kisses them away.

He licks his lips, and Cleo imagines the salty tang on them. "All I've ever wanted was this for me. *You, McCarthy.*"

Bobby lays next to her, and they embrace while Cleo cries into his shoulder. This release has been coming for a long time, so she surrenders. There is a strange peace in the process. She cries for herself, her diagnosis, her gift, Franklin's lost love, and the future. Bobby's future. He shouldn't have to suffer her disease alongside her. It's selfish of her to let him. She cries because she knows she should jump.

Check Please

Cleo wakes up with Bobby asleep beside her. Both are lying above the sheets on her bed, fully dressed. She must have dozed off while sobbing, and then, not wanting to disturb her, Bobby lay here until sleep overcame him. He's too good to be true, Cleo thinks. He's too good for her.

She slides her hand out from under his arm and looks at the clock radio. It's seven o'clock in the evening. "Shit," she won't get back to sleep for hours. But, on the bright side, she does feel lighter. Though still darkened by the fact that she will be a burden to Bobby, her mood is less dire. More practical.

Once the job is done at Ivanpah, she will jump. Period. Bobby will have his life back. She will suffer her misfortune alone. There, she thinks with a nod, done. So that helps alleviate the guilt she's suffered over putting the man she loves into an impossible situation.

Bobby stirs beside her, opening his eyes. "Cleo?" She brushes the hair from his forehead gingerly.

"Hi," she replies, wearing a sympathetic smile. "You look so peaceful when you sleep."

"That is the idea," he says, sitting up. He rubs his eyelids with his fingers and scratches his beard. "Hey, we can still do dinner!" He's happy to see how early it is despite the darkness that has descended upon the city.

"Oh, sure, if you like," Cleo sits up and stretches. "Where to?" She's relieved that they'll go out to eat. She needs something to do.

"Somewhere special," he tells her, looking at his clothes. "I packed a more appropriate outfit. I'll call to see if I can get us in."

Cleo looks at her apparel and goes to her closet. "How fancy are we talking?" She shouts as Bobby leaves the bedroom.

"Fancy," he calls back. So, she pulls her little black dress out and tosses it on the bed.

Bobby doesn't reveal where they're going. The cab takes them across the North Columbus bridge over the Chicago River, a stone's throw from Chicago harbor on Lake Michigan. This is all about location, Cleo thinks. The cab stops in front of Carson's, a restaurant Cleo has never visited.

Bobby is out curbside first and takes Cleo's hand, helping her out. It's cold, and she feels the breeze swoop up her legs, lifting her dress. Her knee-length coat provides the extra weight to keep her dress from reaching her waist. They laugh and enter the atmospheric restaurant. The lights are low, and the scent of wood smoke is inviting. They are seated in a booth next to a bare brick wall. Bobby orders a Pinot Noir straight away.

"So fancy," Cleo says, leaning in.

"Right? But the prices aren't," he winks and unrolls his cutlery to place his napkin on his lap. "I've been here once before. My parents brought me when I got the think-tank placement."

"Downtown living," Cleo says with a smirk. "I bet they come here all the time."

"Nah, they can afford Oriole, Maestro's Steakhouse, Alina, and the like. So, they come here to celebrate the little things," he's being sarcastic, but Cleo wonders if there aren't hurt feelings behind it.

"Well, I love it!" She reaches across the table, and he takes her hand.

"Me too. Besides, the food is amazing!" Bobby opens his menu. "Oh, and I know you like the lighter side of barbeque, so I'd suggest the cedar plank salmon."

Cleo is impressed. He gets her. That comes with knowing each other for ten years. Reviewing the menu, she knows he'll order the filet mignon with au gratin potatoes. Rare. No question. It's funny to her that he's even looking at the menu.

They order, and yes, Cleo requests the salmon, well done with fresh broccoli, and to no one's surprise, Bobby orders the filet mignon.

"Predictable," she mumbles, but loud enough to be heard. The server smiles and pours them each a glass of wine.

"I know what I like," Bobby declares, raising his glass. "To us ... and the success of our joint experiment."

Cleo clinks her glass on his, and they drink. "Wow," Cleo's hand rises to her mouth, "That's super delicious."

"I was going to say the same about you," A wink and Cleo's confidence is soaring. How can someone make someone else feel this good, she wonders?

They enjoy playful conversation until the food arrives when they realize how hungry they are. Cleo cleans her plate, much to Bobby's chagrin, who she knows was hoping to pilfer the leftovers. "No way I wasn't finishing that," Cleo admits.

"Then we'll have to get dessert," Bobby affirms.

"This is a celebration after all," Cleo announces, and Bobby suggests the Key Lime pie and Tiramisu.

After Carsen's, they are tempted to take a walk, but the February winds imply otherwise. So they cab it back to Cleo's apartment in the South Loop and open another bottle of wine.

As much as Cleo is enjoying this time with Bobby, she feels guilty about what she must do. She tells herself that this life will end in a week. She can't be happy if he's unhappy.

"Can you believe I don't even have to assemble the equipment myself?" Bobby's talking about the lasers and is elated. "Still," he says soberly, "I'll have to check their work. The lasers must perform. So, I'll have Jim prepare a test on site Monday evening."

Cleo is caught up in her thoughts, not appreciating the light Bobby is in her life right now. Be present, she tells herself. Fuck. You might as well enjoy the time you have together. Cleo smiles up at him from the couch.

"That sounds like a perfect idea, babe. Then what? You'll come back here, and we'll leave together for Vegas?"

"We'll have to drive ourselves, so we need a solid two days for that," Bobby explains.

"Drive?"

"Yeah, we can't take the lasers on a plane."

"That makes sense," Cleo feels stupid for questioning the driving aspect. She doesn't quite know what to think about a road trip like that, but it's safer than losing the lasers to some security official at the airport.

"I'll rent a van," Bobby tells her. "We can sleep in it if we need to."

"I'm not sleeping in a van when we need to be fresh for Ivanpah," Cleo raises the point, and Bobby agrees.

"Okay, I'll get something good on gas, or maybe an electric car?"

"We need to be realistic, Bobby. What if we can't charge the electric car? The fewer obstacles we create for ourselves, the better," Cleo is not in the mood for Bobby's environmentalist leanings. Not where this is concerned.

"Another good point, McCarthy," he says, drinking from his glass. "Why don't we watch a movie or something?"

Cleo tosses him the 'clicker,' and he slides in next to her on the couch. "How about some classic sci-fi? Bladerunner or Aliens." He searches Cleo's streaming packages and lands on Terminator 2. "Arguably the best of the series," he says, and they settle in for a night of television.

Sunday arrives with a call to Franklin. Cleo explains that Bobby will have the equipment Monday night and that she and Bobby will drive everything to Buffalo Bill's, ensuring no complications. Franklin appreciates this idea and tells her he'll give the green light to his travel agent, minus Cleo and Bobby's airfare.

Cleo confirms she received the email with the Buffalo Bill's Resort & Casino booking number.

"I've managed to secure us two buses for President's Day as well," Franklin adds.

"Perfect, Franklin, you are as good as your word," Cleo tells him, and Bobby nods at her. "I'm going to contact Carri next."

"Good, instill in her the urgency of it," Franklin explains, "we don't want to have to go through all this rigmarole again."

"Amen to that," Cleo couldn't agree more. Her nerves are frayed with all the planning and potential for failure. She's no project manager, so Franklin and Bobby taking the reins have been a blessing. This must work. She can't imagine going through all of it again and explaining it to Franklin, Bobby, and Carri. The thought of it causes her deep anxiety.

"We'll see you at the resort, Franklin," Cleo says, and Franklin hangs up. She falls back onto the bed, staring at the popcorn ceiling. Bobby joins her.

"We got this," he tells her, his confidence inspiring her. "I'm going to catch the eleven o'clock bus back," he says.

Cleo sits up. "Oh, I thought we had all day together?" She's disappointed. He's already dressed and has his backpack on the bed. Bobby takes her face in his hands.

"I want to be at my home base to prepare," he kisses her lips. "Preparedness is next to Godliness."

"I think that's cleanliness, but I get what you're saying." She bumps foreheads with Bobby, and they stand to hug. Then, she walks him to the door. "I love you, Bobby Patel," she tells him.

"I love you back, Cleo McCarthy," Bobby kisses her again, and Cleo watches him saunter down the hallway to the elevators. She waves when she hears the doors slide open, and he waves back.

Cleo closes her door and falls back into it, hating that Bobby ever has to leave. She sighs and makes herself a breakfast of berries and granola.

Road Trip

Bobby parks a pickup truck in front of Cleo's building on Friday night. She laughs when she sees it, previously unable to picture Bobby in something so utilitarian. It has a cap on the truck bed where she supposes the lasers are kept.

"At least it's new," Bobby says, smiling while reading her mind. Cleo laughs louder. Bobby takes her bag, and they embrace with a long kiss. "Can you believe we're doing this?"

"I'm hoping some part of me believes it," Cleo replies, running her fingers along the truck's paint and hopping in the passenger side. Coffee is set in the drink holders, and a bag of chips is neatly placed in the center console. "Roomy," she says. "Aww, you got us coffees?"

"And your favorite, Salt and Vinegar," Bobby pokes the family-size bag. Cleo picks up her coffee to warm her hands. "Buckle up; we've got a ways to go tonight."

"Where are we stopping?"

"Omaha, Nebraska," Bobby says in his best middle-American accent. "It'll take six hours or so, but we have a check-in time, so we'll just burn for Omaha and crash."

"Wow, Nebraska. I've never been there!" Cleo feels energized.

"We're going to see many places we've never seen," Bobby assures her. "Part of the fun of a road trip." He pulls the pickup onto the street and makes his way to the I-290. "We're looking at just under two thousand miles to make Buffalo Bill's."

"Two thousand -" Cleo nearly choked on her coffee, unprepared for such a large number.

Bobby laughs, "Yeah, different than flying, right? Swapping the three and a half hours on a plane for twenty-six on the road." Bobby becomes reflective. "Remember that road trip I took in that nasty work van of Russell's we renovated after I got my bachelor's degree? We went to Seattle, then to Canada, and stayed on Vancouver Island."

"I remember getting a postcard!" Cleo laughs. "Very traditional of you."

"Right?! And then we drove back along the border across Alberta, Saskatchewan, and Manitoba until we hit Northern Ontario, went south, and came back through Minnesota." He drums the steering wheel. "*That* was a trip, McCarthy."

"Uh-huh, you're telling me this because of all the adventures we're about to have?"

"I'm just saying, road trips can be a blast."

"Well, I'm not Russell; please remember that." Cleo drinks her coffee, eyeing the chips. "But I'm not opposed to having fun."

"Yeah, Russell's brand of fun wouldn't float your boat," he replies, winking at her and receiving a disapproving look. "Hey, it didn't float mine either, but he was willing to split the cost, so -"

"Uh-huh, just drive, Bobby." She fingers the chips, the crinkle of the bag making her mouth water.

Bobby picks the bag up and pulls it open, "for Christ's sake, Cleo, just dive in." She does.

They stop in Des Moines, Iowa, to gas up and grab a sub. Cleo is happy for the opportunity to stretch her legs and rub the deep knot forming in her outer thigh. Bobby doesn't offer up an opportunity for Cleo to drive, so she doesn't bring it up. After another one hundred thirty miles, they arrive in Omaha at midnight. They park underground and triple-check the locks on the truck and the cap. Check-in goes smoothly; they strip and fall into bed when they get to their room.

"I appreciate your driving all that way," Cleo says, face in the pillow. Bobby mumbles a response, and they sleep.

Morning is announced by Bobby's phone. It's seven o'clock. Cleo turns over with the pillow firmly curled over her ears. Bobby gets up, and Cleo hears the shower run. She figures she has ten minutes before he forces her up.

Breakfast is quick and greasy in the hotel restaurant. They get two coffees to go, and after checking the truck's cargo, they are back on the road.

"Normally, we would spend a day or two exploring cities and landmarks, but maybe we can come back this way another time to retrace our steps and see the sights?" Bobby suggests.

Cleo thinks it's sweet that he's planning a future with her. Normally, she would be all over it, but she has made up her mind. Looking at Bobby now, she sees a future where that brilliant smile fades along with her body as it surrenders to her disease. She can only picture a future where Bobby is left to manage her when he ought to be enjoying her. And she him. Cleo shakes her head.

"No?" Bobby asks, hurt.

"Oh, sorry, no, I wasn't -" She swallows thickly, "I was thinking of something else." She lays a hand on his, tightening her grip. He won't know this future ever happened once she jumps. He'll have nothing to miss. She will carry that burden alone. Cleo considers Franklin and how devastated he is living so many lives without his wife. But it's the right thing to do. It is. "That's a great idea, babe."

Conversation sometimes lags, but that's to be expected on a twenty-six-hour drive. Then, finally, they pass into Colorado on I-76, where the flats continue to dull Cleo's senses.

"I need to see some water or mountains or something soon," she admits.

"This is why I took the first leg of the drive. Nothing to see, really. You'd probably have dozed off a dozen times by now."

Cleo does her best to look offended. "Are you saying I have no attention span?"

"Attention deficit disorder is what they call it these days," Bobby winks, and it antagonizes Cleo. He flinches when Cleo punches him in the shoulder. "Hey! No distracting the driver."

"I thought Colorado had mountains," she says petulantly, crossing her arms. Then, as they approach Denver, mountains loom in the distance. After gassing up and eating in the city, Cleo takes the wheel. The further west they travel, the bigger the hills and the more majestic the drive. Now, she's regretting driving this portion when she could be taking in the scenery.

"Watch for Elk," Bobby tells her. "They like the salt on the roads. An Elk could kill us if we hit one."

"Nice," Cleo replies. "So glad I took the second leg of the drive." She can see Bobby smiling mischievously in her peripheral.

Snow falls during their crossing over the Loveland ski area. Cleo fears she'll nod off as the falling snow caught in the headlights lures her into a hypnotic state. But Bobby is ever alert and eventually directs Cleo to pull off in Dillon, where he's reserved a room near the reservoir. They grab a late dinner at Bistro North and climb into bed.

Cleo takes the morning drive so she can appreciate what's to come. Then, they gas up again in Glenwood Springs and stretch their legs. The Colorado River winds its way along the valley between mountain ranges. It's picturesque, she thinks. They get an early lunch at a Mexican restaurant, and it's Bobby's turn behind the wheel.

They follow the Colorado River as it runs parallel to the I-70, Cleo enjoying the rugged landscape. Bobby tells her he will drive the remainder of the distance to Buffalo Bill's. Cleo protests, but he's determined to make their destination tonight. Then they'll wake up refreshed rather than driving three more hours to get there on Monday morning.

Cleo calls Franklin, who is at the resort and has gathered the others for a briefing. He tells her eighty-seven have come and hopes it is enough.

"I wish we knew," Cleo replies. "Will we get together in the morning?"

"The buses will be ready to board before noon," he tells her. "Why don't we three meet up for breakfast, and once we arrive at the solar array, we can do formal introductions."

Cleo feels good about the plan and thanks Franklin for his part in helping it come together.

"So, we're all set," she says to Bobby. "We will see Franklin in the morning and the others after breakfast at Ivanpah."

Bobby grunts, his attention on the road. "I'm beat," he admits. "Two more hours, and we'll be there. I can't wait to lie down."

Cleo rubs his shoulder. He's been so good with all of this. She hopes it's worth it, whatever comes.

A Sleepless Night

Sunday night, Cleo and Bobby arrive for a late, late check-in at Buffalo Bill's Resort & Casino, where they leave the pickup in the preferred parking lot as per Bobby's reservations. To have the truck stolen or broken into would end their journey. So, the added security here should help them sleep.

Check-in goes smoothly, and they take their bags to their room. Bobby wants to sleep, and Cleo has a shower before she joins him. He's already out when she slips under the covers.

What will tomorrow bring? She's anxious to be done with all of it but terrified to make the jump when all is said and done. But the longer she puts it off, the more difficult it will be. Experiencing this future with Bobby and being in love is more than she could have hoped. But her Parkinson's isn't going anywhere. Therefore, she can't justify letting Bobby commit to a life of servitude to her.

It's two in the morning when Bobby rolls over to find Cleo crying softly into her pillow. He props himself up on an elbow and pushes her hair from her face.

"What's wrong?" His voice cracks, and he clears his throat.

"Oh, I'm sorry, Bobby. I didn't mean to wake you. Go back to sleep." She turns to her side, facing away from him. Bobby places a hand on her shoulder.

"It's not *nothing*, Cleo. I'm up. Tell me what's wrong," Bobby's tone is sympathetic. Cleo rolls onto her back and turns her head to meet his gaze. The room is softly lit with light pollution from the parking lot.

"It's ... I can't really tell you, Bobby," she sniffles. "It's just - I'm conflicted about something."

"Maybe I can help resolve it?" He smiles sleepily.

Cleo smiles back, her love for him welling up and closing her throat. She shakes her head and closes her eyes. "No," she squeaks. "I can't ask you to make my mind up for me."

"If you give me the problem, I might be able to help you come up with a solution," he doesn't stop trying.

"No," Cleo replies softly, shaking her head into her pillow, "If you knew my conflict, you'd be biased toward the outcome."

"Oh? So, it concerns me?"

"It does, and it doesn't," she explains, thinking it must make no sense to him, her saying that. But it only concerns him in *this* future, not the one she plans to jump to. Because once she jumps and restarts her life from her initiation day, this future never was, so how could it concern Bobby? But, then again, if this future disappears, is it fair to Bobby to rob him of all he's learned? It's a lot to unpack.

"That means it *does* concern me, so you have an obligation to include me," he replies, confusion playing across his handsome features. "Is it about tomorrow?"

"Yes and no," she realizes she's dancing around the subject, feeling frustrated.

"Okay," Bobby rolls onto his back, "I know enough about women not to press the issue further, but if you're having second thoughts about tomorrow, it's a big deal, and we should address it." He places his hands on his chest and closes his eyes.

"I'm going to jump tomorrow," Cleo can hardly believe she's said it out loud, but Bobby deserves to know, she thinks. She owes him that.

Bobby's body flinches, and he sits up, turning the bedside light on. "Why the fuck would you do that?"

Cleo is momentarily startled by his reaction, then slowly sits up. "It's not because I don't love you," she tells him, trying to keep her composure. "It's because I *do* love you."

"More nonsense," he's crossing his arms over his torso, his triceps cutting a sleek shadow on the back of his arm. "Tell me why you would throw away everything we've built." He's hurt and avoiding eye contact, facing straight ahead.

"You deserve to know, Bobby; that's why I'm telling you," She pleads. "I love you."

"That makes no sense," he turns to look at her, "you must realize that makes no sense."

"I get that it makes no sense from your point of view, but from mine, it's my only option."

"You said you were conflicted," he says, tears welling in his eyes. "If you're *conflicted*, let me make a case for not jumping."

"Of course, I'm conflicted, Bobby," Cleo cries, "I *love* you; I love what we've become, but I love you too much to let you suffer my future."

"*Your* future?" Bobby swings his legs around, and his whole body faces her now. "Do you really see your future without me in it?"

"I-I'm sorry, Bobby," she weeps, head down, hands pulling at the sheets. "You can be happy in another future."

"Not without you, Cleo, I can't. I know that now. I'll never be truly happy without you. I'll always feel incomplete if you jump, and we remain just friends. I know I will." His voice trembles. "Please, Cleo, don't." He takes her hands in his, and she leans onto his shoulder.

"You don't deserve the life you're agreeing to," she manages through a heavy chest. "You don't have to suffer alongside me."

"W-what are you talking about?"

"Parkinson's, Bobby, you know what I'll become. You know what it does to a person."

"Jesus, Cleo, *Parkinson's?* That's why you would drop this timeline? To protect *me* from your disease?"

"It's not fair to you," she explains, head still dropped, tears falling on the sheets.

"You don't get to make that choice without me, Cleo," Bobby tells her in no uncertain terms. "I *love* you." He pushes her chin up and lightly forces her face to meet his.

"But," she says, fighting for air, "it's..."

"It's not your choice alone," he tells her, and she feels lighter for hearing it.

"I-It's not?"

"No," Bobby says softly, fingers still holding her delicate chin. "And I will love you through all of it. You must know that."

Cleo nods, "I do know that, Bobby. That's why I must be selfless. To save you from a future you don't deserve."

"I deserve *you*, McCarthy. At your best, at your worst, and everything in between. Don't take that away from me, *please*." Bobby looks helpless to stop her, his eyes a deeper brown behind the tears. She recognizes fear in his expression. Watching this brilliant, strong man she loves suffer like this is heartbreaking.

The empathy and love that overwhelms her in this moment of defenselessness produce a relentless sensation of butterflies caught up in her torso, fluttering against her chest and sternum, pushing her toward him. Cleo lunges for Bobby, and they embrace for a long while. They kiss and connect on a vulnerable, passionate level neither has reached before. It is transcendental. It is good. It is healing.

Ivanpah

Nowhere near as rested as they'd like to be, Cleo and Bobby sit at the café in the resort with Franklin, who looks as tired as they feel. Each has a coffee in front of them with full plates of food.

Cleo feels nauseous from the vapors rising from her scrambled eggs and toast. She wants to eat, to have enough energy to complete their mission, but can't bring herself to lift the fork to her mouth.

Bobby is wolfing his breakfast down while Franklin picks at his. Cleo drinks from her cup, pushing the plate away from her.

"You should eat, Cleo," Bobby says, crunching on jam-covered toast. "It's going to be a long day."

"I've had boxed lunches prepared and loaded on the buses also," Franklin volunteers. "They are very accommodating, Buffalo Bill's."

"So, you have eighty-seven others with you?" Cleo asks Franklin to confirm his numbers. He nods. "Do we think that will be enough?"

"We don't even know why we've brought them all here," Bobby adds, talking out of the side of his mouth while the other side chews.

"Right," Franklin agrees, "We don't know, but the phantoms asked us to bring them, so however many have agreed to come, let's hope it is enough."

"Yes," Cleo forks the too-orange eggs, turning them in the air. "I haven't heard otherwise."

"Right, so you've been in touch with Carri?" Franklin asks, applying peanut butter to his rye.

"Yes," Bobby answers. "She has procured the length of cable we require to hook the lasers up to the power array and accepted and uploaded the software to her system. So we should be good to go once I get the equipment set up and tested."

"Carri has also maneuvered the mirrors to allow the laser light to form the ring," Cleo adds. "But that's going to be part of the test run. To be sure everything aligns."

"Exactly," Bobby says, pouring himself another coffee from the thermos provided on the table. "Once we see the circle take shape, we can fire both lasers in opposite directions and increase the power output until we reach maximum yield."

"And then?" Franklin is keen to know. "What then? You've mentioned Ivanpah hasn't enough power to create a gravity well within the ring laser."

"That's when we wait and see what your phantoms will contribute to the cause," Bobby supposes. "Because without a real push, we won't see a closed timelike curve in application."

Franklin seems uneasy. "It's odd the white noise led us here, where there is not enough energy to complete their request."

Bobby shrugs, "Could be they just saw an opportunity with the mirror arrays." He blows on his coffee. "You're not going to find that setup just anywhere, and with the power available to fire the lasers ... I'd likely have chosen the same."

"So, the energy required to create the gravity well will come from them ... the phantoms?" Franklin lifts the rye to his mouth and nibbles at it.

"We don't know any more than you, Franklin," Cleo reminds him. "Bobby's making an educated guess. They've placed us here, so they must be bringing something to the table."

It's Franklin's turn to shrug. "As long as we've carried out their message, then you're right ... our part is over."

"Exactly," Bobby leans back in his chair, inhaling the aroma of the restaurant. "Now, when are the others boarding the buses?"

"Eleven-thirty," Franklin replies, "sharp." His gaze moves to the window overlooking the parking lot where two luxury coaches await.

"Good, me and Bobby will meet them on-site rather than here," Cleo tells him. "I'd like Carri to be present when we explain what we're doing."

"That's fine; I've briefed them on much of what will transpire," Franklin stands, leaving his toast next to his half-eaten eggs. "But they are all most interested in meeting you."

"Good. Then we'll make the introductions when everyone arrives." Cleo stands next, Bobby following her lead, but not before making a sandwich from her scrambled eggs and toast.

Cleo and Bobby leave their luggage in their room as Franklin booked everyone four days at the resort. Cleo manages to eat half of the egg sandwich Bobby brought along.

They drive the pickup out of the secured parking and pass the two buses as they are being loaded with people, just like Cleo. She asks Bobby to stop for a moment. They're about a football field away. Cleo watches these strangers dressed in their warm-weather outfits board the buses slowly. They don't look agitated or nervous from this vantage point. They merely follow directions.

Cleo sighs heavily and removes her hand from Bobby's forearm. He moves the truck slowly, winding through the massive parking lot, and merges with the highway.

"Almost that time," Bobby says with a hint of excitement. But he is excited. He's eager to see the science happen. Cleo is nervous about the outcome.

"Yup," is all she offers in reply. She's caught up in the scenarios.

"Aww, babe, don't overthink it." He tells her. "Whatever happens today, it'll be fun."

"Fun?" Cleo isn't buying that. But she might as well get into a good headspace. She sighs. "You're right. I'm being too rigid. I need to loosen up."

"Should have had those Bloody Mary's at breakfast," he winks at her. "Like I said: When in Vegas"

"To lost opportunities," she says, lifting her water bottle above her head and then drinking. Bobby laughs at this.

"Don't lose that sense of humor, McCarthy," Bobby says, "It's gotten you through worse than this."

He's right, of course, Cleo thinks. She'd gotten through her Parkinson's diagnosis primarily by laughing about it with him until her first tremor. Then there's time travel. She's had to find the humor in that as well. Without it, she might have gone mad. This is just more of the same to survive the next few hours.

"I love you, Bobby Patel," she says, turning and touching his thigh.

Bobby turns to meet her gaze. "I love *you*, Cleo Maeve McCarthy." He replies brightly.

"Hey!" She says, her voice cracking. "Who told you my middle name?" Her forehead wrinkles as her bottom lip protrudes.

Bobby laughs. "I saw your passport in Toronto. How have I never known that?!"

"You *sneak!* I protect that at all costs." She crosses her arms and pushes back into her seat. "So, what's your middle name?"

"Nah, I don't have one," he looks at Cleo, and she fires a burning stare at him. "Seriously, not on my birth certificate or passport." He removes his passport from his satchel between them and passes it to her. Sure enough, Cleo finds no middle name.

"That's not fair! Middle names are supposed to be this embarrassing thing you try to conceal throughout your natural life," She points out.

"Man, that's sad. I'm sorry your parents didn't love you," Bobby laughs louder, and Cleo joins him.

In mere minutes, they arrive at the gates to the power plant and are let in by a single guard who checks his list for their names against their I.D.

"Okay, follow the white chevrons along the driveway to the main building. Ms. Carri is expecting you," and he waves them on. Cleo fears that it's all too easy. Still, Carri has designed it to be, she reminds herself.

They pull up to the main building, and Carri greets them. She is business casual, as she was when they first met. Her Ivanpah shirt neatly pressed. Carri hugs them both.

"So, here you are," she says, "the others are right behind you?"

"They'll be along in a few minutes," Bobby answers, seeing the cable he will plug the lasers into running along the desert floor from the main building past the first tier of Heliostats.

The second tier creates a perfect circle. "It took me all morning to position the arrays for the lasers to follow," Carri tells them. The second tier is the distance of a football field from the power source, so Bobby gave Carri the specifications for the cables to reach the lasers.

"Yes, your mirror array ought to act as the ultimate ring laser," Bobby sounds encouraging, his hands on his hips. "We can drive out to where the cables end, and I'll get started setting up."

"I'll stay with Carri, Bobby, uh, if you can manage it alone," Cleo says, wanting to be present when the others arrive. Bobby agrees, kisses Cleo, and jumps into the pickup.

Cleo is confident Bobby can manage the lasers' setup as he designed them. He also explained the details to her, but Cleo likely missed much of that. Something about a squeezed light, over forty precision lenses, custom-engineered light detection devices, custom-designed real-time, blah, blah, blah, optimization controls, nonlinear crystals with environmental chambers, something, something, and high-power pulsed lasers hooked up to the array's power outlet. Blah, blah, blah, something, something. It's just another reason to love him, she knows.

Cleo feels anxious as the buses pull in and park, narrowly missing Bobby's cables. Carri takes Cleo's hand and squeezes. Cleo appreciates the support and presses back. Dust blows over them, and Franklin is the first to emerge from the first bus. He waves everyone out and asks that they stand beside the main building in its shade. Carri and Franklin nod at one another, and Carri releases Cleo's hand to hug Franklin.

"It's so good to meet you in person, Franklin," she says with an authentic smile, her teeth bright white against her dark skin, eyes shining. Franklin nods again.

"Carri, wonderful to meet you in the flesh," he turns to Cleo, who feels suddenly bashful as if her favorite Professor is here to grade her accomplishments.

Cleo steps back. "So, what do you think? Enough mirrors for you?"

Franklin turns to take it all in. The place is immense and inspiring. They watch as the buses depart to park beyond the fencing, where the drivers will be blind to the activities to come, as directed. "It's incredible," he replies. "Where is Bobby?"

"Setting up the lasers," Carri explains and turns to greet the others who are mingling in the shade. "This is everyone? Like us, I mean."

Cleo spies Doris, the English woman she met in Rome. Then Sofia from Spain, glad to see they'd both made the trip. She doesn't expect to see Stephan from Paris.

Franklin joins the women. "Yes, all who were available to come. I hope it is enough." He removes his trademark white fedora and approaches the other time travelers. "Greetings again," he starts, "this is Carri; she runs the Ivanpah facility and will enlighten you on the finer points in a moment." Franklin then motions to Cleo.

"This is Cleo McCarthy, the one who speaks to the phantoms and has delivered their message to us."

Cleo gets the distinct and surprising sense that she's in a cult and being touted as a cult of personality. She doesn't seek anyone's affection or admiration and feels terribly uncomfortable with Franklin's introduction. She raises a hand and awkwardly waves all the same. Franklin claps, and the others join in. This is not how she imagined this going.

"Hi, uh," Cleo feels obliged to say something when the awkward applause subsides. "I'm Cleo," Franklin already noted that, *genius*, she reminds herself. "Okay, well, welcome, uh, we're here to, well, I don't exactly know why we've been called here, really. We're going to create a ring laser that, in theory, will create a gravity well that may or may not trigger a time portal," she feels she's rambling, but at least all the information is on point. "We're following directions delivered to me from a future we are, I believe, meant to imitate. Again, the *why* of it is yet to be determined, but Franklin and I are convinced it's the right thing to do."

There is some low-level mumbling passed around the group from which Cleo expects questions. But before she can, Carri is answering a call from her security detail via walkie-talkie.

"A disturbance?" Carri says as if she'd rehearsed it. "Please take everyone to the west array." She nods and winks at Cleo. "Be vigilant. Leave no stone unturned and check in with me at regular intervals." She addresses Cleo and Franklin directly. "The distraction I'd arranged is in full swing. It will keep the limited security I have today busy for hours."

Next, Cleo's phone rings, and it's Bobby. "What's up?" she asks. Bobby asks her to have Carri plug in the cables and power up the program. "Okay," she relays the information to Carri and turns back to the others.

"We're about to test the ring laser, so everyone put on your glasses and masks as provided." Cleo looks at Franklin, and he smiles as the mask falls over his nose and mouth. A precaution after Bobby's simulations showed strong winds and debris flying around.

A whooshing sound is heard, cutting the air above them where the Heliostats stand atop their steel poles eight feet above. Everyone's attention is on the blue laser light forming an increasingly solid shape. Soon, the laser no longer looks as if it is pulsing but takes on a concrete structure. An uneasy hush falls upon the group. Another pulsing laser, red this time, appears and follows a path opposite the first until it, too, forms a solid shape. Now, the laser light appears purple. Cleo feels trapped in a Dyson fan, the air around her pushing down into the earth. It's a bizarre sensation. Her phone rings again with Bobby on the other end. "Beautiful, isn't it?" He says. "Jesus, McCarthy, this is at only a five percent power draw!" He laughs maniacally, and Cleo is reminded of a supervillain. She laughs to herself.

"It is beautiful," she replies, "Is it dangerous?"

"Nah, not yet," he explains, "but when I crank it up for the real thing, we might want to move indoors."

Cleo's loose clothing whips around, sealing against her body as if gasping for breath while grains of sand sting her cheeks and bare arms. Her hair rises and falls in a circular motion, and she gives up trying to tame it. It's a bizarre sensation. But, of course, everything about what they're doing is bizarre. But it works, and that's a feather in their caps.

"I'm going to shut it down," Bobby tells her breathlessly. The lasers revert to a pulse, then as single beams bouncing off the mirrors in either direction until they dissolve.

The group claps, shouts, and whistles as if attending a private light show sans Pink Floyd's Dark Side of the Moon blasting from dozens of speakers. Cleo is impressed as well. Bobby's done it. Their portion of the message is ready to go.

Carri takes the group into the large conference room, where all tour groups end up, and they enjoy the refreshments she has provided. Each is asked to leave their boxed lunches on a table. Cleo and Franklin join Carri in the control room, where the software to run the lasers is up on a screen. Bobby joins them moments later and is congratulated on his excellent work.

"It's absolutely incredible," Franklin tells him, shaking his hand. "Now we know it works; all that's left to do is run it until the phantoms join us."

"Right, well, the lasers were stable at five percent," Bobby replies. "Let's see what twenty percent will get us."

"You'll increase in increments?" Carri asks, concern transforming her smile. "We can't damage the power station."

"Yes, I'll be cautious about increasing the draw incrementally while I monitor the output on-site." Bobby reviews the on-screen content and points at a section that reads IIoT or the Industrial Internet of Things. "You can watch these real-time analytics from here as well. The software designers created all sorts of limits for heat and vibration, so if you see any indicators moving into the red, we'll shut it down."

"Good, I'm glad fail-safes were considered."

"Yeah, seemed prudent," Bobby agrees, wrapping an arm over Cleo's shoulders. Cleo feels a wave of nausea rise into her throat and excuses herself. She finds the washroom they'd initially met Carri in and throws up. Bobby is at the door, knocking.

"You okay?" He asks through the door.

She rinses her mouth in the sink. "Yeah ... well, I just threw up." She hears smooth Jazz entering the bathroom through the intercom speakers. She hadn't noticed it until now. "I'll be out in a bit, Bobby." She hears him grunt and move away. She focuses on the music as it morphs into the familiar white noise. Then, as clear as day, a voice begins to speak. At first, she thinks it's Carri, maybe giving instructions to the group, but then she realizes the voice is much more familiar than that. Feminine, where Carri's voice conveys a more authoritative, masculine tone. Youthful, where Carri's is more refined.

"Cleo, it's *me*," the voice says, and then Cleo understands who 'me' is. It's *her*. It's Cleo's voice talking to her via the white noise. Had it always been her?

"I know this must seem bizarre, but honestly, this whole trip has been bizarre, right?" The voice shares her inflections and angst. It's disorienting. "We don't have much time, Cleo. The Ivanpah plant will be decommissioned and broken down in under a year, never to become operational again," she stresses. "Our window was narrow to achieve this. You're saving all of us, Cleo. Everyone," the other Cleo says, and all Cleo can do is sit on the toilet and listen in awe, mouth agape, curious as to why other Cleo's voice does not sound as if it were being fed through a meat grinder.

"We've completed the closed timelike curve in my future, and we need you to do it in yours. We're fucking up existence, Cleo. It was postulated that the universe would make concessions for time travel. It's not. Our warping of space-time is destructive. It's akin to global climate change on Earth. We didn't think we could make an impression, but it's killing us. *Everything*. It *must* stop!"

Unsure whether she can respond to the other Cleo or if it's just another one-way message, Cleo asks, "How could you have known? With all the minuscule changes in every timeline -"

"That's why it had to be done like this," the other Cleo says. "I've been contacting you in every timeline. In this one, you have pieced my message together and acted. Sending you a singular message and hoping that pieces of it got through has been difficult. But because I'm you, I've had a connection. Not unlike the feeling we experience when we come upon a singularity." Okay, so this isn't a one-way conversation.

Cleo gathers her thoughts, "So, you've accomplished this in your time. Do we just run the lasers at full torque, and then what?"

"Yes, have Bobby – bless his soul - push the limits and have the others meet at the equipment. Then they must jump." Cleo's heart plummets to her stomach at the mention of a jump, and she resists. "Jump? *No.* Why?" She feels a blast of cold from the AC above her raise the hairs on her arms and neck. She'll lose this life. She'll lose her connection with Bobby if she jumps. It's a cruel thing to ask of her.

"It's the only way to stop the destruction of space-time," the other Cleo warns. "It will give the ring laser the energy to create a gravity well in both timelines."

"What, why? What's the science behind that?"

"We'll cancel each other out, Cleo. We'll have repaired the natural order of the universe."

That sounds heavy, Cleo thinks. But if she jumps, she'll lose this future and everything she's worked to keep. "How can you be so sure this will work?"

"My future isn't your future. Mine is more advanced. I'm thirty-seven. That's fourteen years your senior. We have new tech. We discovered this fix. We're monitoring your progress. It's how we're having this conversation."

Cleo can't fight other Cleo on the science; she's not qualified. Of course, she hates the idea of jumping and losing her life with Bobby, but if it's to save the universe, then she can't argue the point—the good of the many and all that. Still, she feels sick over it.

"I'll call Bobby and have him start the lasers," she does so, albeit apprehensively. "Bobby, I've received another message. It's, uh, from myself in another future," she sounds crazy. "The voice in the white noise, it was me all along. We're destroying space-time with our jumping back. The other me is waiting for us to restart and push the lasers to their limit. I'll call Carri to have the others join you there." She can't bring herself to mention the jump.

Bobby is silent on the other end. "Did you get that?" Cleo's angst is beginning to fray her nerves. "What do you think that will do?"

"It sounded too good to be true," Bobby replies. "Time travel at no cost." A pause. "I can only theorize what the outcome will be," Bobby answers her second question, "but if the future *you* is directing us, then I trust her. Do you?"

Cleo pauses just a fraction of a second. "Yes, I trust myself, future me absolutely, past me, meh, but future me knows what's happening." Humor plays down her distress over the jump order.

"Then let's light this sucker up."

Cleo hangs up on Bobby and calls Carri. "Hi, please direct the group to Bobby. I'll be there shortly. I'll let you know what needs to happen when we reach optimal power." Carri accepts the orders and signs off.

"Another thing, Cleo," the other Cleo says, "Where is Franklin?"

"With the others," she replies.

"You need to find him. We had to remove him from the control room," she explains. "Franklin was going to sabotage our efforts as I suspect he will with yours."

"*Franklin?* Why?" This is unexpected. It's ridiculous, actually. Why would Franklin threaten the very mission he's helped along?

"Trust me, Cleo. We don't have time. Ask him yourself. Franklin has always been the common denominator in every timeline. Now *hurry.* Find him. Stop him!"

Cleo stumbles out of the bathroom, heading for the control room where the lasers' software runs the show. Sure enough, Franklin's here with an unconscious Carri at his feet, about to turn the mirrors and break the circle. Franklin spins around, shocked to see her, and points a pistol at Cleo, stopping her at the room's threshold.

"I'm sorry to have misled you, Cleo, but once I learned you were receiving messages from someone across the void, I knew I had to stay close." He wears an expression that simultaneously reminds Cleo of remorse mixed with determination.

"You see, I, too, received messages from myself. He told me what I had to do to maintain my immortality. That this had been attempted many times in other futures."

"Then futures we leave still exist?" She reacts to the concept more than to the pistol pointed at her midsection, stunned over Franklin having assumed the role of the villain in his own story.

"Maybe. What we know is that the messages survive. Once sent, they remain in the cosmic background radiation."

"But none of us want this gift, Franklin. Y-You don't want it." *Does he?*

"I do," he says plainly. "I know that now. It's all I'll ever have."

"Our gift is skewing space-time, Franklin. Did you know that?" She snaps out of her daze to quote the other Cleo. "It's destroying reality. The universe can't compensate for it."

Franklin looks ambushed by this description. Then, he reclaims his composure, describing what *his* white noise explained to him.

"I was directed to seek out all other travelers, keeping a record of them so that when this came, *I* could control the outcome."

"But why all the cloak and dagger if you were only going to stop it?" Cleo's head is spinning, and she feels slightly dizzy.

"Because I didn't understand my message until yours was deciphered. I needed to understand the specifics of your message to piece mine together." Franklin's eyes and the gun are locked on Cleo. He looks fixed, and this frightens her.

"But why not just *kill* me?"

Franklin looks hurt. "I thought you knew me better than that. It isn't something I take lightly - ending a life. And we have become friends."

"Friends don't let space-time tear itself apart at the seams, Franklin." Cleo is tense. If he goes through with this sabotage, will they ever be able to attempt it again?

"How much time is enough, Franklin?" Cleo shouts over the hum of the lasers outside, her hands pushing into the doorway's frame. "You've admitted you should have died with your wife all those years ago. You haven't felt complete without Marla. You don't want to go on forever without her!"

Franklin looks speechless, but she can't read past it. What's he thinking? Will he deny the others their freedom and universal order for his immortality?

"You had your chance, Franklin," Cleo pleads but wants to scream. "And I've had mine," she tells him, distraught at the thought that this timeline will die and, with it, Bobby's love. "We have to jump, Franklin, all at once when that power meter hits red," she points at the screen. "If we don't, it could mean the end of everything."

Franklin's hand holding the pistol waivers. He slumps down on a stool and looks down at the stirring Carri at his feet. "I-I thought my gift was about second chances," he finally says, his gaze returning to Cleo's. "But maybe our gift *is* a curse. Perhaps one opportunity is all we ought to be permitted." His tone carries a sense of defeat. Franklin removes his hat and places it neatly on his knee. He traces the fedora's crown with a long, dark finger that disappears into the pinch, then slides down to circle the brim. It appears to have a calming effect on him.

Cleo nods maniacally, "Yes, that's right, Franklin, that's right, so come with me," her hand is out for him to take, but the overwhelming sadness in his eyes terrifies her. "Please, Franklin -"

"I can't live another day knowing I'll never know her like that again, Cleo," Franklin's expression collapses. There is defeat there, and it is absolute. Cleo flinches. "I'm so sorry. Turn away, Cleo. Please." She doesn't and watches as her friend lifts the gun to his head and fires.

"NO!" Cleo shouts, but Franklin's body has fallen to the hard, concrete floor of the control room with a sickening thud. She rushes to his side, kneeling beside the thick blood collecting around his head. She quickly turns away from the gruesome scene, nausea rising. Tears come instantly. She knows she has no time to mourn this mistake. She feels robbed of a good man and the opportunity to sit with him as life drains from his body.

She thinks this is a monumental mistake, her head shaking in disbelief. She grasps his hand and lifts it to her face, placing it against her lips. It smells of sandalwood and smoke – gunshot residue. She slides his hand to her cheek and cries. Then, realizing the urgency of the moment, standing on trembling legs, Cleo tears herself away from her misguided friend and forces herself up, Franklin's trademark fedora, now speckled in blood, grasped tightly in her hand.

Carri is awake and crawling away from the gruesome scene beside her. Cleo takes her hand and ushers her out of the control room, one arm over her shoulders. They move quickly to the cafeteria despite Cleo supporting Carri's extra weight, where they find the others, and Cleo shouts for them to follow her.

Outside, a violent inrush of warm air nearly rips the fedora from Cleo's hand while the matter around them spins in a blur of activity. Debris and dust are picked up and spun as the outbuildings tremble against the powerful gust being created. The loose sand has depressed and flown away from the naked land within the circle. This spinning force reveals two inches of the concrete footings under the heliostats and buildings. Everyone braces for the worst, kneeling, lying on the earth, holding onto one of the heliostats' support rods, or bracing themselves against a wall. They make themselves small. The protective eyeglasses and breathing masks work handily against the sandstorm that spins relentlessly. Without them, Cleo fears her very breath would be pulled from her lungs, and she would be blinded by the sharp particles blasting against her glasses.

She pushes on, leading the way to the lasers, narrowly missing an unfortunately airborne lizard, and the group follows, albeit reluctantly. Bobby sees her and offers a thumbs-up. She pulls herself beside Bobby, pulls down her mask, and shouts for him to max out the power draw. He nods and increases it to both lasers simultaneously. A high-pitched hum escapes the equipment, and she watches the lights on Bobby's screen go red. Cleo turns to address the group, shouting over the buzz of the lasers for them to jump. They look stunned over the request, so she tells them again more insistently. Still, they haven't been briefed that they would be asked to jump and share a look of confusion. Cleo moves through the group, repeating herself, touching them each on their arms, shoulders, and heads as she moves through the crowd, impressing her will on them.

When she returns to Bobby, she nods at the group, who nod back in unison. She holds up her hand with three fingers raised, counting them down, looks at Bobby, removes her mask again, and tells him, "I love you. I'm sorry," then, feeling like she is leaving her heart in this timeline, jumps.

Ivanpah Part Two

Cleo does not find herself searching for Franklin in the shadows at her apartment on January 17th. She is nowhere, floating or falling or being lifted or turned; she can't tell. There is no reference point, but there is a sense of motion. The place she occupies is white. Just pure white with no edges, corners, or horizons to give a sense of size. It is all at once infinite and claustrophobic.

Cleo feels immediately connected to the white space in a way she's never felt before. It is as if there is no end to herself within this environment. Like her skin and the ether that she moves through are one. She imagines this is what it felt like in the womb, encapsulated in fluid, unaware your body is separate from your mother's. She sways through space and time.

Does she hear voices? Something or someone is trying to communicate with her. She asks for help. She asks for understanding. She asks why. But the answers are lost to this place. This dimension. This wormhole? It could be anything. Anywhere. She is not frightened, but she is uneasy. She'd never experienced this place when she jumped. The jump was instantaneous.

Where's everyone else? Are they each experiencing this? Whatever *this* is. Will she see Franklin on her initiation day now that he has died? Will the act of expecting him there force him to materialize because he existed in her past? So many questions. So much time to think. To contemplate her life up to this point. But no further. She can't think in future scenarios. Even imagining her initiation day is the past.

Cleo, she thinks. *That is my name.* Oh, God, is she losing herself to this place? Maybe her atoms are degrading. Maybe she's in a black hole and will – what was the word Bobby used once to explain the results of jumping into a black hole? ... *Spaghettification.* Where she would be compressed and stretched like a noodle. It's not an intriguing prospect.

Whatever happens, it feels like it's taking forever. Or ... how much time has passed? She has no concept. This place is purgatory.

Perhaps she's being given time to consider her choices. To realize the implications of those choices. It's all terribly introspective.

Maybe this is death? Did the power plant explode? Has the project failed? This scenario is the most upsetting. Bobby wouldn't have survived. All those people they brought to Ivanpah. Dead. Carri. Cleo feels a potent mix of sadness, regret, and guilt for all those lost to her crusade. What was it all for? Did they at least fix what their gift had broken?

She's jumping to conclusions. There's no reason to think she's dead and has taken all those good people with her in a vain attempt to create a gravity well. She's not that dark. And this place, this, nothing ... it's *not* nothing, it's somewhere. Some time. Everywhere. Every time. It's time itself.

The white dims now. It dims and transitions into darkness. Cleo is in shadow and then complete blackness. It is the absence of light. It is the opposite of what she was experiencing. She feels more vulnerable to the darkness than she had to the light. It's difficult to put into words, she decides. She experiences sensations, likening the temperature to a steamy summer night when she couldn't separate herself from her environment. Her body is one with the particles in the atmosphere as she moves through it. Has she lost her body to this place?

Cleo places her hands on her face. She has a body. Or is that the phantom limb sensation people who have lost arms and legs feel for a time after? Is she a ghost? Her sight has returned, having become used to the darkness. Looking at her hand, she's stunned to realize she can see right through it. She bends her perceived neck to focus on her chest and torso. It's gone. All but a faint outline of her material form.

Cleo wants to go back now. She's had enough of this brooding place. She's done what she's done for the betterment of the universal good. So why is she being punished like this? How long has she been floating in the darkness? Every thought feels like a hundred years. Every unanswered question, like a thousand. Or has no time passed at all?

This must be her penance for using her gift, nay, curse. The universe is taking its pound of flesh for her betrayal of its natural laws.

"I understand!" she shouts, but no sound escapes her. No echo accompanies the attempt. Nothing.

"Please ... let me go!" The plea emerges from her like a whimper.

A sunrise lifts the darkness like a heavy blanket pulled over a sphere. The sunrise quickly moves above her and sets behind her. It does so many times, each rotation quicker than the last. It disorients her. Then, the process slows and reverses. Cleo wants to cry out but instead accepts her imagined punishment. Like a petulant child, she'd gone against the natural order to amuse herself in a forbidden playground. This is the universe explaining to her child-self that she was wrong.

"I understand!" she yells again, to no avail. No one is listening. Or, if they are, they have no intention of answering. Cleo is overwhelmed by this unearthly experience. She is a ghost caught in time. Will she experience this for eternity? Will she ever see Bobby again? Will she ever have an opportunity to live a normal life?

A series of unexpected thoughts assail her next: Parkinson's be damned. *I want to live!* I want Bobby in my life. I want to experience all of it. Love, sadness, victories, defeat, pain, joy, all of it. I want *one* life. No do-overs. I want to live!

The space-time distortion shudders, and any motion she's felt ceases. She is hovering in place. Then, finally, the white from before returns, and Cleo senses a deep well of acceptance thunder through her body. She accepts her fate. She wants her life back. She wants to live. Whatever that means for someone with Parkinson's. She wants to live regardless of her disease. She wants to live with her disease. She wants to learn from it. "Teach me," she whispers.

Now, she sees a figure in her peripheral. Then, another in the distance, in front of her. They look alike. Then another pops up next to her, and she turns to see a half dozen more blink into existence in her white space. Cleo gasps into the void. They are her. They are the other Cleos from her alternate futures. They speak as one, the voices erupting in her head.

"One life," they say as a chorus. "One life and no more."

Cleo experiences a jolt of electricity as if she has placed wet hands on an exposed, live wire, and the whiteness fades away to reveal a dusty earth below her palms, instinctively pushing herself up.

She has not left Ivanpah. The laser still closes the loop above her, and the others remain. She looks at Bobby, who is running to her side. He grabs hold of her elbows and rests his forehead against hers.

"That was incredible," he says, breathlessly.

"What was?" She asks, not understanding. Had he experienced what she had? That timeless place.

"Didn't you see it?"

"What, Bobby?" She isn't ready to tell him what she saw, so she watches him return to the lasers, shut them down, and double back to her.

"The gravity well. The others," he explains. "So many others."

"Other what?"

"Time travelers, Cleo, like you. Hundreds appeared, maybe thousands, then blinked out of the gravity well. Travelers from different ages. I saw a Viking!" He laughs giddily. "I saw a flurry of others. Someone from just about every walk of life and era. It was unreal!"

"You saw all that?" Cleo gasps. "You saw others like us?" He hadn't shared her experience. He'd had his own.

"I watched the gravity well materialize and open a portal," he says excitedly. "It was ... magic." His eyes are so large and bright that Cleo feels she could exist inside them.

Cleo watches Bobby move toward the heliostat and remove his phone from its place on the structure.

"Did you record it?" she asks, still shaken by her experience.

Bobby nods, his phone in hand, reviewing the footage. He smiles brightly as only Bobby can, waving Cleo over to him. They watch the winds whip around on his screen as the lasers appear as solid beams of light. The group looks unsure of what they've gotten themselves into. Some are holding onto something; others are reaching for the ground. Then Cleo's order to jump, and then nothing. But the nothing continues to record. It's white noise; the sound and visuals are pixelated. Bobby places a finger on the video's timeline and runs it forward nearly twenty minutes before a picture returns.

"Shit," Bobby mutters. "All the best parts are lost." He looks forlorn. Cleo wraps her arm around him and rests momentarily on his shoulder. She considers the twenty minutes of snow on the screen and concludes that's how long she was in that timeless space.

"Maybe it's for the best," Cleo wonders.

"Uh, I just opened a portal to multiple times," he looks at Cleo in mock shock. "I would have won the Nobel in Physics, but yeah, it's probably for the best." Bobby's sarcasm is peaking, and Cleo can't tell if he's really upset or not.

"It was tearing space-time to pieces, Bobby," Cleo says resignedly.

"So, I shouldn't show my buddies at the think-tank," he replies. Cleo punches him weakly in the arm.

She turns, wide-eyed, to address the others, her role in all this returning to her. Carri joins her and takes her hand. They share a look of knowing.

Cleo turns from Carri's gaze, maintains her hold on Carri's hand, and addresses the group. "We've all just returned from an incredible experience. But it's over," she tells them, voice hoarse, a certainty she feels in her gut makes itself known. "Our gifts have been revoked."

The group, still collecting themselves, some even running their hands along their surroundings or on others, are slowly returning to the now. Then, finally, they acknowledge what Cleo is telling them, nodding and murmuring amongst themselves.

The universe has reclaimed order, Cleo tells them, and she couldn't be happier knowing that she would live out the rest of her days in this future with Bobby. She drops to her knees and bends until her head meets the dirt. Carri kneels beside her, releasing her hand and rubbing her back.

Bobby rushes to her side and sits next to her in the dirt. "Are you alright?"

Cleo looks up at him, a layer of the desert floor attached to her damp forehead; she nods and feels her smile replace a tired frown. "I am."

"The jump – when you all jumped, it was like a burst of energy that amplified the ring laser. It was..." Bobby becomes emotional, one hand pushing back his dark curls. "I'll never experience anything like it again."

Cleo throws her arms around him and pulls him into a bear hug — the group cheers, a delayed realization perhaps, that they are free to live as others do.

Ever After

Remembering a time when she was burdened with an unlimited number of do-overs, Cleo McCarthy finds herself enrapt in the everyday. No longer does she ask herself the question of how much time is enough, knowing that any amount of time spent with loved ones is all the time anyone needs. Be present, be available. Just *be*.

It's a comforting thought. She loves her life and has been on medications to counteract her Parkinson's. She and Bobby were married a year after the Ivanpah event. Trish was her Maid of Honor, and Carri was her bridesmaid.

Now, ten years removed from the impossible life she'd led, Cleo is considering a new drug that has been years in the making. Trials are showing promising results in neurodegenerative diseases, Parkinson's being one of them. For example, neurons that produce dopamine are built by inhibiting a single gene, leading to a complete cessation of tremors and other Parkinson's symptoms in mice.

Bobby, of course, has been all over this since researchers at the University of California first announced it. He is very optimistic, and Cleo is grateful for his optimism every day.

Today, they visit the grave of a friend who had expected to live forever in pursuit of the one thing he'd lost. Franklin's stone is modest. It takes up a single plot in Chicago's Graceland Cemetery in Uptown per his Estate's wishes. The sun is high in the sky, and Cleo imagines Franklin's encouraging warmth as it falls on her shoulders. He will never be the villain in her story. When they had called the police to come to Ivanpah that day and taken ownership of Franklin's remains, they discovered that he had left his worldly possessions in Trust to Cleo in the event of his passing.

It is no small fortune. Franklin was a wealthy man with homes all over the world and charities set up for Cleo to manage. It has been an adventure visiting each home and selling them or arranging property management firms to rent them out. The revenue from each has gone directly into the Foundation in Franklin's name. The Foundation keeps Cleo very busy and gives her life a more profound purpose she might otherwise not have realized. For this alone, she is grateful to Franklin.

Cleo and Bobby remain in Chicago, in Franklin's handsome home in one of the city's upscale lakeshore communities. Cleo has left her graphic design career to commit her time to Franklin's charitable organizations. Bobby's interest in time travel has shifted to vehemently counter the development of the concept after Cleo explained its effects on space-time. His Ivanpah experiment has gone unnoticed, and those who witnessed it remain silent. Otherwise, Bobby works for a successful engineering company where he heads up the physics department.

Cleo has employed those ex-time travelers who showed interest in Franklin's foundation and maintained contact with all of them. Those who did not attend the Ivanpah event have also reportedly lost their ability to time travel. Franklin's dark web website and email have confirmed this. Cleo maintains it for now, just in case.

The Ivanpah array did close its doors, as the other Cleo had promised. Decommissioned; deemed too expensive to maintain. As a result, Carri agreed to move to Chicago to work alongside Cleo as an equal in managing Franklin's estate.

Cleo's particular interest in Stephan, her Parisian time traveler with the dark history of suicide, insisted she visit him as soon as the Ivanpah event had blown over. He was twenty-two when he agreed to her request to be placed in a treatment facility for his depression. He's now a social worker within the organization, making a difference in others' lives.

A butterfly floats gracefully past as Cleo rests one hand on her pregnant belly, the other running over Franklin's stone a final time, rereading the engraving she'd had included.

"A man who knew love, and how much time was enough."

Enjoy the first four chapters from Killing Karma, also by Michael Poeltl

The Karma Killer

You reap what you sow.

Newton's law of universal gravitation states that every particle attracts every other particle in the universe with a force that is directly proportional to the product of their masses. Karma acts similarly in that your experiences are directly proportional to the experiences you put out in the world. Karma transcends the present. It follows you through lifetimes. It is a natural law, and like gravity, it doesn't cease to exist if you don't believe in it. Gravity keeps your feet on the ground, the moon in orbit, and the planets moving around the sun. Karma shares this omnipotent quality. Karma keeps you honest. It carries out cause and effect in its own time, and what you reap, you will sow.

We live in the present, but it is a difficult place for many. Karmic debts are continuously being disbursed in many forms. Some will experience poverty, while others will have great wealth. Some will be sickly, while others can't seem to catch a cold. Some will offer kindness to those who'd showed them a similar kindness in another life. Some will die at the hands of those they'd wronged in a shared past.

Karma goes both ways. It is a perfect accounting system that none can avoid, and like gravity, it is a constant. It works through people unconsciously participating in its greater plan.

No karmic debt ever goes unpaid, but sometimes it needs a nudge.

Karma has a champion.

Chapter 1

Having never seen action, Peter thought he'd avoid the punishing effects of post-traumatic stress disorder, but in hindsight, as a peacekeeper in a foreign land, that reality shouldn't have been far from his mind.

Stationed in Kandahar province in August of 2021, he and his fellow soldiers were ordered to fall back to the airport where embassy and military personnel were being flown out of Afghanistan. The threat Peter was asked to secure was not the encroaching Taliban forces but the citizens who, in fits of despair over their newly won government, begged to be put on planes and evacuated along with the fleeing military personnel and ambassadors who had helped win back their country.

The scene was one of continuous chaos - day and night for many days. Peter stood watch where only chain-link fencing kept people at bay after bombs crumbled the tall cement walls days before. Pleas from the growing crowds to let their children through tugged at his conscience. Hateful cries against the escaping forces leaving them to their fates were soul-crushing. Their voices cracked with anguish under the weight of another Taliban rule. It reminded Peter of the third panel in Hieronymus Bosch's The Garden of Earthly Delights. Chaos. *Hell.* And he had perpetrated that hell for those people:

Pointing rifles and shouting for them to step back. All he wanted to do was help them, but he was a soldier put in a position he hadn't imagined. He relied on his training to steady his nerves. In the moment, it worked. It's what happens after that isn't easily discussed.

Often children were pushed to the front of the terminals to appeal to the soldier's morality. Peter had befriended three of them with what little of the native Pashto he spoke. He had given them candies and water during the calmer moments. When, on that fateful day, a suicide bomber entered the airport, Peter watched those three children become engulfed in the explosion. Rifles fired by frightened soldiers threw hot lead at the crowd who were caught up in a focused charge through the terminal and onto the tarmac in a desperate attempt to escape the chaos and board the military aircraft already moving down the runway. Peter, too, fired on the unfortunate masses – his training overriding his better judgment. His vision had narrowed, and the blood in his ears *thumped, thumped, thumped* against his temples as he instinctively backed away from the stampeding horde. The smell of the detonated explosive and the charred flesh of the innocents permeated his senses. He felt sick to his stomach. It was at that moment he experienced real anxiety for the first time.

His magazine emptied into the air, trying to alter the hoard's trajectory, but the people were not deterred. They fell over the dead, and they fell over the living. They clambered for purchase over one another. The screaming filled Peter's awareness, distorting everyone and everything. He watched helplessly as hundreds stormed the airfield and even leaped onto the landing gear. The aircraft did not falter. A line of bodies on the tarmac followed where the great wheels had run them over. Blood ran like a river collecting in a reservoir where the edge of the runway dipped slightly to the right. The scene was grotesque, and again Peter thought of Bosch's absurd painting.

But that was last year, and Peter vows to get better this year. Several months out of the service, he reconnected with his past love of reading and became store manager of a small but popular bookstore in the Cornerstone Village district of Detroit. He'd chosen a new city a thousand miles removed from his hometown to separate himself from anything that might trigger his PTSD. Peter is something of a recluse. He feels he's lost his knack for developing interpersonal relationships and has trouble trusting people. Besides, who would want to be with a damaged Vet like him? Peter is content, interacting with enough people daily that he is comfortable being alone in the evenings when he is not at the bookstore. He enjoys the occasional conversation featuring reading lists and favorite books but tries not to go beyond those topics. He never speaks of his time overseas unless it is at one of his veteran-sanctioned counseling sessions. At night Peter finds himself back in Kandahar, firing his rifle at civilians. Sometimes he is the civilian being fired upon. Sometimes he is the birdman devouring a human leg in the third panel of Bosch's The Garden of Earthly Delights. PTSD haunts his sleep. It shadows him every second of the day, emerging in his most vulnerable moments. The counseling helps, but it doesn't seem like enough. Maybe nothing ever will be.

After a troubling session with Group, Peter makes his way home, where he rents a two-bedroom apartment above the bookstore he manages. It is an excellent pairing for Peter. He often enters the store during his sleepless nights to read some obscure tome until morning. The potent smell of so many books brings him peace and presence, while reading gives his mind something to focus on. On June 7th, 2022, a young woman enters the bookstore. She seems out of place in Cornerstone Village, but Peter welcomes her patronage. She is lovely, whereas Cornerstone Village is, well, not.

"Hi," the woman looks in her mid-to-late-twenties, Peter guesses. Maybe two years his junior. Her stoic expression does nothing to complement her tiny features. The high-set, messy bun holding her dirty-blonde hair in place adds a sense of resolve flattering her conservative outfit. "I'm Clare," she announces. "Hello, Clare," Peter replies with his customary smile that raises the right side of his face. "I'm Peter."

"I'm here for the book," she continues, seemingly uninterested in his name. She reads the confusion on his face. "I'm Clare? Clare Hastings?" Her eyes locked on Peter's, shifting left to his computer screen as if insisting he finds her there.

Peter thinks her pretty in that mousey, bookish way. He concedes the nonverbal signal, nodding and stepping to his right to pull up the order screen. "Miss Hastings, yes, your book is in," Peter bends down to find the package under the counter. The book is called *The Many Lives of Mr. Jones.* "A curious title," he says.

"It's about his past lives." She says curtly, taking the book from Peter. "Is there a receipt?" Peter looks at the screen again and asks, "would you like that printed or emailed?"

"Printed, please." Peter does so and hands the receipt to Miss Hastings. "Do you have any other books like this on the shelves?" She glances to her left, where four tall, dark wooden racks create five eight-foot aisles filled with books.

"About past lives? No, I don't think we do." Peter has a relationship with all the books in the shop. If he hasn't already read them, he knows what he's ordered. "I've never read a book on that topic. It sounds fascinating."

"You should look it up. There are lots of books on people coming back." The woman stands stock still with the new book flat against her small chest, arms crossing over it.

"From the dead?" Peter teases, finding it strangely easy to talk to this woman.

"From the – no, no," Peter catches the whisper of a smile play across her painted lips. "Well, in a way, I guess that's an apt description. But not like a *zombie*. You die and then come back as another life."

"Like the soul reanimating and so on."

"Right, exactly like that. I've been mesmerized by the genre for years." Peter hadn't expected Clare to open up like this but is enjoying the sound of her voice, husky but feminine. "So much so that I've participated in past life regression." She notes Peter's confusion and continues. "It's where you're hypnotized and asked to relive some of your past lives. It's utterly intriguing. The regressionist even records your session so you can listen to it again and again."

"Hypnotized? That's – is it easy to be hypnotized?"

"She knew I would be easy to put under on account of my imaginative nature. A creative mind is an accepting one." Clare seems surprised at herself for running on like this, and Peter thinks he experiences a genuine smile from her. "It's used as therapy on some people. They say the lives you live when regressing assist in your present somehow. I haven't gone so far as to benefit from that angle, but it works from what I've researched. I suggest it to everyone I meet."

"Does that include me?" Peter asks playfully.

"Of course, we've only just met." Clare moves her hips and tilts her torso slightly in a mock curtsy. "Thank you for ordering the book. I'll certainly be back." She spins on her heels and moves toward the antique glass door.

"Would you give me the number of the, uh, regressionist you used?" The question forms before he can truly process it. "I think I can see myself trying that." Clare turns again, walks back to the counter, lays her book down, and removes a scrap piece of paper from her bag. Peter hands her a pen, and she jotted down an email. He notices her perfume's sweet yet subtle scent as she leans in.

"Send her a note. Her name is Theresa Clement. I'm sure she won't remember me, so it will do you no good to mention my name. It won't get you a discount or anything." She retrieves her book and studies Peter's expression, nods, and turns.

"Thanks?" Peter calls after her, and the bells over the door ring as Clare passes through the threshold. Peter's attention falls to the note. Clare's handwriting is pretty and neat. He types the address into his email client. The PTSD has become a nagging issue of late, and he feels at his wits' end with conventional therapy. Perhaps the road less traveled will offer results?

Chapter 2

The moment Theresa let her guard down and gave life a chance was the moment she knew things would start to get better. Trauma breeds purpose, and it was Theresa's traumatic discovery at her family home on Blackburn Street that put her on a path she hadn't envisioned for herself. When regression therapy was offered as an alternative method to counseling, she felt a spark of recognition. It was inexplicable how the mere suggestion comforted her. She immediately took to the process and decided she would become a past life regressionist herself in a moment of uncharacteristic spontaneity. By 2013 she had completed a course in Lafayette, California. She had plenty of money to pursue whatever path she felt compelled to follow. The course modalities included Hypnotherapy, Reiki, Emotional Freedom Technique, and Bi-lateral Stimulation. These invoked balance, creativity, self-awareness, intuition, and grounding, which quickly accelerated her personal growth. The work and the therapy helped in understanding the guilt she harbored. But it would be a long road to recovery. The training also helped solidify her life path, and Theresa moved back to her parents' home to begin practicing her new career.

By 2018 she had established herself as the premiere regression therapist in her community. She had remodeled the 1960s bungalow she'd grown up in and created an office space from her old bedroom. The International Board for Regression Therapy assisted in guiding her on how she should proceed. Tasteful décor, including candles, salt lamps, oil diffusers, singing bowls, and crystals, gave the space a quality that set her and her clients at ease. A comfortable lounge and weighted blankets offered an additional sense of security during the sessions. It wasn't an easy road convincing people that reliving a past life could assist in bringing emotions and memories from the present to head, but the proof - as they say - is in the pudding.

Theresa found her stride, and the people came. Today she has a steady list of return clients and many one-offs. These come in the form of bachelorette and birthday parties as if she were offering little more than entertainment. But they also come in as serious queries. A small percentage of these become return clients, and this is how she maintains the business.

When Peter arrives for his appointment on June 9th, she reads him immediately. There is a deep well of sadness behind his eyes. *Is it guilt?* She knows that look all too well. There is something else, though. Something closer to the surface. She feels lonely in his presence. He is attractive enough, and just 28-years-old she's noted on the printed form in her hand. Theresa senses a connection to Peter that goes beyond his pain. She will have to meditate on this.

"Hello, Peter," she receives him with a short bow, "please take a seat." Peter bows awkwardly, and she smiles serenely at this. He thanks her and sits on the plush fabric couch beside the door, hands folded on his lap. She notes his discomfort and smiles brightly at him, sitting in the high-backed chair opposite.

"I – uh, thank you for seeing me; I'm new to this." Peter offers nervously.

"Most are, Peter; you don't need to feel uncomfortable with me. I'm not reading your mind or anything," she laughs, and he allows himself a nervous chortle. "What brings you to see me today?"

"Well, I guess my PTSD. From the – uh, Afghanistan."

"Okay, and nothing has changed for you since you filled out the online form? It's the PTSD you want to address with therapy, then?" The question is more of a statement, and she notes the confirmation with a checkmark on the printout. "I can tell you I've performed several regression sessions for this very condition," Theresa explains, quietly acknowledging her struggle with PTSD. Though she will not share her experience with him, she certainly empathizes.

"That's reassuring," Peter admits. "It's been a real issue - getting back into a normal routine. A normal life."

"It's a brave thing to accept new therapies or any at all. You've made a decisive step just coming to this consultation." Theresa celebrates Peter's choice to encourage him further. "You mentioned on the form you've been in Group counseling and attended several one-on-one sessions with psychiatrists. You must have gained some powerful and necessary skills to cope?"

Peter nods yes. "It's been a long road, but I have some tools to get me past certain triggers. Still, it feels as if I'm constantly fighting back the memories. I wonder if I'm going through this for a reason. To overcome some deeper issues. Does that make sense?"

Theresa sits back and nods at Peter, maintaining eye contact. "That's very astute. In my practice, I bring your forgotten past to the forefront to assist in dealing with your present."

"My past lives," Peter says somewhat sarcastically. "I'm sorry, I didn't mean it like that. I'm still trying to get my head around it. I'm not a religious person."

"Then this may resonate with you all the more," she explains. "Regression into a past life is asking a lot of a person experiencing this life. The present is all about what we can see and smell and feel, you know? But in my experience, we've all been here before, and our consciousness has inhabited bodies and lived and learned. It's from past lessons that we can address your PTSD in this life."

"It's certainly a fascinating concept," Peter admits. Theresa notices how he wrings his hands, and she reaches across the coffee table, placing a hand atop his. The wringing stops, and Peter looks up at her. "A habit I developed over the last year." His hands release, and his palms slide over his thighs. Theresa slowly sinks back into her chair. "I've had other strange tics I've managed to overcome, but this one," he pauses, clearly embarrassed, "this one seems to have taken up residency. My hands are so smooth now," he laughs at himself, showing her his palms. "it's kind of ridiculous. I feel like I'm exfoliating myself to death."

"The wringing of hands is a practice of the guilty, Peter. You're not guilty of anything." Theresa uses this to draw out more information on the origins of his PTSD.

"Aren't I?" He looks up at her again and unconsciously returns to the activity. "I kept people from boarding those planes in Kandahar. The bomber and resulting stampede was a result of that."

"I remember seeing that in the news. I'm sorry you feel responsible, but if I recall, you were also protecting others as they boarded those planes to return home."

Peter's expression hardens. "Yes, but the carnage that followed, and for what? Why were we there at all? Spent billions of dollars and so many lives to replace the Taliban with the Taliban. Makes no sense."

"I appreciate what you're saying, Peter, and it's important that you are self-aware of the root cause of your PTSD in the present. It will make choosing the lives you'll face in regression that much easier." Theresa scribbles some notes and returns her attention to Peter. "I'd like to get started as soon as possible. Are you able to come tomorrow anytime between three and seven?"

Peter releases a shaky breath. "I'll be closing the shop at 5:30 tomorrow, so six would work."

"That gives us time then. I'll block off the seven o'clock, and we'll work until we're satisfied with your progress. You may want to clear your evening."

"Will it take that long?"

"I don't like to put a time limit on initial sessions. I want you to find your peace as the trance induction can take up to 45 minutes depending on the person, and then I can better assess timelines moving forward."

"I'm a little terrified over what we'll discover," he admits, studying his hands.

"Don't think of it like that. It's a healing process. Whatever we discover is designed to assist in overcoming your **PTSD.** It helps a person return to a trauma to understand the impact that trauma may be having on their current life or behaviors. Current issues may have their origins in a past life, and so in bringing them forth, we heal. It can be difficult, but I believe that hypnotic regression into your past lives is like tapping into an ethereal teacher, but that teacher is you. It's your spirit."

Peter lets out a sigh, "wow, you really believe in what you do."

"I do, and you'll believe it too." Theresa stands to encourage Peter, who also stands. "Tomorrow then. Six pm." He follows her to the front door, and she opens it for him. He nods and exits her parents' home.

Theresa considers the conversation and notices she has begun to wring her hands. She releases them immediately, straightens her skirt, and thinks, *we're all guilty of something.*

Chapter 3

It was a tough case that ended badly, Harlow recounts. It's the one that got away and has plagued his confidence with every new case he takes on. That was 11 years ago, but the self-doubt has never left him. Having made detective just months before the killings, he approached the scene with youthful ignorance. Sure, he had the training, but this would be his first lead investigation into a double murder. The reporters were chomping at the bit to sensationalize it and at his throat 24/7. His captain at the time had urged him to keep his focus on the investigation and not let anything slip as he fielded questions at the scene.

"Reporters can be ruthless and entitled, Harlow," he'd offered. "Give them nothing they can use to scare the perp into hiding. You've been briefed on this. Just the basic facts. Any evidence, no matter how impressive, cannot be released to the general public."

It was good advice, he remembered, but also a warning. *Don't fuck this up.* The crime was violent and bloody. The residence was in shambles as the perps had ransacked the house for whatever valuables presented themselves. It seemed a classic junkie hit at first sight. Disorganized. Rushed. Probably the murders weren't planned. The couple's lifeless bodies resulted from the murderous home invasion in 2011. Just a couple of meth-heads feeling the pull of their addictions trying front doors until one opened. In his experience, they'd push past any perceived obstacles to their next hit with reckless violence.

Signs of a struggle were everywhere. The broken glass dining table, the lamp, the skin recovered from under the female's fingernails, and the classic defense bruising on both victims' forearms. Eventually, they succumbed to the perp's beatings and hemorrhaged from head trauma not two feet apart on the carpeted dining room floor.

The ensuing investigation gave up one perp's DNA and the fingerprints of both. Neither turned up in the system, so Harlow had little to run with. As the middle-class neighborhood was canvased, others recalled their motion-sensor lights coming on. Some recounted sounds at their doors and windows that night, but no one had a security camera to identify the perps. It was a frustrating start to a brutal crime, and the newspapers were beginning to develop their own hypothesis. It was an embarrassment that stretched on for weeks.

It did end, however. Not with an arrest, but with another double murder. When the newly deceased were fingerprinted, Harlow realized his case was closed. Two tweekers were found in an alley in one of Detroit's less affluent neighborhoods. It was a curious scene. Both bludgeoned to death, needles dangling from their arms. Would he open an investigation on these two murders? Who would care? The city was satisfied to know the murderers were dead. Was it a vigilante who sought out the Clement's murderers? That never went over well at the station. So, Harlow chalked it up as a failure with a satisfactory outcome.

His failure was felt strongest when he delivered the news to the couple's surviving teenager. She breathed a visible sigh of relief over the deaths of her parent's killers, but he felt compelled to ask her about her whereabouts the night before. She offered a curt response that checked out. She berated him for the insinuation and slammed the door in his face, but not before scalding him for the time it took to find those responsible and then having the audacity to accuse her. The victim's daughter was as disappointed in him as he had been in himself.

Still, he was credited as the lead investigator in a closed case. That never sat well with him, but he wouldn't contest it. He just acknowledged the honor and moved forward with his career, one that had flourished under the tutelage of his captain and the work he put into never allowing another case to end the way that one had.

Presently, Harlow is content Detroit has accepted him as one homicide after another is solved through diligent investigative work backed by years of experience. He is a well-decorated detective who has seen it all. At least, that was his assumption until the calling card of a potential serial killer surfaced.

Chapter 4

Peter takes a call from his mother at his apartment over the bookstore. She worries about him. She's always worried about him. She almost lost her mind when he joined the military to follow in his father's footsteps. His father is a mess these days. Peter is sure he'd suffered a similar condition, having served most of his life but was too proud to seek treatment. It wasn't done. His mother was the one who had urged Peter to find help for the trauma he'd experienced. To get help for his PTSD. She is a good mother.

"I'm fine, mom," is his practiced response. "I love the bookstore and am meeting all kinds of people through it." This is offered mainly to satisfy her need for tangible proof. Since he moved a thousand miles away from his family home, she can't just stop in and visit. Besides, she is caretaker to his father now that dementia has robbed him of his independence.

"I am beginning a new therapy tomorrow. Yes, it's going to help. No, I'm not lonely... yes, I'll be sure to do that. Thanks for calling mom. Love you. Remember me to dad. Bye."

He is lonely. But he's hesitant to build a friend base or date until he feels better about himself. The anxiety and sudden panic attacks are not something he can or is willing to explain to an unqualified stranger. For now, he is just going to do his job and concentrate on being better.

The following day Peter takes his coffee down the steps into the bookstore and turns on the lights. He's surprised to see a customer waiting at the door. It's a middle-aged man seemingly dressed for a formal occasion. Peter approaches the glass door and points at his watch. "We're not open for another half hour." He calls to the man.

"You have a book I need," the man shouts his reply, pointing at the display in the picture window. He looks frantic. It's a popular Chic-lit Peter had placed two days ago after receiving a shipment of twenty. This guy doesn't look the Rom-Com type, but Peter's seen stranger pairings with his books. "The thing is, it's a gift for a friend, and I can't get it from Amazon until next week. I'm seeing her tonight. Could I just pop in and pop out?"

The man's explanation offers resolution to Peter's question, and he doesn't see the harm in opening early. He unlocks the door and pulls it open for the older man. The bell rings overhead, and the man snatches up a copy and pays in cash. "Thank you so much. You're a lifesaver. It's her birthday, and this is her favorite author."

Peter nods and offers change for the purchase, but the man waves him off and is out the door in a flash. Peter shrugs and turns his sign from *closed* to *open. Why not?* He saunters off to his counter and logs into the computer. An excellent start to the day, he thinks.

Not ten minutes later, another man, much older, enters with a small dog cradled in his arms. "I'm afraid I've walked her too far today," he explains, an expression of worry lining his already wrinkled face. Peter nods and smiles.

"How can I help you?"

"I hadn't expected to come here today." The elderly man admits, absently staring at Peter. "But that you're open, perhaps a book on dogs, I think. Just a story that involves a dog." The man looks kindly at the ball of white fluff in his arms and notices Peter smiling down at them. "She's fourteen, if you can believe it," the animated little man explains. "Still walks with me daily. Today though," he looks alarmingly around him, "we seem to have miscalculated our route."

Peter has never seen the man in his store before but feels a strange connection to him. Perhaps he's suffering the onset of Alzheimer's or a touch of dementia, like his father. He smells of sandalwood and sweat and looks lost but unwilling to admit it. "I've several books with dogs as the main character if that's what you mean, sir."

"Oh, that would be lovely," he rests a weathered, brown hand on the counter. "I like to read them to Lyla here."

Peter rounds the counter and collects three books that match the man's request from one of the shelves. "We're not normally open quite yet, but this morning has been a busy one," Peter tells him, making conversation. The well-dressed gentleman looks as though he had attempted to shave but forgotten the right side of his face.

He looks inquisitively at the books on the counter, picking each one up and reading the backs.

"And I'm rarely this far from home, so your being open has been a blessing for us both. I'll take all three, please."

"That will be forty-three, twenty-five, please." Peter rings up the books, and the older man pulls out his wallet. His arthritic hands struggle with a card, but he manages one and taps it, taking the bag of books. He looks around the shop a moment longer, and Peter again surfaces from behind his counter, opening the front door. "Would you like me to help you home, sir?"

The man nods emphatically and kisses Lyla's unkempt hair. "That would be very kind of you."

"I can lock up for now. It's no bother." Peter takes the man up the street to a traffic light, where they wait to cross.

"You seem a familiar face, son. Do we know each other?"

"I can't say that we do, sir. I'm Peter."

"I'm, uh, Mohamad." He offers his free hand, and Peter shakes it. It's icy. "You are good to help."

"It's okay; I'm happy to do it." And he is. Peter wants to help. It's what led him to enlist initially. He was not smart enough to become a medical doctor or psychiatrist, and reinforced by his father's stories about how his military career allowed him to serve humanity; he found the direction to do something worthwhile with his life.

The two men chat about the weather while navigating the ten blocks to Mohamad's apartment. There he thanks Peter again, and Peter rushes back to the bookstore.

"It's not like you to be late, Banks," Peter's boss stands at the door rooting through his satchel for the key. It's been over five weeks since Sanderson had shown up at the shop. Peter's been keeping count. "You do still live upstairs, do you not?"

"Sorry, Mr. Sanderson, I had an early customer who needed some assistance -"

"You're paid to sell books, not run errands for others," he snaps. "I have half a dozen hardcovers in my bag preying on my sciatica." Peter unlocks the door and holds it for Mr. Sanderson.

"Won't happen again," Peter promises. Likely it won't, but he'll do the same if it does.

"Place looks clean at least," Sanderson says in a huff, landing the books heavily on the counter. "These will go in the specialty case. Classics worth a mint. Catalog them and put them up on our website immediately. I'll fetch a pretty penny for these."

"Excellent," Peter tries to lighten the mood. Rocky starts with Sanderson never seem to right themselves. He's a wet blanket - a killjoy in his early 60s with two ex-wives and a third who seems intent on leaving him. *Why would anyone marry three times?*

"I'm going to stick around a while today," Sanderson tells him, "Rather be in the books than in the doghouse again." He winks at Peter as if he can relate.

Peter doesn't like Mr. Sanderson, but he doesn't hate him either. They're very different people. He's cheap, and much of Peter's salary goes toward renting the apartment, but it's a situation that works for him for the moment.

PICK UP YOUR COPY OF <u>KILLING KARMA</u> <u>AT AMAZON</u>

Other Books of Fiction by Michael Poeltl

- The Judas Syndrome
- Rebirth (Book 2 of The Judas Syndrome)
- Revelation (Book 3 of The Judas Syndrome)
- Her Past's Present
- Waning Metaphorically (14 Short Stories)
- A.I. Insurrection – The General's War
- Armageddon (Book 2 of the A.I. Series)
- Exodus (Book 3 of the A.I. Series)
- The Blind Affect
- Killing Karma

Young Reader Picture Books

- West of Noreso
- An Angry Earth

Educational Books by Michael Poeltl

- If a Tree Falls in the Forest...
- Energy is Forever, and so are YOU!

About the author

Amazon Author Page: Michael Poeltl Amazon

Facebook Page: Michael.Poeltl.Author

Goodreads Author Page: Goodreads

Instagram: mpoeltl.author

Reviews and requests for interviews are always appreciated!